We've Come for Your Eggs

(And Other Reasons to Annex the North)

Septimus Brown

Look—See—Press

Published by Look—See—Press
Victoria, Canada

For anyone

who still believes in magic.

And free trade.

It Begins with a Pigeon

It was a moderately dark and stormy afternoon when Jorvun Prattlethorn received the letter we'd been awaiting for years. When I first spotted the pigeon, I didn't realize it was a carrier. The wizard only feeds me twice a day, so at first I thought a free snack was conveniently winging right up to my window. Our dank tower overlooks the rainy port of Ravenna, and there are pigeons everywhere, and they're quite tasty. Only a rare few receive the global-positioning and delivery enchantments necessary to get a job in mail distribution.

And so it was that as the bird alighted on my windowsill, I sank teeth and claws into wet grey plumage and we rolled across the cold stone floor.

"Not in the apartment," Jorvun growled at me. "I just tidied up." And then, when he evidently spotted the pigeon's little waterproof backpack, emblazoned with the

Valorican Postal Service logo—which, upon my honour, I swear I hadn't noticed—he added, "Glimm, drop it. Drop it this instant!"

I held his gaze for a moment with some defiance as the pigeon thrashed uselessly in my scaly blue grip, but then I remembered the last time I'd eaten a postie. My boss had to pay a hefty VPS fine, and so he cut my salary down to one meal a day for a week. I nearly starved.

"Fine," I said after releasing the bird, but I didn't relinquish my death glare.

The bird flapped over to the wizard's gnarled workbench, almost knocking over a potion with a sneezing goblin on the label. Behind me, the logs in the fireplace shifted and popped. Jorvun adjusted the pigeon's backpack and smoothed its ruffled feathers while offering a string of half-baked apologies, like *he didn't mean it* and *I understand how that might have been misinterpreted.* He then unclasped the little backpack and pulled out a tightly folded piece of parchment. As soon as he did, the bird gave a furious chirp in my direction and dove back out into the rain.

"Oh my," Jorvun muttered. "Oh wow."

"What is it?" I spread my leathery wings and flapped up to the workbench, right where the pigeon had landed, but with much more grace and poise.

"Oh my," he said again. "It's finally come to this..."

He might not have answered me directly, but something in his tone told me exactly what the small note clutched in his thin fingers was all about. The day had finally come. The day he dreaded and the day I longed for. Well, I suppose it was a day that we both longed for, but for Jorvun it meant a lot of effort and danger and upcoming responsibility. As for me, I was looking forward

CHAPTER ONE

It Begins with a Pigeon

It was a moderately dark and stormy afternoon when Jorvun Prattlethorn received the letter we'd been awaiting for years. When I first spotted the pigeon, I didn't realize it was a carrier. The wizard only feeds me twice a day, so at first I thought a free snack was conveniently winging right up to my window. Our dank tower overlooks the rainy port of Ravenna, and there are pigeons everywhere, and they're quite tasty. Only a rare few receive the global-positioning and delivery enchantments necessary to get a job in mail distribution.

And so it was that as the bird alighted on my windowsill, I sank teeth and claws into wet grey plumage and we rolled across the cold stone floor.

"Not in the apartment," Jorvun growled at me. "I just tidied up." And then, when he evidently spotted the pigeon's little waterproof backpack, emblazoned with the

Valorican Postal Service logo—which, upon my honour, I swear I hadn't noticed—he added, "Glimm, drop it. Drop it this instant!"

I held his gaze for a moment with some defiance as the pigeon thrashed uselessly in my scaly blue grip, but then I remembered the last time I'd eaten a postie. My boss had to pay a hefty VPS fine, and so he cut my salary down to one meal a day for a week. I nearly starved.

"Fine," I said after releasing the bird, but I didn't relinquish my death glare.

The bird flapped over to the wizard's gnarled workbench, almost knocking over a potion with a sneezing goblin on the label. Behind me, the logs in the fireplace shifted and popped. Jorvun adjusted the pigeon's backpack and smoothed its ruffled feathers while offering a string of half-baked apologies, like *he didn't mean it* and *I understand how that might have been misinterpreted.* He then unclasped the little backpack and pulled out a tightly folded piece of parchment. As soon as he did, the bird gave a furious chirp in my direction and dove back out into the rain.

"Oh my," Jorvun muttered. "Oh wow."

"What is it?" I spread my leathery wings and flapped up to the workbench, right where the pigeon had landed, but with much more grace and poise.

"Oh my," he said again. "It's finally come to this..."

He might not have answered me directly, but something in his tone told me exactly what the small note clutched in his thin fingers was all about. The day had finally come. The day he dreaded and the day I longed for. Well, I suppose it was a day that we both longed for, but for Jorvun it meant a lot of effort and danger and upcoming responsibility. As for me, I was looking forward to getting a proper education. The only dragon college in the world is in Frostvale, and when Jorvun first hired me, he promised that the day he became King of the North, he would do everything in his power to help me enroll. It's a competitive program, after all. Oh, to be literate! To be numerate! To be wise in the ways of my ancestors! Could it be that the day had finally arrived? I was over-joyed with the prospect of being an even more helpful fa-miliar to my wizard. In fact, I got so excited that I belched a gout of frostfire that hit the sleeve of Jorvun's tattered black robe.

"What was that for?" He leapt backward, smacking at the ice that had encrusted his elbow and forearm. "You had no right to attack that poor—"

"My apologies," I said. "Complete accident." I'd al-ready forgotten about the pigeon. "Is that... what I think it is?"

The wizard knocked the last chunk of ice off his sleeve, then tossed the letter onto the workbench. He glanced out the window onto the rainy port city, then back at me. He took a deep breath, which puffed him up and straightened his back. It was the first time in ages that he'd seemed somewhat confident, almost hopeful. Or at least less slouchy and miserable. His scraggle of salt-and-pepper hair was, in that moment, less bedhead and more the intentional muss of a younger man with grand designs for the future, even if only for the prospect of a night out at the tavern. His normally dishevelled shirt and tie, usually at odds with the wizard robes, seemed to suggest a personal style that was intentional more than slapdash. With arms at his sides, he wiggled his fingers, clacking his innumerable rings together as if running through a rolodex of spells that might turn mud into gold and set a crown upon his brow. And a haunted light of destiny glinted in his eyes.

"You should never sacrifice what you could be," he said, "for what you are."

"Okay." My guts, devoid of tasty pigeon flesh, clenched in anticipation. "And that means...?"

"My father is planning his succession," Jorvun said at last. "We're going to Frostvale."

CHAPTER TWO

Failed Capitalist, Deadbeat Dad

After his swoon of coronation daydreams passed, Jorvun Prattlethorn flew into a frenzy of preparation. It took most of my energy just to watch him and stay out of his way. Of course, I was also a bundle of nerves just running through all my favourite daydreams about life as a court dragon. And life as a college student. What would it be like to have dragon friends? And dragon teachers? What would it be like to live in a land of delightful ice and snow instead of miserable rain and mist?

My boss packed and unpacked and repacked: suitcases with an array of collared shirts, ties, and mage-appropriate robes; satchels with potions, wands, and dangerous artifacts; a waterproof tote full of magical tomes; and boxes stuffed with linen and kitchenware and dusty board games—all the mundanities of life in a rented wizard tower.

This took the rest of the afternoon and most of the night. Eventually he had to unpack a pillow and blanket because, after all, wizards need their beauty rest. Not that he's much of a beauty. But if Jorvun doesn't get a solid eight hours, his spellcraft can get pretty dodgy, if not downright dangerous. Which is to say, he slept in until the spectre of a sun rose high into the overcast sky over Ravenna. I spent the morning hunting the alleys around our apartment block for rats, since I knew my breakfast was going to be late.

When I finally returned home, unsuccessful and starving, I found him standing at our bedroom window. Not the one I was sitting in when the pigeon dropped by, which faces west, but a smaller window up on our top floor that faces north. And normally the window is shut tight, but this morning Jorvun had it wide open. He hunched, motionless, hands upon the ledge, with his neck cranked forward, as if he was willing the rain to stop. But no—that wasn't it. When I flapped over and landed on his shoulder, he didn't flinch. Didn't even acknowledge me. Just kept on staring.

"What is it?" I whispered.

"Hmmph" was all I got in reply, at least until I dug my claws into his shoulder—very gently, mind you. Miraculously, this seemed to get his attention. "Ow," he said. "I'm thinking. Cut it out."

"Thinking about what, Boss?"

"How to get through that wall," he said.

Hold on a minute. I should probably describe the view out of our bedroom window. Our apartment block is pretty tall. I'm not extremely practised when it comes to counting higher than ten, and there are a good number more than ten floors. Plus our tower adorns the very top. There are a few taller buildings in Ravenna, but not many, so we have an exceptional view. This vista includes the northern quarter of the city, which is where most of the rich people live, all the way up into the hills of Rainier Ridge. Beyond that, you can see the Cascade Inlet over on the left and the Stormbarrow Mountains on the right. Farther still, shimmering faintly on the distant horizon, is the Frostvale barrier wall, an impenetrable monolith of magic, or so Jorvun described it when it first appeared a few months ago.

"Can we fly over it?" I'm not sure why, but I was still whispering.

"Have you ever known me to have wings?" He shook his head, crossed his arms, and I could tell from the wiggle in his lips that he was chewing the inside of his mouth.

"No," I admitted. "I suppose not."

"Besides, if we got up above it, I suspect we'd find that it folds over on itself." He released the window ledge and straightened. "Under too, otherwise the king's army would just tunnel beneath it."

"So it's like an egg," I said.

"Yes, Glimm. Like a giant egg."

Sounds delicious, if you ask me. But no, we weren't on the precipice of a fantastic adventure for endless yolk. We were homeward bound. And that meant snow, ice, and all sorts of wonderful food that I'd never been able to try, eggs included. I mean, I've tried eggs, obviously, but not northern eggs. Or northern pigeons. And lots of other northern things that I'd never even heard of. We just needed to find a way through the wall. Easy, right? Well,

I wasn't worried. My boss is a wizard, after all. Solving impossible problems with dangerous magic is how he puts a tower over our head. Of course, he does occasionally need some advice—and maybe a bit of prodding.

Don't get me wrong—I've never actually been to Frostvale. But that's where my kin are from. Jorvun's too. But while I was born in the familiar trade along the Seaport docks to the south of Ravenna, he was the product of a northern lord's dalliance with a scullery maid. Or so he admitted to me once when he was really drunk. So when I say we were homeward bound, you have to understand that home, for both of us, was a place we had long dreamed of but never visited. Honestly, it seemed pretty stupid to make the trip *after* an impenetrable barrier had blocked off the entire country, but Jorvun is a procrastinator. And all procrastinators come to life in the shadow of a looming deadline, right?

(Please don't tell him that I called him a procrastinator. He'd probably cut me to half rations for a month.)

"How do they eat?" I asked.

Jorvun stiffened for a moment, then held out his wrist, which meant he wanted me off his shoulder. I hopped over. When we were face-to-face, he asked, "What do you mean?"

"I mean, do they have enough food in their giant egg to last forever?" I honestly don't have the first clue about food distribution. We get most of our meat from the butcher shop, but where does the butcher get it? Is there magic involved?

"It's a big country," Jorvun said. "They could probably last forever. But... you have a good point."

"I do?"

"You do." A grin spread across his face, which is

something I wished he wouldn't do. I've never been comfortable with the way humans bare their teeth when they're happy. In the entirety of the animal and monster kingdom, best as I can tell, bared teeth are a threat. "Quite genius, actually."

"And do I... get an extra breakfast for this good idea?"

"Don't get carried away," he said. "It's not that good of an idea. I'm sure I would have come upon it on my own sooner or later. But you're right, breakfast is late. Did you catch any rats?"

"None." I put on my best mopey face and let my wings droop, even though I was excited that he'd finally remembered my breakfast. "I'll have to start hunting cats if they keep outcompeting me."

"Good luck with that," the wizard said as he carried me down the central spiral staircase.

We descended from the bedroom, through the laboratory, and into the kitchen. Jorvun unlocked the food cupboard with the words *aperi sesame*, which sent a tingle of excitement through my bones—in part because I loved the feeling of magic in the air, but more because I was about to be fed. He cracked open a fresh can of newt stew. Clearly my idea had been a good one, because he saved the newt for special occasions, and he definitely gave me a bit extra. While I scarfed, he changed from his tattered black house robe to his new oilskin cloak: chestnut brown, stitched with scarlet thread, and clasped at the top with three ornate bronze buttons. The hood was overlarge and pointed to give an undeniable mage vibe. And then my two favourite features: the shoulders were reinforced with black leather and bronze studs, which gave me an excellent perch, and there were a number of pockets, three of which were big enough for me to crawl inside. I also appreciated that it was made out of basilisk leather rather than the disgustingly trendy option of faux dragonskin.

Once I was nestled in his breast pocket, he took the long flight of stairs down out of the tower, through the heart of the apartment building below, and out into the streets of Ravenna.

"So where are we headed?" I asked as we filtered through the Saturday sidewalk crowds.

"Remember that guy Elric?" Jorvun sidestepped as three small, filthy children careened around the corner.

"Elric Mawkley?" I'm very good with names.

"Exactly."

"Of course I remember him." I stood up in Jorvun's pocket and almost fell out at his feet. "He gave me some boar jerky."

"Hang on." Jorvun held me to his chest as he jogged across the street, narrowly avoiding a rampaging carriage. "Yeah, that's the guy."

"Does he know how food gets into Frostvale?"

"I already know how they get their food," he said.

"How?"

"Their only border is with us, and since our king is threatening to annex them, they've sealed themselves up. But that doesn't mean they aren't trading with Shaelun and Euralis."

"But the egg...?" Sometimes Jorvun doesn't make a lot of sense.

"Ships," he said, as if that clarified anything.

"But... the egg...?"

"There must be a way of opening it, like a sea gate."

The stone walls of the inner city gave way to the

wooden tenements and warehouses of the docks district. Jorvun hurried along the boardwalk until we came to a narrow pathway between two gambling dens that led into Market Square, a courtyard bazaar that smelled of fish and smoked yak and pickled goldines and—trust me, I could go on. I had another question about this sea gate, but it took all my concentration not to drool down the front of Jorvun's oilskin.

The market was packed. There were so many stalls that it left little room for the humans to move between them, especially since there were so many of them standing around, talking about the atmospheric river that had drowned the city all week, about the sun overhead that was promising to poke through the clouds any minute now, and about how the warmth of spring was just around the corner. And no, they didn't mean that the end of winter was literally around the corner, but that it wasn't far off. You really can't take humans at their word.

Jorvun had to zigzag up and down a few narrow aisles before we found our man: Elric Mawkley. He's an awkward-looking guy if I'm going to be completely honest. Kind of soft in the middle, but trying real hard to stand like a statue of himself. Hair like it's always deciding whether to stay or flee—not unlike Jorvun's actually, but a bit straighter and a lighter brown. Eyes that say *I have a plan* and a straight nose that says *I've never been punched for it*. Dresses like a noble who got tricked by a tailor with a sense of humour—half inventor, half wine bar impresario. Crimson shirt, ruffled collar. Waxed felt trench coat, indigo ice-dye. You can tell he used to be rich. You can also tell he thinks he still is.

Anyway, he sells all manner of trinkets and gadgets, most of which he claims to have invented, but I had a pretty decent inspection of his merchant table the last time we were here—between morsels of boar jerky. He's affixed little EMG emblems to many of his products. Elric Mawkley's Gadgets? I suppose that's his attempt at branding. More like rebranding. I could smell the glue holding the emblems in place, and some of them were quite obviously placed over someone else's logo. But who am I to judge?

As we got closer, Jorvun squeezing and grunting his way through the crowd, Elric flipped open a pocket mirror, stared into it for a moment, and then shook his head. Not only that, his lips were moving.

I craned my neck toward Jorvun and blurted: "Is he talking to his own reflection?"

"Shhhh." The wizard pushed me down deeper into his pocket.

"He can't hear me," I protested. The crowd around us provided more than enough noise to blot out my small voice. "Look, he is. He's talking to himself."

"Shut. Up." Jorvun pushed me deeper still into his pocket until only the top of my head was poking out. "We need his help, which will elude us if you offend him."

"To be able to think, you have to risk being offensive," I said.

"Are you quoting me now?" The wizard sounded incredulous, but I could tell he was impressed. "Never mind. No more talking."

"Okay, fine."

"That's still talking," he said. "I won't let him give you a treat if you don't—"

"How dare you..." I said in a quite reasonably annoyed tone. But then I thought better of it and whispered, "Fine."

When we got to within a few feet of Elric's stall, I leapt out of Jorvun's pocket, flew over to the table strewn with trinkets, and landed expertly between a steamless kettle and a self-sorting coin purse.

The ex-noble wannabe inventor jumped in surprise—oops, all apologies—then whispered into his pocket mirror, "Sorry, kiddo, I'll have to call you back. Yes. Yes. Okay, I promise. Yes, I really, really promise this time. Okay. Bye." He slammed the mirror shut and thrust it into his pocket. Then, as if there was nothing strange about talking to his reflection, he bellowed, "Jorvun! Great to see you! And Glimm. Welcome back, little buddy."

I bowed but said nothing. See? I can do what I'm told.

"Elric," Jorvun said in acknowledgement. "How're the kids?"

"Oh, you know." The merchant shrugged while sticking out his bottom lip. I think this body language was meant to imply *all is well* or *no news is good news*, but I could tell he was deflecting. "So what can I do you for?"

"Do you still have those paternity test kits?" my boss asked.

Elric and I both gave him a surprised look. Jorvun definitely hadn't been on a date for as long as I'd been his familiar.

"Sure, sure," Elric said. "I didn't know you had any bastards out there."

"It's for a friend." Jorvun made a face that was half close-lipped smile and half cringe. "I'm also going to need a glamour ring, and... well, some advice."

"Oh?" The inventor had stooped to rummage in a box under his table, but at this he perked up. "The great wizard needs some advice? I don't know how I can help, but I'll certainly try." Then he dipped his head under the table for a moment. "Ah, yes. Here we are." He tossed a small black box in front of us that was labelled *Seed Sense* and (sloppily) affixed with his EMG emblem. He also produced a clattery tin of rings. "How many glamours do you need?"

"Just one." Jorvun grabbed the Seed Sense and slipped it into an inside pocket.

Just one? Hold on a minute. My boss and I have talked at length about our homecoming dreams. Jorvun wants to get back at the father who abandoned him. I want to find the family my egg was stolen from. He wants to sit in a comfy throne and wear a heavy gold crown. I want to try out for dragon sports teams and eat pork dumplings in a college cafeteria. Yet I always imagined that we would achieve our goals with... a party at our backs. Isn't that what adventurers do? Form a party and set out on a quest together? Maybe I was misreading the situation, but Jorvun's request for a single glamour ring made me sit up and pay attention.

"Can't you cast a glamour yourself?" Elric asked.

"Of course I can," Jorvun said. "But a semi-permanent glamour is annoying to maintain, and where I'm going, I'll need all my reserves at the ready."

"Wow, sounds serious." Elric upended the tin into his hand and held out five rings. "Just a gild apiece. The paternity kit is fifty clinks."

"And you're sure they both work?"

"Jorvun, please. You insult my integrity as an inventor of significant reputation. Have you seen my reviews on TavernTalk?"

My boss took one of Elric's rings and then stared at his hands for a moment. He wore so many rings already that he needed to decide which finger would be best for an extra one. But then he grinned and motioned for me to come closer. I did, but warily. That frosted grin again. I'll never shake it. Plus he was giving me mischievous vibes, like I was about to get pranked. Jorvun motioned for me to turn, then he slipped the ring as far as he could up my tail, where he wedged it between two of my smaller osteoderms (tail spikes to the layperson).

"What's the trigger?" Jorvun asked.

"Ah..." Elric checked the underside of the tin, which apparently had a little note to remind him how the rings worked. "*Illume.*"

"Glimm," Jorvun said, "I want you to think of a cat. Bring the image clearly into your mind. Got it? Okay, now say the trigger."

"I thought I'm not supposed to talk," I said.

"You're allowed to talk now."

"Fine," I said. "By the by, Mister Mawkley, do you have any more of that boar jerky? Last time we—"

"Just the trigger, Glimm. Focus on the cat and say the trigger."

Elric gave me a big smile—hideous—but I instantly forgave him since he also patted a pocket in his trench coat to indicate that he did, indeed, have a treat of some kind in there. I wasn't thrilled about being the test subject of a wannabe inventor's merchandise, but I'm pretty easy to buy off. So I conjured my best mental cat—a ragged tabby from the alley beneath our tower—and said the magic word.

Nothing happened, or so I thought, but Jorvun was nodding in appreciation, and Elric was baring his teeth at me again.

"See," Elric said, "as advertised."

I glanced down at myself, and—frost's mercy—I was hairy and horrible. No, thank you. Not interested. It took me about a second and a half to catch my tail and yank the ring off. I tossed it back at Jorvun, shuddered, then remembered the payment I was owed. I tiptoed across the table, picking my way past a folding lantern and auto-bellows, until I stood before Elric, my paw held out expectantly.

"Of course, of course." He retrieved a package from one of his many interior pockets. His trench coat must have had double the compartments as Jorvun's oilskin. But from what I could tell, I wouldn't be able to fit inside any of them. He cracked open the flap of waxed paper, and the smell that issued from its contents made me take a step back. He reached inside and pulled out a stick of deep-fried asparagus. "Here you go, little buddy."

I might have rude thoughts sometimes, or most of the time, but I try not to be rude on the surface. I've found this is especially important when it comes to humans giving me food. If I don't act grateful, they are much less likely to give me another snack in the future. So I did my best to not look horrified at the *vegetable* he handed me.

"Thanks, Mister Mawkley," I managed to say—and I think I even imbued the words with impressive conviction.

Asparagus. Well, at least it wasn't raw. I took my payment back to the other side of the table, where there was enough room for me to plop down and eat.

"By the way," I said, "since I'm allowed to speak now, I think you ought to buy more than one of those rings."

"What are you talking about?" Jorvun scowled at me.

"Well..." I paused to swallow a chunk of greasy vegetable. "For the rest of the party."

"And what do you mean by *the rest of the party*?"

"You weren't planning on taking over Frostvale with only little old me for backup, were you?"

"Taking over Frostvale?" Elric blurted. "You're kidding, right?"

Jorvun's eyelids flared at me in a way that said I'd crossed a line. Maybe I wasn't supposed to mention our mission. Yeah, I thought I remembered him saying something about that before. His parentage and all that—it was supposed to be a secret.

"Keep your voices down," the wizard hissed. "Both of you."

"Sorry, Boss," I whispered. "I didn't mean to reveal anything I wasn't supposed to but... you know, dragon intuition. I think you should buy all of Mister Mawkley's rings."

"Enough," Jorvun growled. "Not another word out of you."

I gave him a bow and went back to my asparagus.

"So, um, do you..." Elric eyed my boss hopefully. "...need a rogue? For whatever reason? I've got plenty of trinkets and gadgets that would be most helpful on a—"

"Just the Seed Sense." My boss scowled. "And the five glamour rings."

"Sorted..." Elric let the word hang in the air for a moment. "And you wanted some advice?"

"Right, yes," Jorvun said. "As you may have guessed, I'm planning—" He leaned closer and lowered his voice. "—on taking a trip north."

"Very exciting." Elric's eyebrows shot skyward like he was just hearing about our quest for the first time. "And yet... isn't that impossible? The wall—"

"I know about the cursed wall." The wizard checked

over one shoulder, then the other. (I could have told him there was no one eavesdropping. I mean, who would even care what these two washed-up bachelors were talking about?) "But they can't have closed all trade routes."

"Well, they have with us."

"Hold your stags," Jorvun said. "I haven't got to the part yet where I want your advice. I *know* the wall is an issue. I *know* they have closed off all trade with Valorica. But they must still be trading with Shaelun. I figure there's a sea gate somewhere up the coast."

"Jorvun..." Elric held up both hands in protest. "I don't know why you'd think I'd have any information about—"

"I wasn't finished," Jorvun snapped. "I wouldn't expect you to know anything about a sea gate. However, you do trade with the Saltborn, right?"

"Ah, that I do." Elric's posture sagged, and his bottom lip again protruded. He was clearly deflated. The advice my boss sought, it turned out, wasn't Elric's knowledge or expertise, but merely a referral. "Yes, the Covenant are regular purchasers of my Barnacle Bombs... ah, among many other things."

"I'm sure." Jorvun steepled his fingers like the cliché wizard he strives to be. "So, can I count on you for an introduction?"

"No problem. No problem at all," Elric said. "But..."

"What's in it for you?"

"Well, I wasn't going to put it that way."

"Lunch," Jorvun said. "Ideally, somewhere the Saltborn frequent."

I immediately perked up. We don't generally have people over to eat. Lunch meant a meal out, and that usually worked in my favour.

"Oh, like today?"

"Like today." The wizard nodded. "To stand up straight with your shoulders back is to accept the terrible responsibility of life."

Jorvun really does like to quote himself. Is that strange? I don't know any other humans as well as I know him, but that strikes me as strange.

"Can you pack up the stall for a couple hours? Or are you expecting a midday rush?"

"Nope, ah. Well, maybe." Elric started gathering up the merchandise spread across his table. "But no. Lunch sounds grand."

CHAPTER THREE

Make Piracy Great Again

Elric finished packing up his stall. Some of his smaller merchandise went into his trench coat pockets, but most went into a holdall backpack. To this he'd affixed an extra-large EMG emblem, which was perhaps the most preposterous of his rebranding attempts. I mean, everyone knows the holdall enchantment is exclusive to the gnomes. But whatever makes you feel better about yourself, Mawkley.

I hopped back into Jorvun's large front pocket, and we followed the inventor out of Market Square and deeper into the docks district. Eventually the boardwalk led us to the busy harbour, where salt-streaked sails flapped from listing masts, their rigging creaking like old bones. Gulls screeched overhead and circled half-loaded cargo barges. I stared at them for a time, wondering what they might taste like. We passed a pair of brawling dockhands rolling through a pile of stinking wet fish, while a nearby bard played an off-key sea shanty to absolutely no one.

A block further on, we came to a large freshly painted mural of the Keelfather, one of the two gods of the Saltborn Covenant. In this particular depiction, the Keelfather towered above a storm-lashed sea, his bare chest the colour of sharkskin and crisscrossed with rope-thick scars, his beard braided with fishhooks and drift-wood beads. In one hand he held a snapped oar like a sceptre, and in the other, he dangled a drowned man by the ankle, water pouring from the corpse's mouth.

"Here we be." Elric pointed at a sign of a fish and frog hanging above a tavern entrance next to the mural. "They call this place the—"

"Let me guess," Jorvun said. "The Fish and Frog?"

"Yes, exactly." The inventor pulled the door open and motioned for us to enter. "A favourite haunt of the Saltborn."

The Fish and Frog was dimly lit and thick with the scent of unwashed human. The floorboards were black-ened and slick from what I assumed was about a century of seawater, spilled grog, and ritual anointings that no mop had ever properly addressed. Nets and barnacle-en-crusted driftwood hung from the ceiling like chandeliers, and in the back corner, a half-rotted figurehead of a long-sunken ship presided over a candlelit shrine to Lady Brine, its mouth stuffed with clinks. Saltborn clergy and pirates clustered around a third of the rough-hewn ta-bles, and another third of the tavern's seats were taken by damp, wide-eyed travellers clutching oversized tankards and trying not to stare too long at the shrine or the tavern's regulars.

Elric directed us to an empty table in the back corner and then scurried off in search of a possible contact among the Saltborn. As we crossed the room, several of the mariner-types glared at us, or so I thought. Or it could be they just had resting glare face. Maybe that's what too much salt air does to human features. I had no idea, but it didn't strike me as the friendliest crowd.

Once Jorvun had taken a seat, I surveyed the nearby tables and the bar, trying to get a sense of what kind of food they served. There didn't seem to be any menus, which in my experience is a bad sign, and in fact almost no one was eating. The Fish and Frog was more of a liquid lunch kind of establishment. But I did spy some bowls of… nuts, maybe. At the table next to ours, a large warrior or paladin (I can never tell them apart) and a fancy-looking young woman with a lute were sharing a sad little sandwich, but I got the impression they'd brought the sandwich with them. The large man kept looking over his shoulder as if he was worried about being caught with contraband snacks.

Eventually Elric came back with a fiery-looking pirate in his wake. She was small, but she stomped over with the aggressive confidence of someone much larger. Like in the way that a cat can seem quite petite and unthreatening and even cute until you try to poach a rat from their alley, and suddenly they are as ferocious as a lion. Not that I've ever met a lion. But you get the idea. She was smartly dressed, certainly more so than most of the other patrons in attendance, in a pristine pearl-covered tunic with gold embroidery. Straight black hair given a lift of body through what was no doubt a diligent grooming routine. And on each hip she wore a bulky scabbard. No, wait—I think the word is *holster*. Jorvun once told me about pirates who carry iron weapons that contain explosive powder and shoot projectiles at their enemy.

The pirate took a seat directly across from my boss, and wow, did she look unhappy to see him. I wasn't sure if they knew each other or if something else was going on, so I hopped out of his pocket, scuttled across the table, and took up a perch on the seatback next to Jorvun. I wanted to be clear of whatever animosity there might be between them. Elric sat across from me.

"Um, ah," the inventor began. "Jorvun, I'd like to introduce Lark Bombast. Lark, this is Jorvun Prattlethorn. He asked for an introduction to a Covenant representative because—"

"And what makes you think—" It was really impressive how much venom she was able to inject into each word. "—any of us wants to consort with an ungodly academic like yourself?"

"Because," Jorvun began, "the enemy of my enemy is my friend." It seemed a pretty condescending way to begin, at least in terms of his tone, but my boss could talk circles around people. "Ever since King Dummkopf threatened to annex Frostvale and they raised their barrier wall in response, all trade has ceased. On top of that, the Saltborn haven't been able to harry Shaelun shipments in years since they started coming across in armadas. And you can't target Valorican vessels or the king will label you as domestic terrorists. Seems to me you're in a pretty situation."

"Pardon my French, but you can fuck right off," she spat. "Do you make it a habit of telling people what they already know?"

"Just acknowledging the context," Jorvun went on. "Look, why don't we begin with some goodwill. Get off on the right foot. Can I buy you a drink? I promised Elric here some lunch, though—" He glanced around the bar. "—I'm not sure this is the most gastronomically appropriate venue to honour our introduction."

My thoughts exactly.

"Brine and blood." She shook her head with eyes wide and unbelieving, her lips in a sneer. "You're a lot. Do you know that? I have no desire to share a drink with you, let alone a meal. The only reason I'm sitting here is because Elric does some occasional business for me. So you better get where you're going, and quick."

"Fine. Fine." Jorvun spread his long fingers across the table between them, then broke eye contact with Lark to glance at Elric. "I'm... um... I have a secret mission."

At this, the warrior-paladin-type at the adjacent table turned to look at us. And in that moment, an idea occurred to me: a strong warrior-paladin-type and a bard-type? Brawn could certainly be helpful in a party. And brains or... What is it that bards offer? I couldn't remember. Resourcefulness, maybe? Hmm.

Without drawing too much attention to myself, I gave the adjacent table a little wave. Jorvun didn't seem to notice—there was too much tension between wizard and pirate for anyone to pay me much notice. Elric cocked his head, just slightly. And Lark's sneer deepened.

"I received word," Jorvun continued, "that Trudera, the Frostvalen king, has been weakened. There is talk of succession. If there was a time to topple their government for the good of Valorica, it is now."

"And you think you're going to do the toppling?" Lark barked a laugh. "You and what army?"

"That's exactly the point. No army. Just me. A lone magical assassin. Like you said, I'm an academic, and the nobility love academics."

"Wow," Elric said. "Just wow."

Two things here: First of all, *topple their government* struck me a bit different than *take over by announcing his royal lineage*. Semantics, maybe. But *for the good of Valorica* was a stretch. What we were after had nothing to do with Valorica. Something about his choice of words made me think my boss was fudging the truth about our quest, possibly to get this pirate lady to do something for him. Second, it seemed Jorvun really was planning on a solo mission. A terrible idea. He might know some great spells, but he's only as good as his last night's sleep. And life on the road wasn't likely to be restful, especially if we had battles and negotiations ahead of us—or even just a lot of walking.

"And how in the name of Lady Brine do you expect me to help?" Lark narrowed her eyes slightly, but not in a suspicious way. And not with the same loathing she had brought to the table. Plus something had changed in her voice. Like she had softened somewhat, and was a tiny bit more interested in hearing what my boss had to say.

"That's where I was hoping to appeal to your expertise." Jorvun bowed his head and flipped his hands over, palms up, fingers still outstretched. "I assume there is a sea gate of some kind so the North can admit the Shaelun trade armadas. I'm looking for a collaborator who can get me there."

Get me there? Sorry, Boss, no. That wasn't good enough. His reign was at stake, which meant my college enrollment was too, and no chance I was going to let my dreams die because of Jorvun's misplaced confidence and ego. So this was where I decided to chime in.

"And come with us!" I shouted with as much enthusiasm as I could muster. Before the wizard could interrupt, I added, "Because we could really use a brilliant woman like you in the party."

"Glimm, please." Jorvun waved me back. "She clearly wants to spend as little time with us as possible. And we don't need help. This is a solo mission. Stealth and fireballs."

Lark didn't respond right away. She stared, unblinking, while something burned behind her eyes. But was it the wizard's spin on our quest that was having this effect on her? Or was it my suggestion? I really hoped it was my suggestion. She seemed very tough. In my estimation, someone you wouldn't want to mess with is exactly who you want in your party.

But just as the pirate opened her mouth to say something, Elric cut in.

"What do you mean by succession?" the inventor asked, as if the conversation hadn't already moved on from that topic.

Jorvun frowned at him like he was confused by Elric's confusion. Since I was feeling particularly helpful, I decided that this was another good opportunity to offer my assistance.

"There's going to be a new king," I said. "Trudera is stepping down, and he doesn't have a known heir, but that's only because he doesn't know—"

"Glimm," Jorvun shouted with unmasked anger.

The rest of my sentence dried up in my throat, and I almost fell off the chairback.

Then he added, with a bit more restraint, "If I wanted your input, I would ask for it."

"So sorry, Boss." I shrank lower and mimed buttoning my mouth shut. Frosted fishguts, if I wasn't stupid sometimes. I had definitely gone too far. My job was simple: don't make the wizard angry. And what had I done?

"Hmmm." Lark raised an eyebrow at me as if she was taking note of my indiscretion, or let's call it a near indiscretion, and for a terrifying second I thought she would ask what I'd been going to say, but she evidently shelved the question and turned her attention back to Jorvun. "I have to admit, wizard, that I like the prospect of this assassination. I doubt you have what it takes to pull it off, but you're right about the Covenant's predicament. No piracy means no sacrifices for our Lord and Lady. These are trying times indeed. So trying, in fact, that I could, perhaps, be persuaded to help a blasphemer like yourself. For a price, of course."

"I can pay," Jorvun said quietly.

"But what exactly are you proposing?" she asked. "That I sail you to the sea gate, drop you off, and you tread water until an armada comes along? And then swim to shore?"

"I would purchase a small vessel, perhaps a rowboat or a dinghy with a simple sail. If it's not too large, I have a spell I can use to shield myself from view."

"Intriguing," Lark said. It seemed she had actually come around and was now properly considering this plan. "I think the dinghy would be a better option. The barrier comes out around the Saturna Keys, so a rowboat would be a backbreaking endeavor."

"I'm in," Elric blurted.

Brilliant! I wasn't sure if I'd gotten through to the pirate, but Elric could be useful in a pinch.

"Excuse me?" Jorvun sat back in his seat.

Lark also swung on the inventor with a look of surprise. I suppose I did too, but I was a bit distracted since I'd noticed again that the warrior-paladin-type at the next table was listening to our conversation. Actually, now his bard-type friend was too. I waved at them again, then mimed marching and sword fighting.

"This is exactly what I need," Elric said. "I mean, what would my kids think if they knew their dad was on a mission like that, fighting for the glory and honour of Valorica? And think of the money!" He hesitated and held up a hand since it was quite apparent that my boss was about to cut in. "I don't mean your money, Jorvun. Of course not. But Dummkopf is sure to reward us—"

"This is a solo mission," Jorvun said with finality. "One assassin will be better able to slip in without raising alarm, and besides—"

"What if you get caught on day one?" Elric barreled onward. "You'll have no one there to help you. And I can be extremely helpful. Or at least, my gadgets and trinkets can. I'm not necessarily good in a fight, but I can pick a lock. And I can be pretty sneaky."

I wasn't going to take additional risks with my lunch by agreeing with Elric, so instead I nodded emphatically and gave him two claws up.

"This is ridiculous," Jorvun said. "Elric, please."

"I think he's right," Lark said with a sly smile—a reasonable smile in which her lips stayed appropriately tight over her teeth. "What you're proposing is an important quest, if you can pull it off, and you're more likely to succeed with a solid team at your back. You're right that this is no mission for an army. Stealth and guile over brute force."

"And what..." My boss shook his head as he looked

back and forth between the inventor and the pirate. This so-called lunch, still sorely devoid of food, wasn't going in a direction either of us had expected. "Are you suggesting that you want to join me as well?"

"Yes," Lark said, "as a matter of fact, but keep your heretic voice down. Look, I don't want to work with an academic, not if I don't have to. But what you said earlier is true. We haven't had a good sacrifice since that cursed wall went up. Our coffers are running dry too. My Lord and Lady come before everything else, even my reservations about consorting with blasphemers. If I can help you overthrow the Frostvalen king, then I can see their worship restored."

Absolutely perfect. I kept nodding and putting out the best *gathering the team* vibes that I could muster.

"Crust on a cracker," Jorvun said.

Just then the bartender, a lanky woman with sea-glass earrings and a nose like a ship's prow, walked up to our table. "Are y'all going to sit there talking and taking up space all afternoon without ordering anything?" And then she noticed Lark among us and added, "Sorry, Bombast. Didn't see you there."

"Please," Jorvun said, "let's have a round of... whatever's your strongest."

"Coming right up."

While the bartender had the wizard's attention, I again took the opportunity to motion at the adjacent table.

Jorvun waited until the bartender was back behind the bar before he continued. "Okay, let's say for a second that I'm entertaining this idea," he grumbled. "A small party rather than a lone assassin. I'll admit that some gadgets and pistols might come in handy, but my concern is—"

There was a thump and shuffle from the table next to us, and a moment later the warrior-paladin-type and the bard-type were looming over us. Amazing! It worked! Jorvun stopped mid-sentence.

"Sounds like a fantastic mission," the bard-type said.

"Really honourable," the warrior-paladin-type said.

"I'm Fox Tattleby." The woman in the scarlet doublet bowed low and then thrust a thumb at her friend. "And this is Xander Bonesmith. I'm a bard. He's a paladin."

Bard. Paladin. See? I'm pretty astute.

"Order of the Holy Dose," the paladin clarified.

"What in nine hells is actually going on right now?" Jorvun moaned.

"Looks like you've got a party coming together." Lark grinned, and with teeth this time—ugh.

"Something about this," Elric said, "feels like fate. Doesn't it?"

At this point the bartender came back with three tankards full of a light green liquid topped with dark green bits. Seaweed, maybe? She glanced at the newcomers to our table and asked if we needed anything else.

"Yes," Lark said. "Two more of those. On the wizard's tab."

Jorvun moaned again and slid his chair a few inches backward. For a moment I thought he might turn and run right out of the tavern.

"Does anyone even know these two?" he asked a moment later.

"We're new in town," the paladin said. "Looking for work, actually."

"We have references," the bard added.

"References." Jorvun shook his head, and not one little twitch but a slow shaking, back and forth, back and forth, like he was wrestling with his own thoughts as much as the intentions that had just been heaped upon him.

Whenever possible, I try to be a helpful familiar. And clearly my boss was struggling. When someone is struggling, it's important to help them, right? Sure, I was supposed to keep quiet, and my lunch—maybe even dinner—was already in jeopardy. But what am I here for if not to offer what little assistance I can muster? Fate—yes indeed, Elric. I couldn't have said it better myself. Something about this scenario felt like an eventuality more than a possibility. And maybe, in some small way, I would help make it possible.

"Boss," I started. And despite the death glare he shot at me, I was undeterred. "It does occur to me that there are now five of you, and earlier, at the market, you did buy five of those rings."

"You need to keep your scaly little mouth shut," Jorvun hissed, but there was no fury behind his words.

He knew I was right. I knew I was right. The party was formed. We were going to Frostvale to *topple* the government and put my boss on the throne, even if that last part was a secret.

But why was it a secret? I'd have to ask him at some point.

CHAPTER FOUR

Death, Lies, and Supplements

Jorvun didn't immediately give in, but as the tankards of green booze went down, conversation between the five adventurers flowed more freely, and soon they were all offering hypotheticals about the dangers they might face in the North and the strategies they would employ to overcome them. Lark ordered another round, again on the wizard's tab, but he didn't protest. His improved mood was a promising sign that he had forgotten my interference.

With the second round polished off, we departed the Fish and Frog for a more appropriate luncheon locale. I'd never known my boss to be particularly generous, but I supposed some drinks and food and any other expenses necessary to make the mission possible were an invest-ment in his would-be rule of Frostvale. So maybe it doesn't count as generosity after all. Jorvun still hadn't mentioned the real reason for the trip. That seemed like a mistake from where I was sitting—perched upon his re-inforced leather shoulder. Sooner or later, the truth would have to come out. Right?

Lark led us to a wharfside eatery with a nice view of Cascade Bay, with many more than ten boats of all sizes coming and going. The sun had made an appearance, and the day was warming up pleasantly. As a creature of the North, I prefer ice and snow, of course, but warm and dry is definitely preferable to rain. We grabbed a table for six at the edge of a busy patio—I leapt off Jorvun's shoulder and took the empty chair next to Elric. The others might be willing to give me a bit of their lunch, but the inventor had already proven himself a reliable source. Speaking of which, a quick glance at the other patrons told me this place served fish and chips. Fantastic. I mean, chips if I must, but battered and deep-fried fish? Any day of the week.

By the time everyone ordered, I'd decided that I needed one last bit of reassurance about this party, and that my boss was in fact going to allow them all to join us. My college education was at stake, after all.

"So, Xander," I said. "I notice you are unarmed. You do have a fancy paladin sword or something that you would be bringing on this adventure?"

Jorvun shot me a look to let me know I was interfering again, but he didn't say anything, which meant he didn't entirely disapprove. As cute as I am, even I needed to pass a job interview to land in the wizard's employ.

"Not a sword, no," Xander said. "My beloved Truth Hammer is an oversized mace. And is she ever a beauty. Somewhat bulky to carry around town though, and besides, she tends to bring unwanted attention from the local constabulary."

"Very exciting," I said. "And what about you, Fox? I have the general impression that bards are resourceful, but how do you fare in a fight?"

"Resourceful is an understatement." The bard stood, spread her arms wide, and slowly looked around the table at each of us. "Many of you might not know this, but we study all martial traditions in the school of bardic hermeneutics—even the arcane arts."

Hermeneutics? I wasn't sure what that meant, but it certainly sounded fascinating and deadly. I thought a follow-up question was in order, but apparently I'd done enough to light the interview fires. Jorvun was ready to take over.

"Clever little pet, isn't he?" Jorvun gave an awkward laugh.

Yes indeed, it was time for me to fade into the background. That awkwardness told me I'd bruised his ego a bit, which isn't what I'd set out to do. Managing the wizard's fragility is also a part of my job, and usually I'm pretty good at it, but there was a lot on the line. Anyway, it was seeming, at least, like I'd helped him over the hump of considering a party for this adventure to considering *this* party. Mission accomplished? I certainly hoped so.

"I have to assume, based on your accents, that you two are from the Midwest," the wizard said. "So what brings you to Ravenna?"

"Journalism," Fox answered without hesitation, then sat back down.

Xander took a moment longer to consider his response, then said, "Eggs, mostly."

"Eggs?" Lark asked.

"Order of the Holy Dose," Xander said. "We're not

just an order. We're also a network of entrepreneurs, and I'm in charge of the whole operation. It's an ingenious structure—a portion of the sales from each recruit goes to the person who recruited them, and a portion of that commission goes to the person who recruited *them*, and so on, up six levels. Which means I'm invested in everyone's success, and everyone is quite evangelical about the business. In fact, if any of you wanted to get on board, I'd be happy to—"

"Eggs," Jorvun reminded him.

"Oh, right." The barrel-chested paladin tapped a crest in the centre of his hauberk. Until this point, I hadn't looked that closely at it, but it seemed to portray a flexed arm holding a chicken egg. "The Order of the Holy Dose sells supplements and potions for a variety of ailments and battlefield necessities. And it's all triple tested. Everything from Alpha Power to Sleepy Time Edibles to Divine Fiber Blend. I've got plenty of samples back at our—"

Just then two medium-sized children came running from the kitchen with plates of steaming fish. You'll have to forgive me as I'm terrible at guessing the ages of human offspring. But these were at least old enough to balance a tray of food. Conversation paused as they handed out the fare—and did it ever smell delightful.

Honestly, this paladin can take his sweet time getting to the point. I hoped he wouldn't be like that in battle. With food so near at hand, I decided to be helpful.

"Eggs," I repeated for my boss.

"Yes, yes." Xander stuffed a few chips in his mouth, which he seemed to swallow without chewing. "Eggs are the base of all our products. As you know, ever since the barrier wall went up, the entire country is facing a shortage. And then there's the ongoing wave of hen pox.

Definitely not helping anything. But the bigger problem is that we used to import half of our eggs from the North. It was bad enough when Dummkopf put tariffs on everything, but now we can't afford to make most of our supplement line. The profit margin is too narrow. We're essentially out of business. So when we heard you talking about Frostvale—well, let me tell you."

"So it's a pyramid?" Elric asked.

"Sorry, what?" Jorvun swung back to the inventor.

"His business structure," he said. "I'm an entrepreneur myself, and I think it's just fascinating. What a scheme! It really sells itself."

"Oh, sure," Xander said. "I hadn't pictured it like that, but I suppose you're right. And here's the real irony— we've even developed a cure for hen pox, but we can't get it out to the poor birds who need it. Honestly, if—"

"What about you, Fox?" Jorvun cut in. "Are you part of this sales pyramid?"

"Oh no." Fox Tattleby set down the lump of fish she'd been nibbling and wiped her hands on her pants. "I used to be in sales, and I was fantastic at it, but ultimately it just wasn't my jam. Didn't speak to my heart. One day I had to admit that I'm a storyteller, no way around it. And that led me to journalism. Freelancer at present, but I've been offered a network deal."

When she said this, Xander's face flashed with a curious expression. Almost an eye roll, but subtle, like he'd started to roll his eyes but then checked himself.

"So why are you looking for work?" Jorvun asked.

"Oh, I mean, it's a longshot offer, and it's not with MaxNews. That's my dream placement."

"Then I suppose," the wizard pressed on, "you will want to chronicle our mission."

"Absolutely." Fox picked up her lute and struck a

dramatic chord. "This is the story of a lifetime, assuming we survive."

"Yes." Jorvun nodded slowly as he prodded at a piece of fish with one of his chips. "If we survive..."

By this point I struggled to follow much of the conversation. The sight and smell of food all around me was just too much. I sidled over to Elric until I was right at the edge of my chair, trying to get his attention. He wasn't picking up my cue at all. I considered hopping up onto the table and maybe even planting myself in front of his plate, but I didn't think my boss would appreciate that. He doesn't mind me getting an occasional treat, and by occasional I mean nothing more than one snack per day outside my regularly scheduled meals. Maybe he thinks that I'll be a better employee if I'm hungry all the time.

No, I had to be subtle, so instead I resorted to poking Elric and miming, which means I sprawled across my chair, made a face like I was dying, and then pointed at my mouth. The inventor got the message. Greasy batter and whitefish! I was surrounded by brave adventurers, it seemed, all willing to risk their lives for our chance to visit my homeland, but Elric was the true hero of my afternoon.

Once my boss was apparently satisfied with his party, he called an end to our little get-together. Blessed be the blizzards of the North! We would all head off to do what needed doing in preparation for a long voyage, which meant packing bags, saying farewells, and registering a last will and testament with the Ministry of Inheritance. Everyone agreed to meet outside the big marina at the end of Aurora Street at dawn, which I thought was pretty auspicious, but no one else seemed to notice the connection.

WE'VE COME FOR YOUR EGGS

Since Jorvun had packed the night before, all that was left for him to do was arrange a couple wagons to take the larger portion of his furniture and belongings to a storage yard in the Seward District. That left one large chest of clothing (shirts, ties, slacks, wizardly robes, and a variety of footwear for different occasions), a medium-sized chest of spellbooks, a small chest of potions and alchemical supplies, and a duffle bag full of tins of food for yours truly. He tucked away some emergency essentials in the smaller pockets of his oilskin, including a few wands, scrolls, and his bank card.

I got to enjoy a final dinner at my favourite window, watching the sun set on our cozy tower while imagining that my can of bison curds and gravy was from the spoils of a fresh kill, and then we said goodbye to all that was familiar. Another wagon transported us along with Jorvun's luggage to the Shadowland Inn, right across the street from the Aurora Marina.

What a day!

And as I curled up at the foot of a plush king-size bed, awaiting pleasant dreams of the frosty North and entirely under the assumption that my earlier indiscretion had been forgotten, my boss nudged me with his foot.

"Glimm—" By the way he said my name, I knew it was serious. "—you just about ruined everything for me today. Do you realize that?"

"Oh..." I feigned a yawn and did my best to adopt a convincingly innocent expression. "How?"

"I've told you before—it's a secret that Trudera is my father. No one can find out about this, do you understand?"

"Sure, I remember. But—"

"No buts. None of these people would have joined us if they knew the mission was for me to take my proper place as King of the North. To them, Frostvale is the enemy."

"The enemy? But that's impossible! Frostvale and Valorica are allies, aren't they?"

"Not anymore. It doesn't take much to change the sentiment between two nations," the wizard explained. "That's why we have to pretend we are going there *on behalf* of Valorica."

"So we have to lie?" Let's get this straight. Lying is something that humans do all the time, but it seems pretty inappropriate to me. And I wasn't sure lying was covered in my contract.

"Yes, for my safety," he said. "And for the good of the North."

"Okay, okay." It still didn't feel right to me, but this was the guy who fed me, after all. I needed him if I was ever going to get into dragon college, and so it made sense that the North needed him too. I held up my right paw like how I'd seen humans hold up their hand to make a promise. "I won't say anything about your father. From now on, I will pretend that our goal is to help Valorica... um, what's the word again?"

"Annex."

"Right. I will pretend our goal is to help Valorica annex Frostvale."

"That's great, Glimm." Jorvun blinked at me affectionately—much preferable to a smile—and snuggled beneath the downy blankets. "If you fulfill your obligations every day, you don't need to worry about the future."

He was quoting himself again, but I was fine with it, even if his lofty pronouncements didn't completely make sense. My stomach was mostly full, the blanket and mattress beneath me were as soft as a cloud, the room was warm and dry, and tomorrow our great adventure would begin.

CHAPTER FIVE

Don't Worry About the Future

Imagine this: a plush king-sized bed with satiny sheets (not actual satin, of course—we were across the street from the docks) and down blankets and pillows, a room that was not too warm or too cold, a light rain tapping on the window, not a sound in the streets all night, and... my boss couldn't sleep. Unbelievable. And of course, when he can't sleep, I don't get to either—not because of a psychic or even empathic link, but because he has to tell me over and over again throughout the night that he's restless, that he can't quiet his brain, that he can't drift off. Do I really need to know? In what world does waking up your familiar with insomnia complaints in any way help the insomnia?

There was actually a brief stretch in which he did drift off. Maybe an hour or two. And I knew he was sleeping because he was dream-whimpering. A fairly common experience. In addition to the whimpering, he was also muttering, "Daddy... Daddy, I'm right over here." Once upon a time, I found his abandonment issues to be endearing, if sad. A human might call this *humanizing,* but from my perspective, that term doesn't cut it. Anyway, after a night of much-interrupted sleep, it was downright annoying.

When predawn finally arrived, he was a wreck, and I was in a foul mood, let me tell you. Of all the nights to fail at his beauty rest! He was almost certainly going to need magic today, and chances were now pretty damn good that the wizard was going to be a strugglecart. Over breakfast (which thankfully was on time and a decent portion of skitterling roast), I asked him why he hadn't taken a sleeping draught. Jorvun looked at me blankly and then said he hadn't thought of it until it was too late and that it would have jeopardized his morning. Hmm. Honestly, the morning, afternoon, and evening were in jeopardy, and there was no way I would have let him sleep in.

Okay, okay. Time for me to let it go. We had a grand adventure ahead of us, and my education was on the line. If Jorvun's reliability was now in question, I would have to be as sharp as my teeth.

When we got to the fog-shrouded marina, Lark was already waiting for us. She was dressed the same as yesterday—tunic decorated in gold and pearls, black weatherworn boots, twin holsters—and she was travelling light, with just a canvas bag over one shoulder and a small duffle bag that clinked when she set it down.

"Good morning," she said without much enthusiasm as she eyed the porter crossing the street behind us with a dolly loaded with Jorvun's luggage. "How do you intend on carrying all that once we're in Frostvale?"

"I plan on hiring a cart," Jorvun said through a yawn.

"It's not really giving *stealth assassin*, if you know what I mean."

"That's not the plan anymore, is it," the wizard snapped. "We're rocking up with a small army."

The porter, a slight young elf, parked the dolly next to a small loading crane, gave my boss a glance that seemed to assess whether Jorvun was the type to tip, apparently decided not, and headed back across the street.

"Sure." The pirate shook her head as she pulled the canvas bag off her shoulder. "Anyway, I have a favour to ask. To ensure you are, um, treated with the respect you deserve aboard my ship, I think it's best if you look a bit less academic."

"What are you talking about?" Jorvun pulled his oil-skin tighter around him and did up the top bronze clasp to conceal his collared shirt and tie. "It's not like I'm wearing one of my robes."

"You might as well be," Lark said. "That hood screams wizard, not to mention those narrow side pockets that can only be meant to contain wands. And I'm pretty sure those are sigils engraved into your buttons. Oh, and you have a familiar, which definitely tips the scales."

"Excuse me?" I blurted. "You want to do what to my scales?"

"It's an expression, Glimm," my boss said under his breath.

I flapped off Jorvun's shoulder to land on the nearby loading crane. A gull and three sparrows perched atop a storage shed behind Lark. I gave them my best I've-al-ready-eaten wave, but they still looked nervous. Well, not the gull.

"Here." Lark held out the canvas bag. "I brought you some deckhand leathers and a saltcloak. I really think you ought to—"

"And where am I supposed to get changed?" The wizard looked back at the inn across the street. "I've already checked out, and I don't think the housekeeping staff would appreciate—"

"Just change right here," she said. "There's literally no one around."

However, that wasn't entirely true. Just as Lark said this, Fox and Xander came around the corner with a loaded pushcart.

When Jorvun was packing the night before, I hadn't really considered his choices, nor how difficult a lot of luggage might be to deal with once we got to Frostvale. I'd never been on an adventure like this, nor on a boat, so I didn't have a point of reference. But what Lark had said made sense—as did her one duffle bag. Yet here was the brawn and bard duo, and they seemed to have brought everything they owned in the world: six large chests, a massive cauldron, two collapsible deck chairs, a beach umbrella, and three instrument cases (judging by the shape, containing a harp, a saxophone, and the lute we had seen yesterday). Atop the pile was a massive black maul and robust leather harness. Wow.

"What the hell, guys?" Lark's mouth hung open wide enough for a pigeon to fly down her throat.

"Oh no" was all Jorvun could manage.

"Good morning, fellow adventurers," Xander bellowed.

"Can't wait to get started," Fox added with a hideously toothful grin.

"This…" Jorvun motioned vaguely at their mountain of equipment. "What is all this?"

"My supplement inventory, mostly." Xander nodded enthusiastically. "I'm going to have you all in tiptop shape. I've got protein shakes and creatine snacks to buff us up, Sleepy Time Edibles for the insomniacs, Divine Fiber Blend to keep us all regular, and my newest formulation, triple tested, is Alpha Power, for whenever we need to charge into battle without any hesitation. And those are just my top sellers. Plenty more I'm excited to tell you all about. Oh and of course I brought my apothecary gear for replenishing the supply. So that includes my drying rack, my—"

"Edibles for insomniacs?" I muttered. "Could come in handy for sure."

"Oh, there you are." Fox waved up at me. "Hi, Glimm."

"Okay, stop." Jorvun paused and closed his eyes for a moment. "I get it. I get it. But the thing is—"

"It's too godsdamn much," Lark said.

"What do you mean?" Xander looked at Fox as if for moral support, but the bard just shrugged.

"We're going to be sailing on a dinghy," I chimed in. "And I'm pretty sure *dinghy* means *very small boat*."

"Exactly," my boss said.

"You've got a lot of stuff too." Fox pointed at the pile of chests behind us.

"She has a point," Lark said.

"Good morning, team," Elric shouted from behind them.

Given the luggage predicament, I was at first

impressed that he was carrying only his holdall backpack over one shoulder. But a moment later, a teetering cart came into view, along with four children who pushed and pulled it along.

"We're fucked," Lark said, then added, "if y'all will excuse my French."

The rest of us stared in a tableau of curiosity and confusion as Elric directed the children by name—one girl and three boys, from quarter-human size up to half-grown, or thereabouts—to unload his two cherrywood trunks, six monogrammed leather valises, enchanted espresso machine, self-heating footbath, foldable jukebox, cocktail kit with crystal tumblers, fey-powered travel fridge, and wind-up grappling hook launcher.

"Cool hook launcher." Xander whistled to emphasize his enthusiasm.

When the children finished their task, Elric said, "I'd like to introduce you to a few of my kids. This is Wren Two, Tob, Bram Three, and Jax. Say hello, kids."

The kids did not say hello.

"Okay, well. Thanks for getting up so early to see your Pops off on his big adventure." The inventor knelt down and held his arms wide. "Hugs?"

Wren Two stepped forward with a palm extended.

"Right, right." Elric dug into his pocket. "Now what did I promise you again? Three clinks apiece?"

Wren Two scowled. Tob shook his head in dismay.

"You definitely promised us five," said Jax.

"Of course I did. Here you go." Elric dropped some coins into each child's hand, then got back into hug position.

They did not indulge him. The children pocketed their money, took up their positions again around the now-empty cart, and set off into the morning streets.

Jorvun watched this interaction with a quiet intensity and, it seemed, a certain glistening in his eyes.

"Little rascals!" The inventor tried to laugh off the slight as he stood and faced us. "But this here mission and what we're about to accomplish—wow. They are sure going to be proud of their Pops when they find out."

"And yet—" Lark shook her head at all the trunks and luggage spread across the marina entrance. "—with how y'all unbelievers have packed, our mission is dead in the water."

"I have a deity." Xander reached for the sky in a strange flexed pose. "My Lady Panacea."

"Sorry, Xander," she said. "But you still packed like an idiot. And wearing full armour? At sea? You're definitely going to take that off before we depart. Have none of you been on a boat before?"

"I've been on hundreds of boats," Fox said. "Back when I was in the Merchant Marines, I used to—"

"Lark's right." Jorvun made a slow circuit around each pile while he thoughtfully stroked at his shaved chin. "But you're going to pay a price for every bloody thing you do and everything you don't do."

What did that even mean? Another vague tagline meant to sound philosophical. I supposed he was trying to dig his ego out after realizing that he'd fallen into the same idiotic trench. Like: I may have made bad choices, but I'm not going to take them back, and I'll try to reinforce my pompous sense of superior intelligence in the process. Okay, wow. I was definitely still grouchy from lack of sleep.

"Thanks for acknowledging that I'm right," Lark said. "But what are we going to do about it? The original plan has sunk. We'd be hard-pressed to get even one of y'all's loads onto a sailing dinghy, at least one that can be stowed on my deck. And even then, my winches couldn't handle a dinghy loaded with all this stuff, and we couldn't transfer it all out in the chop. Do you see the problem?"

Xander frowned a bit and blinked gravely. Elric bit his lip while assessing his pile. Fox shrugged like this was a scenario she had already met and conquered in the Merchant Marines. Jorvun nodded with all his sage wisdom, but I could tell he was at a loss.

"I guess you'll have to leave a bunch of this stuff behind," I said.

"Easy for you to say, little buddy." Elric took up position in front of his pile with arms crossed. "I need all this stuff. Not just for me, but for the mission. And I plan on being instrumental."

"Speaking of instruments," Fox chimed in, "you can't expect a bard to travel without the tools of inspiration."

"The Frostvalenites are out to get us," Xander said. "This isn't a game. We're going to need every last drop of supplemental power that I'm packing."

No one said anything for a while. My boss took a long look at his own pile of so-called essentials. A bell tolled somewhere out in the bay.

"Okay, new plan," Jorvun said. "I also need all my stuff for this mission. Even if everyone else packed light, the dinghy plan still isn't going to work. So instead, we don't catch a ride aboard Lark's ship. I'll just buy us a large dinghy, or a small sailboat, or whatever will accommodate our numbers and equipment." He glanced back at Lark. "Would that fly?"

"And I don't need to explain to my crew why I've brought an academic aboard?" Lark hooted and slapped her thigh. "Sounds fantastic. I'll go let them know right now. And in fact, I'm so in favour of this idea, I think I can swing you a deal with the purchase." She paused for a moment to raise an eyebrow at my boss. "You do realize this is going to be costly."

"I'm putting my life savings into this mission," Jorvun said. "And besides, I'll be able to sell the boat once we arrive."

"But then how will we get back?" Xander asked.

"Don't worry about that," the wizard said. "When we're done with Frostvale, the barrier wall will be a distant memory. We just need to get to Fangcover City, do the job, and then we can come back overland to Ravenna."

"But wait a minute," I was forced to cut in, and despite Jorvun's scowl, I proceeded. "You originally made it sound like your spell, to hide the boat or whatever, like when the Shaelun armada arrives, requires a small vessel. Are you going to be able to cloak a bigger sailboat and all of this stuff?"

"Of course, Glimm." My boss puffed up his chest and tilted his chin skyward. "Like I always say, work as hard as you possibly can on at least one thing and see what happens."

"See what happens?" I shot back.

"I am a master wizard, and I have all the resources I need." He stifled a yawn, then continued. "I appreciate your concern, but if you'd like a nice dinner tonight, I suggest you stop second-guessing my abilities."

Not all that reassuring, to be honest, but what do I know. I'm just a familiar. And sure, he's a master wizard. There was a lot riding on this gambit, but I supposed I had to trust him.

"That's settled then," Lark said. "Hang tight. We'll be off before the sun breaks the Stormbarrow. And no time to lose. We should reach the sea gate before four o'clock to make sure we're well ahead of the Shaelun."

"And they arrive daily?" Jorvun asked.

"Most days," Lark said. "Actually, even more regularly now since trade with Valorica has dried up."

"Perfect." The wizard bowed to the pirate—quite a gesture, if you ask me. "Then let's not delay."

"This is already shaping up to be an epic story." Fox pulled a small leather-bound scriptlet from inside her scarlet doublet and jotted a couple notes.

We lost a couple hours to the procurement process, during which time I hunted pigeons and sparrows and rats all around the docks. Unsuccessfully, but at least it gave me a way to pass the time that kept my mind off the mission's first failure. On one paw, I worried that the team's lack of foresight in planning could be the first note in a theme of incompetence. On the other paw, I was pleased that my boss was able to arrive at an accommodating compromise—and without losing his cool. I supposed he was adopting some regal airs and an overall diplomatic vibe, which of course he would need as King of the North.

Jorvun ended up purchasing a stormleaf cutter: the *Brine Whisperer*. She was a seaworthy if unglamorous coastal sailboat built for fishing runs and smuggling hauls. She had a single mast with a well-worn mainsail and a staysail that had been hastily patched in a few places with mismatched fabric. Good enough for our purposes? Lark seemed to think so. The hull was pine and ironwood, stained salt-grey and crusted with barnacles below the waterline. A weathered cuddy cabin offered just enough shelter for two to sleep shoulder to shoulder, which was fine since we wouldn't be sleeping aboard. The deck was cluttered with cleats, crunchy old rope, and frayed fishing net, which the party used to tie down all the gear.

Lark got us underway without much effort. No one else knew what was what—not even Fox, who had supposedly been a Merchant Marine. But *pull that rope* and *tie this line to that cleat* were about the extent of her instructions. Xander was the most eager of her assistants, and he almost looked like a proper sailor now that he'd changed out of his armour into a simple combo of leather and linen. Yet I was pretty sure Lark could have sailed the cutter without any help. I took up position at the top of the mast, which gave me a fantastic view of Cascade Bay, with fog simmering off the water as the sun pushed through the grey haze of morning. All around us were gulls and ducks and cormorants, though they kept their distance when they spotted me on my perch, and myriad boats speckled the inlet, setting off on voyages of their own or just rowing out to cast a hopeful net.

The farther north we sailed, the more rugged and wild the world became. Ravenna was all I had ever known. I mean, I'd been hatched in Seaport, which is a day's travel by horse cart to the south, and that's where Jorvun first hired me, but my memories of that time are dim. So this was my first real taste of the outside world, and it was wonderful. The forested islands of Tideglass Sound gave way to open water and broader channels, where the wind bit sharper and the sea grew more ambitious. Low clouds dragged across the Stormbarrow Mountains to either side—jagged snow-capped spines to the west, rolling tree-clad peaks to the east. On and on we sailed, until out past the last scattered isles, the channel widened again into the open strait, the Maelreach, and the colour of the sea darkened with it. And ahead of us, growing ever closer, was the shimmering barrier wall that concealed the land of my birth.

Once we entered the Maelreach, we had to sail east and then northeast, for the wall extended out and around a number of Frostvalen islands. The biggest, which we ran alongside for most of the day, is called Fangcover Island. This is a strange name for the island, or so Jorvun once explained, because the massive port city known as Fangcover isn't actually on the island—it's back on the mainland. And it was to the City of Fangcover that we were headed.

For most of the day we skirted the barrier wall. It was a dazzling array of colours that swirled and danced and fuzzed. It also thrummed with magic, deep inside my bones, in a way that was as beautiful as the dazzling colours. So much power! I'd never felt an arcane current like this before. Not even close. Lark kept the *Brine Whisperer* a good distance from the edge, just in case, but from my perch, I could see that Jorvun was right about the barrier descending down below the surface. I couldn't confirm that it was a giant egg, not unless I wanted to exhaust myself in flight. And actually, I wasn't sure I could fly that high. The barrier was taller than a mountain.

Fangcover Island was visible through the wall. Not super clearly, but I could make out a rocky shoreline, trees, and rolling hills. I have to admit, I was a bit surprised that it wasn't covered in snow. That's the image I'd always had in mind when I thought of Frostvale, but I supposed we weren't that far away from Ravenna. I'd pictured people running around with woolly winter hats and mittens on, and everywhere little dragons like me luxuriating on snowy rooftops and munching on icicles. But I had read somewhere that Frostvale was an even larger nation than Valorica, so it stood to reason that there was a range of terrains and climates. Still, I was a bit disappointed. When would I get to experience true cold?

As we rounded the westernmost tip of Fangcover Island and followed the barrier wall north, Lark explained how the Saltborn Covenant had been harrying some of the trade armadas from Shaelun—not successfully, mind you, but Lady Brine and Keelfather demanded blood, so they had to make an effort at least. This meant she knew exactly where the sea gate was located. After another couple hours on a northward tack (a new sailing term I had just learned), we came to a place where the barrier wall danced in a different pattern from everywhere else around it. All day I'd been mesmerized by the beauty of the random shimmering fractal patterns, but here the colours were ordered, structured into a massive arch of interlocking geometric shapes that danced in unison, left and right, left and right. I glided down from the top of the mast to land on the wizard's shoulder.

"This is it," Lark declared. "Welcome to the sea gate."

"It's like a giant metronome," Fox said in complete awe.

"By the dose." Xander made a reverent gesture by tapping his forehead, bowing, and flexing both his large arms in front of him like he was crushing someone in a hug.

"I might have an idea..." Jorvun mumbled. He studied the patterns for a time, then dug into the chest that contained all his magical tomes.

"What kind of idea?" I asked.

"Glimm, I need you to go on a scouting mission for us." He sat cross-legged upon the deck with a book bound in black leather in his lap—a book I was pretty sure I recognized. "Get as high up as you can and fly west."

"To look for the armada? Sure," I said. And yet, I had to press. Not that I could read, but I was pretty sure that this book was the one full of unlocking spells. And I didn't need wizardry training to guess that Frostvale was smart enough to lock their sea gate with a spell that couldn't be undone by a single wizard running on less than half a night's sleep. I hopped down onto the deck and faced him. "But you didn't answer my question."

"Are you my familiar?" My boss looked up from the pages with a warning across his face. "Or is it the other way around?"

"I just..." *Careful, Glimm,* I told myself. His expression made it clear that my dinner was in jeopardy. "Fine," I said after a moment. It wasn't fine, really. Sometimes he would treat me like we were collaborators. Sometimes he'd even ask me for advice. But when other people were around, I was just supposed to shut up and follow orders. "I just want to make sure you conserve your strength."

"Excuse me?" Jorvun slammed the book shut.

"You didn't get much sleep last night." *Not a good idea, Glimm. Shut your stupid mouth.* Half of my brain was saying this, at least. The other half was eminently concerned about my educational prospects. "Plus you said that you could only cloak a small dinghy. Maybe you can find a way to boost that spell, but I don't think it's wise to waste your magic trying to unlock—"

"*How. Dare. You.*" My boss stood and towered over me. "First of all, you're illiterate. You don't know what I'm looking up in this book. Second, I am the wielder of arcane power, not you. I know what I'm capable of. Third, I don't appreciate your condescending tone, especially in front of—" He gestured to the others, who were standing around with their mouths hanging open, apart from Elric, who was still staring at the sea gate. "—our, ah, colleagues. Fourth, if you thought you were getting dinner tonight—forget it!"

"Great." I shook my head, partly at him and partly at myself. I was all too familiar with his ego, so I should have known better than to question him like I did. Dumb, dumb, dumb. On most days, I had a pretty decent diplomacy score, but clearly the grouchiness from lack of sleep still hadn't left me. And now I'd be going to bed hungry. A hundred times dumb.

"So... what's a retro gnome?" Elric asked, apparently oblivious.

"A metronome," Fox said quietly. "A thing for keeping rhythm. Nothing to do with gnomes."

Jorvun glared at me. I stared back, trying to think of something I could say to ease the tension between us.

"You're still here," my boss growled. "You want to forfeit dinner all week?"

"Fine," I said again and then took to the sky.

CHAPTER SIX

Glimm to the Rescue

The thing about Jorvun is he's the only person I've ever really known. The memories I have of Seaport, where he found and hired me, are all pretty vague. There were probably some other dragons in the familiar market, but if there were, I can't recall. Apart from a few alley cats I competed with around the tower and would occasionally talk to, I'd never really had any friends. That's not to say I was lonely. Not really. Jorvun kept me pretty busy, helping with his many experiments, going on shopping trips, and visiting people like Elric on occasion, even if he didn't need to buy anything from him. But when I stopped to think about it—not that I literally stopped, since I was winging my way skyward in search of a Shae-lun trade armada—Jorvun didn't really have any friends. All we had was each other.

That made it hard to stay mad at him. Don't get me wrong, I was still mad. For sure. No dinner? For my first night in Frostvale? This was my homecoming. It definitely didn't seem right that I wouldn't be able to celebrate the occasion with an interesting meal. No dinner also meant that I would have another bad night's sleep, even if we managed to get to an inn. And that was assuming my boss was actually going to pull off whatever cloaking or unlocking spell he had in mind.

Anyway, I flapped and flapped and flapped, but I was so internalized with anger that I barely took in my surroundings. Until I did. Wow, it was pretty spectacular. The *Brine Whisperer* was far beneath me, a little bobbing patch of brown and white in a vast blanket of deep, dark blue. The barrier wall stretched far below and above, but from up here, I could now see where it eventually curved back over on itself—the top of the egg. And through the wall was my homeland—lush green rolling hills rising to mountains somewhere in the middle of Fangcover Island. I could also spot a few boats on the other side of the wall, about the same size as our stormleaf, or so it seemed from my height. Fishing probably.

Frosted fish. My stomach clenched with the reminder of my lost dinner. Frosted wizard.

At a certain height, I found an even air current that I could casually drift on. Almost no effort at all. Still no armada in sight, and I wasn't concerned about finding my way back to the stormleaf as the sea gate gave me a pretty clear beacon. So I took a rest, just drifting along, catching updrafts, and delighting in the view. Humans could do a lot of interesting things with all their technology and spells and enchantments, but they couldn't just flap their wings and see the world from this perspective. For that I felt pretty lucky. A couple times I got so comfortable up there that I started to nod off. That was certainly interesting, because I would have thought that falling asleep while flying would be a terrible idea—that I would fall straight back down to the sea. But in fact, my body seemed to know what to do. And no doubt if I did mess up and started to fall, I'd wake up immediately. So I gave in and had a little nap.

When I awoke, the sun was a bit lower in the sky. At this time of year, sunset was around seven o'clock, so it must have been about five. Lark had wanted to arrive at the sea gate by four, and maybe we had been a little bit early. Again, judging by the sun—I didn't own a watch. So I'd been on my scouting mission for about an hour. I yawned and checked the horizon. Oh—maybe that was something! I could make out a distant blur far off to the west. But I also spotted something directly below me—a patch of white and brown upon the water. The armada, if it was actually the armada, wasn't going to be here right away, so I decided to swoop down and investigate.

After dropping half my altitude, it was clear that the white spots were in fact gulls. Intriguing. Some were sitting on bobbing debris, a tangle of logs and garbage, while others flapped around them, and still others were diving and splashing around in the water. Very intriguing. When I was about the height of the *Brine Whisperer*'s mast above them, I realized they were feeding. There was a massive school of little fish, all right near the surface. Easy pickings, if you didn't mind getting wet.

I landed on a big log in the middle of the flock, which sent the gulls scattering and squawking at me. How to explain to a bunch of birds that I wasn't a threat? I doubted they could speak Valorican. Apart from pigeons, birds tend not to learn human languages. Oh shoot— what would the people in Frostvale speak? Jorvun had never said anything about having to learn a new language. Was it possible they spoke Valorican too? They must, or he would have mentioned it for sure. But did they call it Valorican? That would be odd if they did.

Anyway, waving at the gulls didn't seem to help, so I did my best to look relaxed and unthreatening. After a while they apparently realized that I was the same size as them. They settled down around me and went back to their feast.

Fish. How could I get myself some fish? I really didn't want to get wet, but I also didn't want to go without dinner. And it was pretty much dinnertime. Securing my own meal would be such a victory, not just for my stomach, but also in my feud with Jorvun. My meals were a power he wielded over me, so whenever I had the chance to find food on my own, it was like I could become my own boss, if even for an hour. Wet versus hungry. The gulls all had feathers, which I would have thought could get soaked like a blanket in the wash, but that didn't seem to be the case. After they dove for a fish, they just landed on the little island of logs and garbage and ate their snack: no big deal. Maybe feathers are more like scales than fur. Since I also didn't have any fur, I could only be wet for a few seconds, right? And then I'd have a fish.

Okay, I was going to do it. I had to do it. First, I spent a few minutes watching the gulls, trying to learn from them. Spot a fish, dive in, grab it in their mouth. But did I want a mouthful of seawater? Maybe better to use my back paws for the snag. Just like catching a mouse in the alley. My front limbs are pretty short. Helpful for eating, and I suppose if I ever learned to read, I could hold up a book if it didn't weigh too much, but my back legs are longer, more powerful, and I have retractable talons that would come in handy. The little fish did look pretty slippery.

Taking a lead from the gulls, I flapped up to about twice Jorvun's height above the water. Of course this scared the gulls again, and they did another round of scattering and squawking. Whatever. The fish teemed around the little garbage platform. I dropped down, back feet first, and hit the frigid water. Pretty horrifyingly cold. And I was totally unsuccessful.

After three more attempts I was shivering so much my teeth were chattering, and that made me wonder what the difference was between water cold and snow cold. I'm from Frostvale! I come from a land of ice! It must have just been the wet that was getting to me. I'd never liked the damp and drizzle and downpours of Ravenna. Yes, that had to be it. Water cold was just something else. It wouldn't have bothered me as much if I had a tasty little fish to distract me. For a while I watched the gulls again. Going in headfirst did seem to make sense. Eyes watching fish right next to their beaks. Had to make targeting easier. But I really didn't want a mouthful of seawater. That's when another idea occurred to me. These frosted gulls could share—or should. Shouldn't they? Here I was, a visitor to their little feeding platform, and they hadn't even offered me a snack. How rude! And let me tell you, these birds were pretty plump. They definitely had room within their subsistence efforts for a little generosity.

Once my teeth stopped chattering and shivers stopped racking my body, I did my best to stay perfectly still. The gulls were keeping their distance from me, but little by little, they seemed to relax and forget about my presence. All I had to do was wait for one to pluck a fresh little snack from the sea and—

My opportunity was at hand! A gull flapped down right next to me with a particularly large morsel of shining and wriggling black fish flesh, which it set down on the log and secured with one webbed foot. *Dear sir or madam gull—can anyone tell the difference?—I apologize in advance.* Without otherwise moving a muscle, I horked out a gout of frostfire at the fish. It was instantly frozen in place, all the wriggle gone out of it. The gull screamed and leapt into the air, shaking its icy foot with terror and rage. The other gulls also screamed and launched into flappy hysteria all around me. But no problem—I had acquired my dinner.

Okay, problem: as I took my first delicious bite of frosted fish, the gulls started diving at me, snapping their beaks and trying to steal the fish back. Again, no hospitality whatsoever. I shot a couple more gouts of frostfire at them, mere warning shots, which bought me a bit of space while I hurriedly gobbled and crunched up my fish. A couple times they managed to peck me, so I unfurled my wings and roared at them. Let's be real, it's a pretty sad roar. Jorvun says it's cute. But it seemed to get the point across to the gulls that I wasn't messing around.

With the fish's head saved for last—crunchy and amazing—I decided against overstaying my welcome, so I roared again, then launched into the sky. The gulls came at me, even more brazen in the air, and they were nimble on the wing, so it took a few more warning shots before I was able to get away. But get away I did, with a full belly. And honestly, now that the ordeal was over, I had to admit that it was pretty exciting to have to fight for my meal like that.

WE'VE COME FOR YOUR EGGS

Time to gain some distance and check on the—frost's mercy. The armada. I'd had my back to it the entire time, and it was a lot closer now. So close, in fact, that they could probably see it from the deck of the *Brine Whisperer*. In other words, my scouting mission was a failure. What's the point of being a scout if you don't get back in time to let your party know what's coming? News is meant to be new. Old news is history. Was that one of Jorvun's expressions? Maybe not, but I thought I'd heard it somewhere.

When I got back to the stormleaf, which had drifted a bit north of the sea gate, I circled overhead to assess the state of the party. Or more precisely, the state of the wizard. The trade armada was definitely in sight. Lark was watching the incoming fleet through a spyglass. Fox was taking notes in her scriptlet. Xander was in the middle of a stretching routine. Elric was at the back of the boat, talking into his pocket mirror again. And my boss was still sitting cross-legged upon the deck with a book in his lap as if he'd never moved. It was, however, a different book. His eyes were closed, and he was already chanting the spell—I couldn't quite hear the words, but the emanations of magic wafted up to me like billowing smoke.

I alighted upon the top of the mast, thinking I could just remain anonymous in all this, but I apparently made the tiniest rattle when I landed, and attuned, as a good pirate ought to be, to the song of her ship, Lark looked up at me immediately.

"Hey, little guy." She waved. "Welcome back."

Jorvun didn't open his eyes, but a scowl crept over his face. Frosted fishlips. I didn't like the look of that. Fish victory aside, he could still follow through on his threat to deny me dinner for the rest of the week. And this time I supposed I deserved my punishment. No, hold on. I didn't deserve to be denied dinner for a week. No one deserves that. But whereas he was at first completely inappropriately mad at me for offering him perfectly sound advice, now he had a legitimate reason to be disappointed. Scout fail and all that.

I waved back and considered flapping down to hang out on Lark's shoulder since she didn't seem to be angry with me, but then I decided I'd rather stay where I was. It wasn't like there was anything I could do to help at this point. Maybe I could join in on Xander's stretching routine. Maybe I could eavesdrop on Elric talking to himself. Both of these options could be entertaining, but the dread churning around in my chest sapped my will.

Jorvun's spell was slow to take effect. But with each repetition of the chant, I could feel the fabric of his intent stitching together. He was drawing power up out of his umbrix, which is like a wizard's magical heart. Eventually, a faint haze appeared around the front of the boat—the bow, I think Lark had called it. Or the prow? Something like that. Anyway, the hazy spell clung to the front part where someone had carved a likeness of Lady Brine, like she was up there keeping watch for us. I supposed that Jorvun's spell was originally going to cloak the entire boat, but since the stormleaf was a good deal larger than he'd been anticipating, and since his lack of sleep was no doubt another complicating factor, he resorted to obscuring one section of the *Brine Whisperer*—that part that was immediately visible to the armada. But did that account for their perspective? The trade ships were much, much larger, which meant they were looking down on us from a height. Wouldn't they still be able to see the ass end of our boat? And wouldn't they still be able to see the mast? I tried not to panic, even if my education was at stake. The sun was low on the horizon now, about an hour off sunset, so probably two hours before we could count on the dark for cover. And the armada was almost on top of us.

Besides, the others didn't seem to be worried. The magical development had gotten them excited—they all gathered next to Lark at the helm and, careful not to disturb the wizard, whispered about the adventure we were about to embark upon. Of course, we had already embarked that morning, but it was true that getting through the sea gate was a threshold that would make or break this mission. Frost's mercy that it would be the former.

"I'm thrilled to think of the blood that can again be spilled into the sea," Lark said, "if we can reinstate trade with the North."

"I can't wait for the chance to prove myself heroic and honourable," Elric said. "You know, to my children."

"Just think of all the eggs that will again flow southward," Xander said, "ready to be made into miraculous supplements."

"And what an honour," Fox said, "to be able to share our story with the world."

The wind was picking up a bit, which made it hard to catch everything they were saying, so I decided to stop moping atop the mast and take up a nearer perch on the roof of the cuddy cabin. Lark glanced over her shoulder and shot me a big smile. Yup, full teeth. I might have to talk to her about that eventually. But for now, though disconcerting, her smile was welcome, as if she guessed how I was feeling after my altercation with Jorvun and wanted to reassure me. I flapped over and landed on her shoulder. She gave me a little scritch behind the ear before returning her attention to the big steering wheel.

"Remind me again," Lark whispered to me, "what is it the wizard wants out of this mission?"

I stiffened, though I tried not to. This was a dangerous topic. The subject of Jorvun's big lie. And did I ever hate the idea of lying, especially to someone being so nice to me. I glanced over at my boss—I could now make out the words of his chant.

"*Fadere, obscure, mantella sneekum.*" He paused to take a deliberate breath between each repetition. "*Fadere, obscure, mantella sneekum.*"

"To conquer Frostvale," I said to Lark. That was the truth, right?

"Yeah, but why?" The wind gusted a bit harder, and she spun the wheel back and forth, trying to compensate. "Like, we all have specific reasons for joining the party. What is it about the barrier wall or the trade disruption that would get an academic in knots?"

"*Fadere, obscure, mantella sneekum.*"

"In knots?"

"It's an expression," she said. "I just mean, what is it that's motivating him?"

"*Fadere, obscure, mantella sneekum.*"

"He's a wizard," I said carefully. "Aren't they all about acquiring power and knowledge and stuff?"

"Fucking wind—excuse my French. Xander!" Back and forth on the wheel. "We need to make a sail correction."

Despite Lark's work at the helm, the boat had turned toward the south, which meant the hazy cloak Jorvun was trying to raise, if it was even working, was no longer covering the part of the boat that faced the armada. Not a good development, but at least it spared me from having to answer more of the pirate's questions.

"*Fadere, obscure, mantella sneekum.*"

"Wizard," the pirate hissed through gritted teeth. "Any chance of getting your spell to wrap around the whole boat?"

Jorvun didn't answer, which was not surprising since he was in the middle of a chant. If he stopped, the entire spell could collapse. But his eyes did flick open. He glanced first at Lark and then forward to the haze that had wrapped around no more than a third of our boat.

The wind picked up even more, and though Lark was able to get the stormleaf turned back to face the armada, we were slowly drifting southward into their path. It seemed to me that we wanted to be off to the side. That way the sea gate could open, the armada could pass through it, and we would then follow them in.

"*Fadere, obscure, mantella sneekum.*"

"I think the dragon was right," Xander whispered to Fox. "He used up too much of his magic trying to unlock the sea gate."

Did I hear that correctly? First of all, I was right, which was nice in a way. But also, I was right! The idiot wizard *had* attempted unlocking spells. When I was off fighting with gulls, he had been wasting his precious umbrix power on efforts that had pretty much zero chance of working. Couldn't he feel the sheer power smouldering off the barrier wall? I couldn't believe it. No wonder our cloaking spell was so weak and so... partial. My educational prospects were receding with each moment. And there I was, completely helpless to do anything about it.

But was I completely helpless? Probably, but I had to at least try something. Hmm. I picked a shard of fishbone from between two of my back teeth while I thought about that. I was no magic user. I couldn't hide the boat. I couldn't do anything about the wind. If there was another solution, I felt like it had to be in one of the wizard's spellbooks. Not that he would have enough power left to pull off anything interesting. What did that leave us? Elric's rebranded trinkets? Unlikely. Diplomacy?

"*Fadere, obscure, mantella sneekum.*"

Oh, now there was a thought. Diplomacy. I've been told I'm pretty cute, and I've definitely helped the wizard with interpersonal conflicts in the past. Did that mean I was capable of diplomacy? And if so, how could that help in our current situation?

I could... fly over to the armada... and... ask them for help? Ask permission to follow them through the sea gate? But what reason would I give? They were probably on strict orders not to let any Valoricans into Frostvale. Then again, I wasn't really Valorican. And neither was Jorvun! I could tell them that we were... refugees? Or exiles? Yes, exiles. I'd tell them that we were exiles trying to get home. This was pretty brilliant, right?

But what about the others? Would they be willing to lie and say they were exiles? And was I willing to lie on their behalf? Hopefully I could use careful wording to avoid the lie. Okay. It did feel like I had a plan coming together. And I had to do something soon because the *Brine Whisperer* was almost in front of the sea gate. The armada would soon be right on top of us.

And then I thought of something that would make it much easier for me to avoid lying.

"Jorvun," I shouted as I flapped over to land on the deck in front of my boss. "It's not working. You know it's not working. Stop the spell—I have an idea."

"Fadere, obscure, mantella sneekum." The wizard looked up only long enough to make my heart skip a beat, then he went on chanting, only louder. *"Fadere, obscure, mantella sneekum."*

"Your glamour rings," I went on. Heedless! Dinner be damned! "You should all put them on. Make yourselves look like Frostvalenites. Like... Frostvalen fisherfolk."

"Fadere, obscure, mantella sneekum." Jorvun was now almost yelling his chant.

"I will fly up to the armada and explain," I said. "I'll tell them that... that we're exiles. That we're just trying to get home."

He shut his eyes extra tight, as if that could make me go away. I took a quick glance over my shoulder to confirm that—yup—his angry chanting wasn't having any additional effect. Our cloak was too small. The armada would soon be able to see the back half of the stormleaf, and then it would be impossible to convince them that we were legitimately trying to get home.

"I think Glimm has a point," Elric said.

Jorvun ignored him. *"Fadere, obscure, mantella sneekum."*

"I agree," Lark chimed in. "It's a pretty good plan."

Amazing! I had support! Perhaps I could be good at diplomacy stuff. Maybe not when it came to my boss, but at least I had won over two people.

"Totally a good plan," Xander said.

Three people!

"Fadere, obscure, mantella sneekum."

"Yeah." Fox stepped forward, scriptlet in hand. "This is quite an exciting development, and—"

Four!

"Fadere, obscure—" Jorvun's chanting ended with a growl, and he slammed his tome down upon the deck. Almost right on top of my tail if I hadn't jumped back in time. Furious. Yup, he wasn't taking this well. But you know what, I wasn't about to let his ego dash our plans for the future.

"The rings, Boss." I pointed at a small pocket in his oilskin, where I was pretty sure he had put them. "There isn't much time."

"How. Dare. You." He shoved his book to the side and stood so he could tower over me. "My spell was coming together. I could have hidden the entire boat, I just needed a few more—"

Minutes? That was probably what he was about to say. But he was interrupted by a thunderous sound from behind us: clacking, whirling, grinding. Everyone spun around as the sea gate's locking mechanism released and the huge arch unfolded from the top, dropping straight down into the deep, dark sea.

CHAPTER SEVEN

How Not to Break into a Kingdom

Were there any dragon physicists in the world? I wasn't sure. Maybe with the right education. And that's why this mission was so important to me. Depending on what I ended up studying, I could take my life in so many different directions. But at this point in time, I was no physicist, so I was at a bit of a loss to explain what happened next.

The arch of the sea gate, as I've already noted, *unfolded* from top to bottom. That's the best word I can think of to describe it. How does a magical barrier wall actually work? And what is it made out of? I had no idea. But the effect of this unfolding was a great wave, and not like a splash. It seemed there was more water on the inside than the outside, just waiting to rush out. And rush out it certainly did.

The wave that came forth from the gate was about half the height of the *Brine Whisperer*'s mast. Since we were directly in its path, I knew right away that it was going to wash over the entire boat. Not that I'm an experienced sailor, but I was pretty sure it wasn't going to end well. Also, I'd had enough salty wet-cold for one day, so I took to the air. Was that cowardly of me? It's not like there was anything I could do to help the others. And it wasn't like I made a conscious decision to flee the approaching calamity. Instinct and reflexes. A giant wave was about to smash into the stormleaf, so I got the frost out of there.

In the ensuing moments before the wave struck, Elric shouted, "My inventory!" Xander dashed across the deck to grab a satchel of supplements. Fox froze in place and screamed. Jorvun shouted something about his legacy. And Lark just crossed her arms and muttered, "Godsdamn academics."

The *Brine Whisperer* didn't whisper when the wave arrived; it groaned and cracked. The five humans were all washed overboard in an instant, as were the chests and luggage. The mast splintered and fell. The cuddy cabin was torn right off its foundation, exposing the boat's insides, which burbled up a bunch of air as it filled with water. The stormleaf didn't sink as fast as I thought it would, but since most of the hull was ironwood, sink it did. I wondered for a moment if the wave was going to cause damage to the approaching armada, but it dissipated very quickly as it spread out in all directions. Clearly, being right in front of the sea gate as it opened was a bad idea. The change in wind seemed partly to blame, but if Jorvun's spell had done what it was supposed to do, it stood to reason that Lark would have been able to keep us off to the side.

Well, whatever.

After the ocean had calmed—somewhat, it was still windy—I flew back and forth between party members, helping them to locate floating debris that they could cling to. They all looked pretty angry and soggy and cold. And for Jorvun, make that extra angry. He was cursing and growling and, between curses and growls, spitting out seawater. Eventually I found each of them a plank of wood from the smashed cabin or a piece of mast to hold on to. Good thing the entire boat hadn't been made of ironwood. One of Fox's instrument cases—the lute— was floating nearby, so I landed on it and tried to steady myself. When they had all paddled and flutter-boarded themselves into a sad little circle, Jorvun let his fury explode.

"Piss on a poptart," he cursed. "I can't believe I ever allowed myself to be talked into bringing you *idiots* along on this mission." He paused to spout some more sea-water—it was evidently difficult to talk in choppy waves. "Just me and a little dinghy. That was the plan. But you had to bring all this *shit* along with you, and then the pi-rate—the one with so-called sailing expertise—parks us right in front of the sea gate. How the hell did you ever think that was a good idea?"

"You slimy, pompous, blaspheming academic piece of—"

"Now, now," Xander cut in. "We're going to make a terrible situation worse by throwing insults around."

"Worse?" Jorvun coughed and took another wave in the mouth. "We're doomed. We're dead. We're in the di-rect path of a Shaelun armada, and if we aren't drowned in their wake, we're too far out to make it to land without dying of hypothermia first, assuming we can swim through the sea gate before it closes."

To make matters worse, the sun would soon drop over the edge of the world. I was pretty sure that any time of day was terrible for a shipwreck, but in the gathering twilight? Yeah, it seemed to add to the dilemma.

"If you're certain we're doomed, I could put you out of your misery right now." Lark had managed to get one of her blasters out of its holster. She raised it out of the water and pointed it at my boss. "We could call it a final sacrifice to my Lord and Lady."

"You seem to have forgotten," I piped up, "that I have a plan."

No one heeded me. But I guess they were in full-on panic mode, so it made sense.

"What will my kids think of me now?" Elric sobbed.

"No need to panic," Fox said. "I was in a similar situation back when I was in the Navy."

"I thought you were in the Merchant Marines," I said.

"Oh, that was years later." She squinted and looked into the sky as if remembering a time long past. "But yes, in my first Navy tour—"

"Hold that thought," I said.

Jorvun had pulled a wand out of one of his oilskin pockets and was aiming it at Lark. Lark had thumbed a little lever on the back of her blaster, and the weapon made a threatening click. This whole situation was getting uglier by the minute. I had to do something, and fast. So I stood up as best I could on the bobbing lute case, sucked in a full breath of air, and roared.

"Aw, that was so cute," Xander said.

I'd meant to sound ferocious, or deadly serious, but at least I had their attention.

"You're right, it's not a great situation," I said. "The plan didn't work out. But if you two will stop pointing weapons at each other for a second and listen, our mission can still proceed."

Jorvun and Lark glanced at me, but neither was willing to take their eyes off the other for long.

"Come on," Elric said. "Shooting each other in the face isn't going to solve anything."

"Listen to the inventor," I said. "I'm going to get us out of this mess. But first you have to put your weapons away."

"I'm willing to listen to you," Lark said, "but I'm not putting mine down first."

"Well neither am I," Jorvun said.

"Boss, let's be reasonable here. You were the one who started shouting at everyone and blaming this on Lark." The lute case wobbled down the side of a wave, and I almost lost my footing for a moment. "You don't want to admit it, but this is also your fault. The cloaking spell wasn't going to cut it. She was doing her best to keep the stormleaf pointed toward the armada so they couldn't see us. If you had been able to hide the entire boat like you said you would, we wouldn't have been pushed in front of the gate."

"I can't even believe—" A wave washed right over his head, and he came up spitting. But hey, at least he was now looking at me instead of the pirate.

"You can be mad at me later," I said. "It doesn't really matter at this point. You're all in the water, and I have a plan to get you out—and through the sea gate. But first I need you to put the wand away."

Jorvun didn't come right out and agree to listen to me, and he definitely didn't stop glaring, but he lowered his wand. When he did, Lark unclicked the lever thingy on her blaster.

"Great. That's a start," I said. "Now put the weapons away. You're going to need your hands free."

A long, tense moment passed in which we all bobbed on the waves and waited as the wizard and pirate wrestled with their mutually wounded pride. But slowly, eventually, they both pulled their weapons back under the water and returned them to pocket and holster.

"Thanks, Glimm." Lark was again clutching her plank of wood with two weaponless hands. "You've got a level head, and I appreciate it. So what's your plan?"

"Jorvun has five glamour rings," I said. "I want you all to put them on and make yourselves look like Frostvalen fisherfolk. I'll go explain to the armada that you were caught outside the barrier wall and have been trying to get home." It was technically true, at least for me and Jorvun. "Who knows, the shipwreck part of the story might even help. They might not have been willing to take a chance on helping us if the boat was intact."

"That's fantastic, little buddy," Xander said.

"More or less what I was going to suggest," Fox said.

"First tavern we come to," Elric said, "I'm buying Glimm some roast mutton."

"I'm not wild about putting on a heretic ring," Lark said, "but for the sake of the group, I'll do it."

My boss grumbled, wiped water out of his eyes, spat out a bit more brine, then finally nodded. He reached below the sea, made a few faces as he dug around in his pockets, and then produced the five rings that, only yesterday, I'd convinced him to purchase in the Ravenna market.

How long ago and how far away that now seemed.

WE'VE COME FOR YOUR EGGS

Well, the first stage was complete. Now it was time to put my diplomacy to the test.

One massive dreadhull led the rest of the armada, which followed alongside each other in twos and threes. As I winged my way over to this flagship, I realized that none of them had sails. They chugged along by some other means of propulsion, which explained the low thrumming from deep inside the hull, and maybe also the thick smoke puffing from four tall chimney towers that at first I mistook for masts. Each ship in the armada was a bit different. The flagship was broad and tall, an iron-ribbed vessel with a hull that flared outward like the open jaws of a fish. It had the faint curve of the old galleons I used to watch sail into Cascade Bay, but none of their ornamentation. Instead, thick plating lined the sides, bolted in overlapping rows like scales. Rust streaks bled from the seams.

Four sailors stood up at the front—at the bow-prow place—watching the waves and perhaps assessing their approach to the sea gate. One was talking into a little pocket mirror just like Elric's. How odd! Even though Jorvun told me to shut up about the mirror, I was going to have to broach the topic. That was just too curious. This sailor was repeating a series of numbers and names, something like four-Mike-six and Juliet-two-Charlie. Complete nonsense. I was forced to conclude that there was something wrong with him, and so I alighted on the ship's handrail closer to the others.

"Greetings, Shaelun traders," I said. "My name is Glimm, and my friends need your help."

The three sailors nearest me stood chatting in a semicircle, their long coats flapping in the wind. Their uniforms were the colour of the dark sea, trimmed with maroon piping and bearing a curling crest over the heart that resembled a coiled serpent. Their collars were high, their cuffs buttoned in silver, and each wore a deep green sash wrapped diagonally across the torso. The woman in the middle—taller than the others, with a white streak in her hair and a rigid posture—had epaulets on her shoulders and a polished silver chain draped from one pocket to the other. The officer in charge, most likely.

There was something in their faces too—broad cheekbones, sharp eyes—that reminded me of the folks in the Shae district back in Ravenna, but their hair was cropped shorter, and each of them wore a silver circlet that curved above the ears and across the forehead.

No one looked particularly thrilled to see a dragon land on the handrail.

"Shipwreck," I blurted and waved my paws frantically. "Dead ahead."

The officer pulled a spyglass from her belt and, leaning over the front of the boat, scanned the sea. When she finally spotted my party, she said a few words in the Shaelun tongue. That set the other officers into motion. They ran back up the deck, shouting orders of their own. So far, so good.

"Where," the officer asked me with a slight accent to her words, "are your friends from?"

"I'm from Frostvale," I said. "My boss is too. We were trying to get back home, but there's this barrier wall now, and when the sea gate opened—"

"The wall has been up for months," she said. "Where were you this whole time?"

"Um..." I swallowed hard. Jorvun would probably want me to lie, but what lie would even make sense? Where could we possibly have been? "In Ravenna."

"Interesting. And what were you doing in Ravenna?"

"Oh, you know…" Frost's mercy. What was I supposed to say? Diplomacy was a bit more difficult than I'd expected. I was supposed to say something about the party being fisherfolk. Lost at sea? For months? That just didn't seem plausible. So instead I blurted the best thing I could come up with. "Hunting pigeons, mostly."

"Pigeons." She cocked her head and held out her arm for me to perch on. "I see."

I didn't like the sound of that, but I hopped over to land on her forearm. She spun about on her heel and marched us to the middle of the deck, where her crew was lowering two lifeboats with a powerful loading crane. One of the lifeboats had four sailors in it, and the other was empty.

I might not have succeeded in framing our cover story as I'd been hoping to, but at least the party was about to be plucked out of that icy water.

As the lifeboats made their long descent from the heights of the dreadhull deck down to the darkening sea, a deafening horn sounded, followed by a series of flashing magic-powered lights from the top of a middeck structure that I guessed was the dreadhull equivalent of a cuddy cabin. The command centre? Maybe. It was a blocky wheelhouse encased in glass and slate-grey panels, with metal tubes and rotating signal lights bristling from its roof. The rumbling propulsion system eased off, and in a moment it seemed we were slowing down. The ships immediately behind us in the armada responded with two toots on their own horns and more flashing lights. Then the ones behind them did the same. It was a noisy and yet effective way to make sure they didn't all crash into us as we stopped to rescue my boss and new friends.

As we waited, the officer brought me to an iron post with a lantern on top and crossbars for hanging ropes and raincloaks and visi-vests. She lifted me up to one of the crossbars that had nothing on it.

"Stay here," she said in a snarky tone that reminded me of my wizard. "You'll be safer and less distracting."

This perch gave me a decent view of the middeck. There were two more loading cranes mounted toward the other side of the ship—starboard, if I'm remembering correctly—and at the back. The stern? I was really starting to sound like a Saltborn with all this new lingo. Lantern posts like the one I perched on formed a U-shaped perimeter around the inner deck, which was piled with crates of various sizes and boxes of chain with links bigger than my head. The lanterns glowed with a steady light, not at all like the flickering of a regular lantern, and they radiated the same quiet magic as the big light atop the command centre that had flashed at the other ships. And all around, sailors hurried in every direction.

There really was a lot to take in. So much bustle, and not just from the sailors operating the crane and watching the progress of the lifeboats below. It seemed everyone else was getting ready for the port ahead. Fangcover City, probably. How exciting. To think that we would soon be walking around in Frostvale, just as I'd always dreamed. I got to wondering about the dragon college and whether it was in Fangcover or somewhere else, and what would be required before I could submit my application. These imaginings swept me up, because before I knew it, the crane was rattling once again—Jorvun and the rest of the party were ascending the long climb up to the deck. I waved at them with unrestrained excitement. Success! I had saved them from complete disaster!

WE'VE COME FOR YOUR EGGS

By the time they were hoisted about halfway, a crowd had gathered. About a dozen sailors assembled next to the crane, dressed in a darker, sleeker version of the regular crew's uniform—trimmed in scarlet instead of maroon, with high collars fastened by metal clasps. They didn't wear the green sashes like the others, but instead had wide leather belts hung with all sorts of tools and oddments: stubby batons, coiled cord, metal rings, and what looked like socketed rods with faintly glowing runes. I assumed they must be from engineering.

However, my assumption turned out to be quite incorrect. When the two lifeboats were at last deposited on deck, the crowd surrounding my friends flexed with the poise of cats about to pounce. On top of that, they now all had their batons in hand in a way that was giving *security detail*. Definitely not engineers.

As the party stepped out of the boat and into the dreadhull's lamplight—shivering, dripping, with arms clutched across their chests—I was at first confused about their appearance, but then I remembered the glamour rings. Jorvun's wizardly outfit had morphed into slightly mismatched denim pants and shirt, a slick black raincloak, and a brown fishing hat embroidered with *Langford Strong* across the front—with a couple fishhooks dangling from the narrow brim for what, I had to admit, was an impressive flourish.

Lark was perhaps even closer to the mark. I mean, I didn't actually know what a Frostvalenite should look like, and Jorvun presumably had a good idea, but there was a varying spectrum here in terms of costume. She sported a worn waxed-canvas coat, dark green with a high collar and interior quilted in red, with rough oil-stained trousers tucked into sturdy work boots. And on her head she wore a wool winter hat—the kind with ear flaps and a leather strap that went under the chin, though this was currently unfastened in a way that made her seem relaxed and even charismatic.

The other three, however, fell on the other end of the spectrum.

Fox had opted for some kind of sports uniform—a thick blue jersey with a stylized black and white whale across the chest and the number 16 on the back, and she wore one of those floppy winter hats with a giant pom-pom on top and braided tassels that hung down past her shoulders. And all of this at odds with the lute case she clutched under one arm. Xander, by contrast, was going full lumberjack: bushy brown beard, red-and-black flannel overshirt, and thick leather suspenders holding up a pair of canvas trousers.

And then there was Elric. Oh, Elric. He wore a gleaming white parka with fur lining far too plush (though currently soggy) to be practical, paired with clunky fur-trimmed snow boots that went nearly to his knees. Mittens—actual mittens—dangled from his cuffs on toddler-style strings, and a matching scarf covered his lower face like he was preparing for a blizzard, not a brisk sea breeze.

So yes, varying degrees of believability. But would the Shaelun security team be able to tell the difference? That was the real question.

"Your pet," the officer said as she stepped toward the party, arms clasped behind her back, "claims you are from Frostvale."

Pet? How offensive. I wanted to offer a correction but decided to hold my tongue. I could let her know about my illustrious job title later.

"Correct," Jorvun said as the rest nodded vigorously behind him. "We were out fishing when the wall went up. We've been trying to get home ever since."

The officer cocked her head with a puzzled expression, then glanced around at the party, looking each of them up and down.

"I'm from Langford originally." Jorvun grinned with all his teeth—why??—and pointed at his hat. "But we've been working out of the Port of Fangcover for about five years."

"And what business did you have in Ravenna?"

"Oh, we..." Jorvun pressed his lips together and shook his head in a way that I could tell was meant to be dismissively relaxed but seemed like—well, like bad acting. "...we stopped in there about a week ago for a re-supply, but—"

"I'm unconvinced." The officer drew a small circle in the air—apparently a signal for the security detail because five of them closed in and grabbed each of the party by the arm.

At this point Jorvun locked on to me with a glare, like clearly I had spun a story that he hadn't been able to guess, but honestly, he should know that I'm not able to lie like him. Right? Whatever. He was mad again, and once more it wasn't really my fault. How many times could I piss him off in one day? I was starting to think that the stress of travel was putting a serious strain on our relationship.

"Hey, what's going on?" Xander bellowed, which brought two more security personnel to his side.

"We're having a particularly terrible day," Elric whined. "Please, just help us get back home."

"I've been a resident of Fangcover my entire life,"

Fox said with quite a convincing casual air. "I started my career as a circus clown but turned to the maritime arts after an unfortunate encounter with one of the lions. Left me quite traumatized, actually."

Lark, meanwhile, just shook her head—resigned, it seemed, to the direction this was all turning.

"You've concocted some interesting stories," the officer said. "Quite entertaining, in fact. So entertaining that I've decided not to throw you back into the sea. Actually, that's against protocol, as much as I wish it wasn't. I am obliged to turn you over to the port authority, regardless of whether I believe your story. And I don't believe it, by the way, and not just because the little dragon already told me you've been *living* in Ravenna, but because of your accents. I may not be a native speaker, but your *outs* and *abouts*, sir," she said to Jorvun, really stressing the *ow* of each word, "are a dead giveaway. And if I can tell? Well, port authority will have you pegged as Valorican spies in about two flaps of a sail."

Crap. This was not good. And here I thought I'd managed to pull off a heroic rescue. I mean, at least it wasn't just the Ravenna detail that tipped her off. I was admittedly relieved that Jorvun's accent was also to blame. And how odd that he'd gapped on such an important detail. He's a scholar, after all. Shouldn't he have known there was a difference in accent? Ugh. Anyway, the situation was taking a dark turn. Better than them drowning outside the sea gate, though. Still, I couldn't see how they could get out of this situation. Jorvun's magic was taxed, and even if it wasn't, would he be able to come up with a quick spell that could neutralize all these guards? Lark presumably had her blasters hidden beneath the glamour. Elric probably had a couple trinkets secreted away somewhere. But Xander had no weapon, and even if Fox could get out her lute, I wasn't sure what she would be able to achieve with it. She did say something back at the Fish and Frog about studying martial traditions, bardic hermeneutics, and arcane something or other, but I found myself putting less and less faith in her grand claims.

So... what to do? The reality was: they were probably going to get locked up until we arrived at port, and then they'd be locked up somewhere ashore until this port authority could interrogate them. And if they couldn't convince this Shaelun officer of their cover story, then they'd probably be locked up for good. Jorvun would be denied the throne he'd long dreamed of, and my chances of getting into dragon college would be dashed. I needed a new plan, and quick. I needed to—

Nope. Denied. As I was straining my brain to come up with something, I hadn't noticed a guard slip around behind me. She grabbed me by the neck and, though I managed to spit out two gouts of unaimed frostfire, stuffed me in a sack.

But you know what? As terrible as our situation was, there was one nice thing to come out of all this. As the guard carrying my sack stomped off across the deck, Jorvun shouted with undeniable panic in his voice: "You let him go! You let him go right now!"

Wow. It had really been a rough day. I'd lost track of how many times my boss had been angry with me. But even after everything that happened, he still cared. That was something, right?

CHAPTER EIGHT

The Magic of Friendship

The sack-wielding security guard carried me across the deck and down a few flights of stairs into the depths of the dreadhull's hold. I did my best to gauge what direction we went—right, then left, then right, then left? But it's not easy when you're swinging back and forth in darkness. A lock clicked and clunked. A door opened and closed. The smell in the air was different here, even filtered through the burlap—straw, fur, feathers, and maybe... manure?

The guard took me deep into the room and then paused. Jangling. Clinking. A creak. Whatever she was doing, it was one-handed since she still held on to the top of my sack. I considered blasting at her with some frost-fire to make her drop the sack. But then again, she probably had one of those nasty batons. Getting smashed in the face didn't seem like much fun. And yet, maybe this was my last chance to get free. I needed to do something—

But then she shoved my sack into a small space and set me down. As I scrambled out and into the dim light, she slammed the door on a cramped iron cage, turned a key in the lock, and walked away. My opportunity for a final attempt at escape had come and gone. I tried to shout something at her, but my words just came out as an ineffectual roar.

Caged!! The indignity of it. The disrespect. The dashing of my college dreams. To be separated from my boss. To land my new friends in such circumstances. Maybe Jorvun had messed up with the accent, but I had also messed up. Why couldn't I tell a small lie? Not that I really wanted to lie, but I could definitely see its usefulness. If I had spun a super convincing story, maybe the accent thing wouldn't have been an issue. If only I was better at diplomacy. If only...

This was where I broke down into tears. A mess of regret and grief. I had let everyone down. I had let myself down. It was no consolation that I could feel the magic thrum of the barrier wall pass overhead as the dreadhull, evidently, slid through the sea gate. Sure, I might have arrived in my homeland, but if I was a prisoner, what did it matter? Just when I thought my emotions would swallow me whole, a soft little voice interrupted my meltdown.

"If it's any consolation, I've heard they treat pets pretty well in Frostvale."

I blinked several times to clear my vision and turned toward the voice. At that moment, the room I was caged within sharpened into focus. I was in a cargo hold lined with metal cages of every size, some stacked two or three high. Lanterns swayed from hooks along the bulkhead, their warm light casting dancing shadows across scaled hides, twitching ears, and eyes that glinted in every col-our imaginable. Some creatures slept curled up, others paced or glared, and a few blinked at me with what I could only describe as professional courtesy. Chains clinked, wings rustled, and a spark fizzled as something small and electric sneezed.

In the nearest cage, a few feet away from me, was a small flickerkit, something like a black-and-tan tabby cat but with mottled brown moth wings and silver antennae.

"Pets?" I tried to disguise the disdain in my voice, since I know there's nothing wrong with being a mere pet. Some creatures love it.

"Pets, yes." The flickerkit smiled—by crinkling her nose and squinting her bright green eyes, because animals and monsters know the score. "My name's Aneko. What's yours?"

Aneko spoke with an accent similar to the officer I'd met on deck. Accents! They really were a clear indication of provenance. I still couldn't believe that Jorvun had messed this up.

"Glimm," I said. "Nice to meet you, Aneko, despite the circumstances."

"How is it that you've joined us so late in the journey?" She blinked at me warmly and cocked her head. "Did your owner surrender you or something?"

"Owner? Um, no. I've never had an owner. I'm a familiar, not a pet. I have an employer, but there was a misunderstanding, sort of, and he's been taken captive."

"A familiar! Of course," she said. "I've never actually heard of a pet dragon. What sorts of spells do you know?"

"Spells? No, sorry, I think you're mistaken." I picked up the burlap sack that I'd crawled out of, then folded it twice to make a little mat for me to sit on. "A familiar works for a wizard, kind of like a helper, and sometimes an advisor."

"Oh, strange." Her antennae twitched as she gave that some thought. "I met a little dragon like you back in Yenzhou, only pink instead of blue—you're quite pretty, by the way—and he said his wizard was teaching him some magic. Like an apprentice or something."

"Thanks for the compliment." I bowed. "But as a boy dragon, I think *handsome* is preferable to *pretty*. Not that I really mind, but that's what my boss told me."

"Oh." She frowned at me for a moment, then shrugged. "My apologies. You learn something new every day."

"Anyway, I'm not really sure," I said. "Wizards don't tend to get along very well. Maybe some familiars have an umbrix and others don't, just like with humans. But not me. I'm more of the advisor type."

"Well, isn't this lovely." Aneko did a quick circuit of her cage, unfolded and refolded her wings, and then curled up in a tight little ball. "I'm not sure how much of the journey is left, but it's nice to have someone to talk to."

Was this the end of my adventures with Jorvun? Should I be as content as this flickerkit to curl up and see what fate awaited me in the pet markets of Fangcover? Would I actually end up as a pet—*owned* by someone rather than a proper employee? And what, exactly, was the difference? Even less food perhaps? Would I be kept in a cage all the time? Would I be expected to do stupid tricks?

The best response I could give Aneko was a despondent nod. Nice conversation. And meanwhile my boss and friends were being shoved roughly into a prison cell in some other dark hold of the dreadhull—awaiting an even darker prison cell in some dungeon. No, this wasn't a fate—for me or any of us—that I was willing to curl up and accept. But busting out of a solid iron cage? And then this room? And then freeing the party? And then escaping the dreadhull? Didn't seem plausible. I was just one small dragon. And clearly my diplomacy skills couldn't be relied on. What else did I have apart from some sharp claws and frostfire?

I took another look around the room—with less panic this time. My cage was more or less in the middle, along a central aisle. Since I couldn't count above ten, I did four separate counts while looking out from each side of my cage. More than ten animals and monsters in each direction. Make of that what you will. I felt terrible for all these poor souls, destined to be owned by someone. I also felt terrible for them in the present moment, locked up in small, uncomfortable spaces for such a long journey. No bedding even. And there was that *smell*. Excrement? Urine? That made me stop and wonder where the bathroom was. There must have been a sailor who came around at regular intervals to let them out to do their business. But... where? I couldn't see—

And that's when I noticed a small pile of brown pellets in the corner of Aneko's cage. Frost's mercy. It was poop. She had to poop *inside her cage?* And just go on sitting there next to it? What a complete lack of respect the sailors had for these passengers. What an unthinkable insult to their dignity. I wasn't sure how long the rest of the trip would be, through the sea gate and past Fangcover Island, all the way to the mainland, but I might well have to do business of some kind over the next several hours. Seriously, seriously unthinkable.

Okay, Glimm. It was time to come up with a plan. An iron cage. An impossible situation. But was it impossible? First things first, I gave my cage door a good rattle. It did seem pretty strong. What if I froze the lock? Could I shatter it with enough frostfire? Worth a try.

So I huffed, I puffed, and I spat out as much concentrated ice at the back of the lock as I could muster. I spat and wheezed and spat until my head spun and the cold spread through the rest of my cage. Good thing I had my burlap mat to sit on. While I was still looking forward to the ice and cold of my homeland, I had to admit that sitting around on frosty metal wasn't comfortable. Metal-cold must be a particular type of cold, like wet-cold, that I just wasn't into.

"Too bad our cages aren't a bit closer," Aneko said. "I might be able to help you with that."

Help me? I wasn't sure what she meant. Anyway. I was running low on frostfire reserves, so I threw myself against the cage door. Nothing. I plopped down on my backside, using my tail for stability, and kicked the door with my hind legs over and over again. The clanging was quite loud, and after a while a few voices from the room shouted for me to be quiet—to stop making such a ruckus. How could they be so complicit in their own subjugation? I rolled over onto my mat and sniffed, trying to hold back my tears. Crying wasn't going to get me anywhere closer to freedom.

"I guess you really don't want to be a pet," Aneko said.

"No," I said between stifled sobs. "Do you?"

"Some say it's better than being feral." She moved closer, right up to the side of her cage, as if a couple inches of extra proximity was all the support she could offer. "Owners don't let you go hungry—I mean, assuming they are good ones. But most people get a pet because they want a companion. So they should love you and even spoil you. Maybe buy you toys and take you on forest walks."

"But don't you have any ambitions, other than to be owned and spoiled?"

"I mean... it would be amazing to get a job as a lamplighter." Aneko wiggled her tail out of the cage and stretched it out like she was reaching for me—I hadn't noticed before, but the tip of her tail wasn't furry like the rest of her. It was capped in a little cone, shiny and dark, almost like a tooth or claw. She gave it a flick—and a small flame issued from the end. "I am absolutely entranced by fire. By lamps too. Light in the darkness—it really calls to me. So yeah, I think working as a lamplighter would be great."

"That does sound great." I gripped the bars of my cage. Another wave of tears threatened, so I took a deep breath and swallowed hard. "I really want that for you."

"Being a familiar sounds like the best thing ever, though. Learning magic? I wish."

"I already told you," I said, "familiars don't necessarily learn magic." Was this flickerkit a bit daft or what? "In fact, I've never heard of a magical familiar."

"How many familiars have you met?"

"Well, none, I guess. But I'm sure my boss would have—"

"So you've never actually tried?" She hopped up onto all fours with her tail flicking behind her. With each flick, a few tiny sparks shot out of the end.

"No, but... I wouldn't know where to start."

"Fair enough, I guess." Her tail drooped and she sat back down. "I wouldn't either."

I fell back into hopeless daydreams of escape. A flickerkit with a flametail could be helpful. We could maybe... start a fire or something. That could be a good distraction. Although I wouldn't want to do that in this hold and get any of the animals or monsters hurt. Well, I didn't want *anyone* to get hurt. Okay, maybe the sailors a bit, but that was mostly my anger talking. I supposed they were just doing their job, following orders. But if Jorvun ever gave me an order to lock someone up in a cage? I'd tell him to go hex himself.

My cage was up on a table, so about the height of a half-grown human from the floor. I wondered if I could shimmy my cage off the edge. The floor below was wood, but it looked like it might be ironwood, so maybe it was hard enough to break the structure, especially if it impacted at an angle. Sitting around waiting to be sold into pet-hood didn't seem like much fun, so I set to work, hind legs planted, thrusting my weight forward over and over again. I suppose I looked like I was doing a strange dance. The expression on Aneko's face was one of confused amusement.

Bit by bit, my cage slid closer and closer to the edge. With a final thrust, I toppled over the side and hit the ground with a tremendous crash. Not only did the cage smash against the floor, I smashed against the inside of the cage. It took me a few moments to recover from the stun. And...?

My cage had landed upside down. Sturdy iron bars were as sturdy as ever. No apparent structural damage. I howled in frustration, which is like a roar, but more mournful. In response, I received another few shouts of criticism from other creatures in the room.

From up above me, Aneko whispered, "Nice effort!"

Ugh. This really was hopeless. If only the flickerkit were right. Magic would come in really handy right now. If Jorvun was here, he'd pull out an *aperi sesame* and the lock would click right open. If only it could be that easy.

But it couldn't, could it?

Nope. No chance. If there was any possibility of little ol' Glimm being magical, Jorvun would have told me. No doubt, he would have been delighted to share his craft with me. I was his employee, but let's be realistic—I was also his best friend. Make that only friend. We spent all our time together. He confided his deepest longings and secrets in me. Who else knew that he was a Frostvalenite? Well, apart from the spy who had sent him the missive about Trudera's coming succession. And whoever had told him about his parentage in the first place. But I'd never met these people. Anyone and everyone in our day-to-day life had no idea that the great Jorvun Prattlethorn was actually the bastard son of Justice Trudera, King of the North.

And think of all the non-work-related activities we did together: him walking through the park with me riding on his shoulder, going for seaside picnics, debating Jungian psychology, playing chess—though, admittedly, we stopped playing once I figured out how to beat him. Absolutely, definitely, we were boss and employee, but we were also good friends.

So, my dear little flickerkit, there was not an icicle's chance in hell that my friend-boss wouldn't have told me that I was capable of magic. Nil, zero, zip. And just because I didn't want the awkward question to linger any longer than it already had, I would prove it. I stood as tall as the cage would allow and pointed my front paw at the lock.

"*Aperi sesame*," I said.

Holy sleet. Imagine my surprise, relief, horror, excitement, and shock. The frosted door to my cage popped open.

CHAPTER NINE

The Great Pet Rebellion

"You did it! You did it!" Aneko jumped up and down in her cage.

I flapped twice to land on the table beside her, then, breathless from astonishment, whispered the words of the spell again. In my first attempt, I hadn't been expecting it to work—quite the opposite—so I hadn't prepped myself for what I might feel if it did. This time, however, I noticed a burbling somewhere deep inside me, a rising of power, like a spiral of magic that shot up through my guts and came charging out my mouth. Was that burble and spiral coming from my—my umbrix? It had to be, right? If I could say the words and the magic obeyed me, then I had the requisite arcane organ.

Her lock released. A moment later she joined me on the tabletop and threw her paws around me. I hugged her back, but I did so shakily and with a quivering breath in my lungs. I was free. I was... magical. But that also meant

I was... betrayed? No, that wasn't the only conclusion. Jorvun just hadn't realized. It hadn't occurred to him. Magical potential was probably as uncommon in dragons as it was in humans. And maybe he'd assumed that I would try to use magic at some point, because why wouldn't I want to emulate my boss and role model? And since I never did—since I never let him know that I'd discovered my talent—he'd just automatically concluded it wasn't a possibility for me. Plus he probably didn't want to get my hopes up. Yeah, that made sense. He had just been protecting me from feelings of inadequacy or failure. Wow, when I thought about it that way, it really confirmed what a great guy he was.

"So," I said when the flickerkit finally released me, "how about we break out of this place and find you a job as a lamplighter?"

"Whoa." Her green eyes opened wide, and she stared off over my shoulder at the imagined possibility of her future. "I mean, that would be the best. But it's also a bit daunting, you know? I wouldn't have the first clue where to begin looking for a job. I don't know much about Frostvale. And we're still on this boat. We're still locked in this hold, and—"

"It turns out locks aren't a problem."

"I guess so." She plopped her butt down and chewed thoughtfully on a claw. "What was your plan—after getting out of the cage?"

"I hadn't considered it fully," I said. "But it did occur to me that a diversion would help. You can make a flame, so for example, if we started a fire somewhere, a bunch of sailors would be required to put it out. Then, while they're doing that, we could sneak around a bit easier."

A look of (slightly) evil excitement swept over her face as her tail tip ignited. She held the flame between us.

"Not in here, though." I motioned at the other cages. "I wouldn't want any of these fine creatures to get hurt."

"Oh, of course." She extinguished the flame and gave a little nonchalant chuckle as if to say that she had just been joking—sort of.

"How long do you think we have before someone comes to check on us?"

"We get fed once per day, and that was a few hours ago. So I think we're fine—unless they capture any more errant dragons like yourself."

"Once per day?" I shook my head in dismay. "That's barbaric."

"Tell me about it. That's one reason why most of us are looking forward to the prospect of petdom."

"I wish we could rescue everyone," I said.

"You know any other spells that might help?"

"Hmmm." I plopped down next to her and dangled my hind legs off the edge of the table. "I'll have to give that some thought. I'm not used to the idea of solving problems with magic." I swung my legs back and forth for a bit. "Nope, nothing is occurring to me. This is really a lot to think about. Maybe I will come up with a spell when a more specific problem presents itself."

"Okay, so what's our first step?"

"Diversion, part one."

Along the wall next to the hold entrance was a long workbench. I flew over and landed on it, which gave me a good view of the entire room. I stood as tall as I could and shouted at all the creatures trapped in the tens and tens of cages.

"Dear friends! I apologize that I was making a racket earlier that some of you found disturbing. And I apologize if me addressing you right now is also disturbing, but

I have a proposal that many of you will want to hear." As I spoke, Aneko flapped over on her delicate moth wings and landed next to me. "I have managed to escape from my cage, and I have set my new friend free as well. Next, I will open all of your cages. If you are happy to stay put and get sold into the Fangcover pet trade, that's fine. Just stay in your cage. But if you want to escape, I'd like to offer you an opportunity. If you don't really care either way but would like a chance to participate in some fun chaos, then those of us who want to escape would really appreciate your help."

There were so many shouts and exclamations in response to my address that I had to wait for a few moments for everyone to calm down before I could continue.

"I have to admit," I went on, "that I don't have a formal plan. But I do have some human allies who are being held in another part of the boat. After I release you, I will go and free them. Then, together, we will figure out a way off this dreadhull. For those of you with wings, escape should be no problem. For those without, we will do our best to figure something out. In the meantime, here is what I need you to do: When the cages are unlocked and the hold door is open, charge out of here and run all over the place. Don't stop running and scrambling about. Try to get the sailors to chase you, but whatever you do, don't let them catch you. If you can buy me enough time to rescue my friends, then there is a much greater chance for everyone to get away."

Next to me, Aneko threw her front paws over her head and cheered. Many—if not most—of the caged creatures shouted back with undeniable excitement. I guess I was pretty good at delivering a rousing speech! I might

still need to work on my diplomacy, but I figured my cha-
risma score had to be pretty decent.

Okay, now to open all the cages. I could fly around
and repeat the spell tens and tens of times, but that
would take a while. I paused to consider what my boss
would do. I'd seen him take a simple spell and multiply it
to several targets. One time he bought a couple pounds
of peas from the farmers' market near our tower. He got
frustrated shelling them manually and then came up with
a phrase that popped all the peas out of their shells at
once. It hadn't actually made his work that much easier,
though, since the peas shot out everywhere and we spent
ages picking them all up off the floor. But anyway, I was
pretty sure I remembered what affix he'd used.

With my front paws held out, I tried to imagine
every lock in the room popping open.

"Aperi... sesame... omnis!"

Bam! Every cage in the room clicked in unison. The
animals within roared in response and immediately dove
out of captivity. Pure chaos. Wow, magic was unbelieva-
bly fun. And pretty easy, I have to say. Of course you need
to put in the work to learn the spells, but I'd been listening to magical phrases for years. I'd been studying magic
without even realizing it.

For a moment, I just stood there, taking in the exhil-
aration. Two jade shroomlings were doing a little dance
on top of a cage. A cloud weasel was running laps around
a long table, leaving puffs of mist in his wake. A squibbit
was climbing up the walls with the help of tentacle suc-
tion toes. Three potbellied golems were turning themselves into earthen balls and rolling up and down the
aisles between cages. A jungleroo was hanging upside
down from an overhead support beam by her prehensile
tail. Like I said, pure chaos.

It was time for action. I spread my wings to glide down in front of the exit—one more lock to deal with—but the muscles in my back felt weirdly weak, so I wasn't quite able to catch the air resistance I was expecting. I hit the ground hard and bit my tongue. That was weird. I took a couple steps forward, flexing my wings in and out, and the world dimmed for a moment. I had to stop and take a few breaths to steady myself.

"Are you okay?" Aneko fluttered down next to me.

"I think so," I said. "Just a bit tired suddenly."

"That was a big spell you just did."

"Yes, I suppose that's it." This frosted flickerkit was surprisingly worldly for a pet. She'd guessed that I could do magic, and she seemed to know something about the mechanics of arcane power. "I've seen my boss get drained from overtaxing his umbrix. But he can pull off some pretty big spells before it noticeably affects him."

"Well, you're still pretty small." She linked front legs with me, and we walked over to the door. "And it's your first day as a spellcaster. How old are you anyway?"

"I'm not really sure," I said. "More than ten, but that's as high as I can count."

"Oh. Okay." She gave me a cute nod with wide eyes like that somehow surprised her. "I would have guessed younger, but what do I know."

"How old are you?"

"In my family, we keep a moon count," she said. "By that reckoning, I'm four hundred twenty-two. Which would make me..." She did a quick calculation on her claws. (Impressive—she knew how to count *and* do math?) "...about forty-three years old."

I was going to ask her how many tens were in forty-three, but we'd arrived at the door. Time to carpe the diem, as Jorvun liked to say. Hopefully one more spell wouldn't knock me out. I took another deep breath, imagining just the smallest bubble of power coming up from my umbrix, and pointed at the door.

"*Aperi sesame*," I whispered.

Click! Honestly, this magic thing was just too much fun. It wasn't without a cost, though. That was becoming painfully obvious. As the door swung open and the first wave of freed creatures stampeded out of the hold, I had to cling to Aneko for a few moments to gather my strength. I wasn't destroyed by the effort, but doing anything in a hurry would be tough, and I didn't think I could pull off any more magic until I'd had a chance to rest. Whatever came next, I would have to rely on my wits—and on my new friend.

"Let's do this," Aneko said.

"First things first. We need to find my humans."

The newly freed creatures thundered to the right, chasing the fresh tang of salt air. I grabbed Aneko's paw and pulled her left, away from the stampede, down a corridor dimly lit by overhead magical lanterns swinging on chains. The bulkheads were riveted iron, painted the colour of mouldy parchment and slick with condensation. Hissing pipes crisscrossed the low ceiling, and the floorboards creaked with the motion of the ship.

This part of the dreadhull was quieter, but not still. Shouts echoed from somewhere above. Doors trembled in their frames as boots thundered overhead. Aneko and I hugged the shadows, sticking close to the wall, slipping past narrow hatches marked with signs I wished I could read. At one junction with steep stairs leading up, the sign included a symbol of a wheel, which made me think it led to the helm. No matter how much chaos the stampede of creatures created, I couldn't imagine the pilot or pilots leaving their station. And the brig would probably be in the most dungeon-ish part of the ship. Next we paused at a junction where two more corridors split off in opposite directions, one with a staircase leading down.

A trio of sailors hurried past the far end, shouting in Shaelun. One of them carried a net. Another had a baton that crackled faintly with static. I flattened myself against a crate marked with what I assumed was a warning sigil—three green triangles in a circle—and held my breath. Aneko tucked in beside me, her tail flicking softly against my leg. Once the sailors passed, we crept on.

The deeper into the ship we went, the worse it smelled. Wet iron. Old mop water? Aneko wrinkled her nose but said nothing. We passed a cluttered storage alcove where we had to duck behind a cracked barrel and wait for another two sailors to rush by.

When the coast was clear again, we turned another corner and came upon a bulkhead door half ajar and swaying with the ship's motion. I peeked through: a narrow stairwell led farther down. We descended, carefully, quietly, my claws slipping once on the edge of a tread. I still felt weak, but my strength was slowly returning. At the bottom was a final corridor, wider, warmer, and even danker than the last. Faint music warbled from somewhere up ahead. At regular intervals, there were side passages and inset alcoves, some framed with low arches, others marked with brass stenciling.

We came to a doorway that was open just a crack. Inside: triple-stacked bunks and a long bench strewn with personal effects. Crew quarters. Two small portholes gave us a view of water and coastline—presumably the shore of Fangcover Island. No one in sight. Next was a long, open room packed with linen bins, folded cots, and wall-mounted racks of uniforms.

I padded forward and poked my head around the final corner.

Bingo. The brig.

The hallway ended with a small guard station. Batons and manacles hung from one wall. A small shiny box about the size of a roast chicken sat atop a small table between two stools. (*Glimm, stop thinking about roast chicken.*) It pulsed faintly with magic. That's where the music was coming from. Underneath the table was an instrument case—Fox's lute, apparently. But I didn't see anything else that had been confiscated, so that must have meant the glamour rings were still doing their job. Standing in the middle of the small room were two guards, the ones who wore all black—long coats with high collars, leather gloves, and heavy belts with "tools" that weren't just for show. Neither looked bored. Neither looked like someone I wanted to fight in my current depleted state. Scratch that—I would never want to fight these two.

Beyond the guards were two doors fitted with iron bars. The room on the right appeared empty, but through the bars on the left, I could make out a couple of winter boots trimmed in white fur. That would be Elric. And next to the boots... it looked like someone was seated on the floor: a shoulder and arm, dark green with a flash of red. It was Lark. I stooped down so I could see more of her. She was saying something, gesturing vaguely, and she must have been whispering because I couldn't hear the words. Then she glanced through the bars and we locked eyes. I gave her a little wave and then held a claw up to my mouth. Of course she shot me a full-tooth grin when she waved back.

Aneko leaned in close. "Plan?"

I nudged her backward, down the dank corridor, and into an alcove where a large pipe ran from ceiling to floor.

"A couple thoughts," I said. "First, I'm having some weird feelings about... the magic thing. My boss can be a bit sensitive, so I think I ought to find the right time to let him know that I can cast spells."

"What? Then how are we going to get them out of there?"

"He's a wizard. He can cast it himself. And besides, it's a jail. Wizards end up in jail sometimes, right? So the lock is probably extra strong. Or something. Anyway, I'm sure we'll figure it out."

"What about the guards?" Aneko peered around the pipe to make sure the hallway was still clear.

"My first thought was that I could get them to chase me," I said, "but I'm still pretty tired. So how about that second diversion?"

She flicked out a spark from the tip of her tail and nodded eagerly.

"Come on."

We scurried back up the corridor to the empty barracks. The mattresses and bedding looked pretty flammable, so Aneko positioned her tail tip underneath a bottom bunk.

"I suppose we could use some frostfire to get this going," she said. "But then again, we don't want to burn up the entire ship."

I frowned at her but decided against saying anything. Clearly she just didn't know what frostfire was.

Her flame was small, so while we waited for a blaze to catch, I surveyed the room. And good thing I did. Right behind us, next to the door, was a fire-suppression canister. Hmm. Rather than correct her on the properties of my breath weapon, I would instead demonstrate! I blasted the canister with a few gouts of frostfire to make sure it was stuck to the wall. Then, once the mattress was crackling and billowing smoke, we dashed back up the hallway and took up our hiding place again in the alcove behind the pipe.

The smoke was black and smelled horrific, and it didn't take long before one of the guards muttered something and clomped up the corridor to investigate. When he got to the barracks and saw the fire, which must have been roaring, he shouted to his colleague. A second pair of boots ran past. We'd done it! Our opportunity had arrived. We scrambled out of our hiding place, around the corner, and skidded to a stop in front of the cell door.

"Your rescue party has arrived." I gave a grand bow.

On the other side of the bars, the pirate clapped, the bard whooped, the paladin fist-pumped, the wannabe inventor rogue did a little dance, and the wizard nodded like I'd done a reasonably good job.

"Jorvun, quick," I hissed, "can you unlock this thing?"

"It's warded." He shook his head.

"Frosted fishbrains," I said. "I was worried about something like that." Actually, I was a bit relieved, and maybe that was inappropriate at a time like this, but at least there was less of a chance that I'd need to use my own magic again right away. "Any other ideas?"

"I could shoot the lock," Lark suggested. "Not sure it would do the trick though, and it might ricochet and hit one of us."

"Also pretty noisy," I said.

"Who's your cute little friend?" Lark asked.

"Oh, this is Aneko. Aneko, this is Lark, Jorvun, Elric, Fox, and Xander."

"I think we need to hurry," Aneko said.

"I've got some lockpicks," Elric said. "But I don't think I can reach the lock from here. What about you, buddy? Do you know how to use these?" He held out some oddly bent iron sticks.

No idea is what I would have said, but Aneko stepped forward and grabbed them.

"Yup," she said. "It's been a few years, but I think I can manage. Glimm, give me a boost?"

"Cute *and* street smart," Lark said. "Where did you meet this doll?"

I stood as tall as I could underneath the door handle. Aneko gave two flutters of her moth wings and landed on my shoulders. She could just reach. After a few twists and rattles and clicks, she hopped back down.

"There you be," she said with a flourish.

Jorvun was the first to stride out of the prison cell. He glanced around the guard area, sniffed at the smoke, then spun on his heel. His oilskin, currently disguised by the glamour ring as a slick black raincoat, flapped about him.

"It seems something on the ship has caught fire," he said.

"Actually," I said, "it was Aneko who—"

"We should take advantage of this distraction," Jorvun blustered on, "and make for the life rafts."

I was pretty used to Jorvun talking over me. But... no *thank you?* Not a single word of a rescue well done? It wasn't like I needed congratulations or felt like I was owed a pat on the head, but it did seem a bit rude that he wasn't willing to acknowledge my efforts to this point, nor that Aneko and I might know something about the current situation.

"Well, we released several tens of creatures," I piped up, "they are now running around up on—"

"Prepare yourselves for a fight," Jorvun said. "Nothing and no one will stand between us and freedom."

"Hold on," Elric said. "I think Glimm is trying to tell us something."

"Thanks." I cleared my throat and tried to stand a bit taller. "We loosed a number of creatures who are all running around up on the deck to create a distraction. Aneko started the fire for a second distraction to get the guards away from the brig. We should hurry and sneak past them before they put it out. But rushing up to the deck might not be the best idea. There will be a lot of sailors and guards up there trying to deal with the creatures."

"Nice job, little guy," Lark said.

"Exactly what I would have done," Fox said.

Elric and Xander both gave me a thumbs-up.

"Okay," I started, "so here's what I think—"

"Yes, wonderful." Jorvun cleared his throat with impatience. Someone's ego was obviously sore. "But it doesn't really matter. We have my spells and Lark's blasters. Xander can find a weapon on the way. Hopefully Elric has a useful gadget in one of his pockets. And Fox... well, um, I think we just need to strike fast and hard."

Fox retrieved her lute case from under the table and wielded it like it was an oversized blaster.

"And what about the rest of the armada?" I asked. "Even if you manage to fight your way to a life raft, they could easily call for other ships to send people after us."

The wizard's lip twitched, and I felt a threat coming about future dinners, but Elric spoke up before my boss could get his angry words together.

"Why don't we just hide?" The inventor held up his hand as if to show us his glamour ring, even though it was currently obscured by his fancy alpine costume. "We'll just make ourselves look like boxes. We're not far from Fangcover. We'll get loaded off with the rest of the cargo, and then we can slip away."

"That won't work," Lark said. "The port authority uses anti-magic scanners. They will see through the illusion right away."

"That's true," Fox said. "I used to operate an anti-magic scanner when I was in the Merchant Marines."

A loud thump reverberated down the hallway, maybe coming from the barracks.

"I don't mean to rush this meeting along," Aneko said, "but we really need to hurry."

"Exactly," Jorvun said. "Some sense at last. Your little friend would make a decent familiar."

Ouch. Low blow. This was getting stupid. Escaping the ship was going to be difficult no matter what, but it certainly didn't help that Jorvun had worked himself up into such a mood. Okay, so he did lose a lot of money and most of his possessions in the stormleaf shipwreck, and he did get imprisoned, and he did just get saved by a miniature dragon and flickerkit, but now was not the time to be having a tantrum.

"So the plan is to just run out there blasters a-blazin' and hope for the best?" Lark asked.

"I don't see that we have any other option," Jorvun replied.

But he didn't charge forward. None of them did.

They just stood there nodding slowly, like they knew it was a terrible plan, but there were no other options to consider. Frost's mercy, how I wished I was better at planning. Create a diversion or two? Check. Bust out the party? Check. But then what? And what about all the creatures, especially those without wings, who wanted to escape the dreadhull? No, there simply had to be another way off this ship—to get across the sea and over to that rolling green shoreline that I'd glimpsed through the porthole in the barracks.

Another loud thump from up the corridor. Were they trying to free the fire-suppression canister that I'd iced to the wall? Holy sleet. We really needed to get moving.

But wait a minute—that was it! Fangcover Island wasn't far away. Maybe too far to swim, given how cold the water was, but if there was a way to get us closer...

"The helm!" I squeaked, then tried again with a bit less excitement. "The helm."

"What about the helm?" Lark asked.

"I know how to get there. We passed it on the way down to find you. It's probably not heavily guarded, what with a horde of creatures running around and causing trouble on deck. It would be much easier for you to over-power a pilot or two, right? Then we just steer the boat directly at the island. Crash into it. Jump overboard. Or... climb down with a rope. Whatever. The point is, if we can crash the boat into the island, then the creatures can all jump off at the same time we do. We can bring the diver-sion with us!"

Jorvun's eyes narrowed, and for a second it seemed like he would come back with a reason why my plan was impossible, but then his fingers shot up to his chin for an autonomic scratch of his salt-and-pepper stubble. That told me without a doubt he was considering my proposal. Win!

"Glimm, my new friend—" Aneko swung a paw over my shoulder. "—that's brilliant."

"Abso-fucking-lutely," Lark said. "If you'll excuse my French."

"I was just going to ask if you knew where the helm was," Fox said.

"I really need to get myself an anti-magic scanner," Elric said.

"Well, let's do this thing," Xander bellowed.

Ugh. He wasn't one for stealth. But with a quick glance around the corner, I confirmed that thick smoke was still pouring out of the barracks. Less than before, but the fire certainly wasn't out. And then another thump echoed up the hallway—this one followed by a crunch. If they had the canister off the wall, the fire would be out in moments.

"Hurry!" I shout-whispered. "Follow me!" And with that, I flapped with all my spell-sapped strength up the corridor. There was one more thing I could do to buy us time.

If one or both of the guards were working to get the fire-suppression canister off the wall, then that meant they would be right near the door, and that meant they'd spot us immediately as the party ran by. Not a great start. So with all the speed I could muster, which admittedly was a lot less than normal, I winged up to the door of the barracks. Sure enough, one of the guards was right there, and he gasped when he saw me. But I didn't give him time to react. I grabbed the door handle and heaved backward. As soon as it was shut, I spit frostfire in short bursts up and down the edge of the frame. And at the knob. The party all ran past me with Aneko in the lead.

On the other side, the sailors were shouting and kicking at the door, which made me realize they were trapped in there with the fire and smoke. It seemed to be mostly out, but with the door shut, they would soon run out of air. Obviously I didn't want them to get hurt, so I stopped short of completely trapping them in. It was a frightening estimation that I had to make, because if they got out too quickly, we'd be in trouble, but if my ice was too effective, they could end up dead. So I held off for a moment and just watched the door as they hammered on the other side of it. The ice seal was cracking—okay, it looked like they would be free in a couple more kicks. As my party disappeared up into the stairwell, I gave the door one more gout and then hurried to catch up.

It seemed a much shorter trip back to the sign we had passed with the wheel on it. Isn't that always the case? When you're seeking, the way always seems longer somehow, and then the way back is quick. Anyway, everyone agreed that the wheel was a pretty clear indication of the helm, so once more Aneko and I were showered in thanks and congratulations. Not from Jorvun, but he at least nodded when the others spoke our praises. But he wasn't going to have us shorties steal any more of his potential authority and glory.

"Everyone behind me," he hissed. "Stay as quiet as possible."

Sure thing! I definitely didn't want to lead the party into a fight. Was it going to be a fight? Yikes. I'd never been in a fight before. How would I react? What would I do? Of course I wanted to escape, and I wanted the same for my friends and for all the creatures I'd set free, but was I willing to hurt someone to achieve that? No, I didn't think I was. But did fighting always have to mean hurting? Were there other ways that you could win a fight without causing harm?

In that moment, with these thoughts churning in my mind, I wanted to shout for Jorvun to stop. I wanted to ask him if he had a plan that didn't involve throwing fire and shooting blasters at people. But it was too late for that. He had already dashed halfway up the stairs. Plus, Aneko and I were at the rear, racing to keep up with the rest of them. At least—and this was a small consolation— if anyone got hurt, it wouldn't be me doing the hurting. But was that really true? It was little ol' Glimm who had suggested this course of action, so really—

Nope, no time to finish that thought. Jorvun bounded up the last few stairs, threw open the door, and leapt inside. Xander was right behind him, gulping down the bright red contents of a small vial that he had pulled from somewhere within his glamoured lumberjack attire. We all scrambled in after them.

And there it was—the helm.

The pilothouse towered like a glass cage above the deck, thick iron panels speckled with rust reinforced smaller windows on the sides, and a big curved windshield stretched wide across the front and back like a pair of wraparound spectacles. Tubes and signal lights jutted from the roof, a couple still blinking in warning rhythm, and steam curled up from a vent near the rear wall. The room smelled like metal filings and burnt oil.

Two Shaelun crew members turned at once to gape at us—a pilot clutching the ship's massive steering wheel and the commanding officer I'd met before, the tall woman with the white streak in her hair and eyes like cold flint. She still had that silver circlet over her brow, though it was crooked now, and there was soot on one side of her face. Her coat was unbuttoned, and her sash hung loose. The pilot was younger, round-faced, eyes wide—his left eye magnified even wider with the lens of a monocle. With one hand still on the helm, he smashed a little red button on a pedestal to his left.

Uh-oh. It was a loud horn, and not the same as the one that had been used to signal to the other ships in the armada. This one was a call for help.

"Somno!" Jorvun shouted with one arm forward. *"Duad!"* The words rattled through the space with sharp emanations of arcane power. A pale shimmer rushed from his fingers and rolled through the air like morning mist. It struck both of them, and just like that—they collapsed where they stood. The monocle rolled across the metal floor with a lonely clink.

I blinked.

That was... efficient.

I filed the words away immediately. *Somno.* Simple. Elegant. No one got hurt. Just a little nap. And *duad.* Did that mean *two* in the ancient tongue? Yes, I thought it did. Noted!

Elric and Xander dragged the unconscious pilot and officer off to the side to get them out of our way.

"Still breathing," Lark said with a nod, but something about her tone made me think she was disappointed by this fact. "I suppose that works."

Jorvun cleared his throat and straightened his raincoat like someone had applauded. No one had. But maybe we should have. He looked... satisfied. Just a flicker of pride behind the squint and the scruff. And he glanced at me, not with his recent sour disdain, but with—well, with something a bit softer. Recognition, maybe. Or relief. Not exactly an apology, but I'd take it.

I turned toward the window.

From this height, the dreadhull's deck stretched out in all its chaotic glory. Though it was now fully dark, a nearly full moon hung over the water to the east, and the many lanterns across the deck illuminated the scene. The cargo cranes swung like lazy giants, unattended. Loose rope snapped against the railings. A stack of shipping crates had been knocked clean over—some smashed open, revealing straw bedding, feed sacks, and what looked like a half-crushed drum of rice.

And darting through it all—my liberated friends.

Three jade shroomlings were tripping sailors by bounding between their legs. Pugzips zigzagged through puddles, snapping at sailor boots with tiny electrical zaps. A whole cluster of jungleroos bounced from box to box, using their tails to vault the gap between railings. A pair of hawktoads took wing from the upper rigging, one leaving a splatter on a chimney tower that would proba-bly take weeks to clean. The potbellied golems were roll-ing back and forth across the deck like oversized bowling balls. The sailors, bless them, were absolutely losing it—yelling, diving, scrambling around with net poles and ba-tons, tripping over each other in a full-on magical me-nagerie stampede.

And we had brought the storm right to the bridge.

"Okay," I said. "So, uh, this is working."

"And it's all thanks to you, kiddo." Lark had already taken the helm and was steering the massive ship to star-board, right at the rocky shores of Fangcover Island. "Everyone, hold on to something."

And with that, she grabbed a lever beside the

steering wheel and slid it forward as far as it could go. Immediately, the dreadhull picked up speed. From somewhere behind us, other ships from the armada sounded their horns as if to warn the flagship that we were veering dangerously off course.

Jorvun stood at the windshield surveying the chaos, nodding to himself, looking quite vindicated. Our mission wasn't a complete failure after all. Who knows what would happen next, but at least the party wasn't headed for a prison sentence. Maybe—just maybe—he would still get the chance to sit upon the Frostvalen throne. And, of course, I would get to head off to dragon college. The dream was still alive.

Until—

Shouting from behind us.

A thundering of boots.

A squad of armoured guards surged up the stairs to the helm station, weapons drawn. Blades. Batons. Arcane shackles.

Okay, now what? We were outnumbered. Out-armed. Cornered.

First things first: shut the door.

"Xander," I shrieked. "Help me close this!"

The door was heavy, for me at least, but the paladin slammed it shut in the faces of the approaching guards just in time. And with what force! Wow. He seemed strong to begin with, but Xander's muscles were bulging more than normal. There didn't seem to be a locking mechanism, so I sealed the edges with frostfire while he held it shut.

"The glamour rings!" I yelped. "Quick, make yourselves look like Shaelun sailors!"

"Another stroke of genius, Glimm." Okay, you won't

believe who said this. It was Jorvun! Jorvun called my idea *genius*. I almost passed out in surprise.

One by one, the party closed their eyes to concentrate and then said the trigger word: *illume*. Their (mostly) ridiculous Frostvalen attire vanished and was replaced by the slick uniforms of the Shaelun armada.

And that's the exact moment the dreadhull crashed into the coast. It was quite an impact. Every one of us was sprawled on the floor. While the rest of us shook off the stun, Aneko fluttered up to sit atop the steering wheel.

"Now we just need a way out of this room," she said. "Anyone have a way of smashing the window?"

Lark growled with delight as she clambered back to her feet and unholstered her blasters, which was weird since you couldn't even see they were there beneath her glamour, but sure enough, they were. Everyone plugged their ears while she aimed and fired at the glass windshield. It spiderwebbed, then shattered, and the wind roared in with a howl.

"But wait," Elric said as he peered at the deck below us. "How do we get down?"

Fair enough. Aneko and I were the only ones with wings.

"Leave that to me." Jorvun's renewed pride came through with each word. *"Pluma poffo... omnis."* And with that, he leapt through the window and glided softly down to the deck below.

Honestly, he didn't need to target me and Aneko with the spell, but whatever. It was kind of fun to float through the air without flapping my wings.

"Let's go!" Aneko cried with absolute glee in her voice.

And down we went—across the deck, through the

chaos, and then right over the side of the dreadhull. As the party drifted ahead of me to the rocky beach below, I flapped twice, lulled in place with the lingering lightness of Jorvun's spell, and turned to all the creatures still running about the deck. For a moment, I wondered how they would get down to the shore without magical help, and I even considered whether I could manage a sneaky cast of my own. But then I realized that the ship had crunched into a rocky bluff that was only a couple feet below the prow. It made a perfect little bridge for their escape.

With as much volume as I could muster, I roared.

"Friends! Now is the time to flee!" I pointed toward the front of the dreadhull. "Into the forests! Let's get the frost out of here!"

This was happening.

Ice me sideways.

We'd really done it.

CHAPTER TEN

Follow Me (I Think?)

As we dashed into the nighttime woods of Fangcover Island, I gave a final wave to the horde of creatures liberated from the dreadhull. Where would their paths lead from here? Would they find professions rather than the subordination of petdom? Or would they live wild somewhere in this rugged landscape? Though our journeys would no doubt lead us in different directions, I wished there was some way we could keep in touch.

But this was no time to get sentimental. In addition to the creatures, Shaelun guards were also scrambling over the gunwale—some with nets in hand, intent on recovering their fleeing cargo, and others with... blasters? Were those actual blasters they were aiming at—?

There were two loud *cracks* and puffs of smoke, followed by an immediate *zip* and *thwack* as projectiles slammed into the tree trunks on either side of us. Okay, no time for lollygagging. I dove behind a rock and then hurried into the trees. Everyone was running (or flapping) apart from Lark, who dropped down to one knee, took aim, and returned fire. From somewhere behind us, a soldier shouted in pain. I glanced over my shoulder in time to see him stumble backward, clutching his chest, and fall from the rocky shore into the sea.

"That one's for you, Lady Brine." Lark cackled, then kissed the barrel of her blaster before taking two more shots.

I'm not sure if any of the guards were brave enough to pursue us after that. They didn't fire at us again, and as we pushed deeper into the dark woods, we could no longer hear their shouts. Although, that might have been partly on account of how deafening the blaster fire was. What a reckless, frightening weapon. As I flew ahead of the party, doing my best to pick a moonlit path for them that wasn't completely overgrown, I kept imagining the guard fall backward into the sea. Was he dead? A blaster shot to the chest was no insignificant injury. But they had to have healers among their numbers. Yes—I reassured myself more than once—his colleagues would pluck him out of the water and get him back aboard so a healer could mend the wound. Right? It was a win-win, in that case, since Lark got to have her gruesome sacrifice for the Saltborn Covenant, and we got to escape without, um, permanently hurting anyone. Ugh. I sure hoped that was the case.

As we pressed on through the trees, the dark fell heavy around us. The forest floor, blanketed in a thick tangle of marsh ferns and knotted brushroot, made the party's every step a battle. Branches clawed at their glamoured uniforms, and unseen nettle thorns sliced at their ankles. The farther inland we travelled, the more mist snagged low along the ground, swirling around tree trunks banded in silvermoss and fat clusters of bellcap fungus.

"What was that?" Xander asked every time a twig snapped or an old drift pine groaned in the wind.

Fox and Aneko took turns reassuring him. I wasn't sure if he was rattled from the battle or if he was just afraid of the dark.

I stayed low, navigating from one sliver of moonlight to the next, picking a path that slanted uphill toward where the trees thinned slightly. The salt tang of the sea was replaced by the sharp resin scent of cedaris and blackspike fir—though we had travelled from Valorica to Frostvale, not much was different from the forests around Ravenna. Behind me, Aneko fluttered silently, but the others—especially Xander, who kept muttering about shadow assassins—were less subtle. Still, the crashing of surf and the shouting of Shaelun voices were long behind us now.

We climbed a steep rise, then descended into a gully with a stream somewhere below us that bubbled in the darkness. When the trees finally opened onto a mossy ledge overlooking a gorge of tangled deadfall and mist, I dropped down into the thick carpet and motioned the others forward. The ledge, sheltered by a curtain of hanging witchlock vines and hidden from the slopes behind us, seemed like a decent enough place to hide. Good enough for tonight.

Since it had been a hurried journey through the woods, and considerable effort for those afoot, the party sat down on the ledge for a time to recover their strength and let the reality of our new situation set in. As we discussed the events of the day, which began amicably at first, Fox got out her lute and picked her way into a pleasant little melody.

"Just to get this straight," Elric said, "we're on Fangcover Island, but the City of Fangcover is not actually on the island?"

"That's correct," Jorvun said. "It's a bit of a mystery how that happened. From what I read, the great capital is a day's sail from the southern tip. And I should clarify— I *think* we're on Fangcover Island. Based on the maps I studied and how long we were in that brig, it makes sense that is where we've ended up, but it's hard to say for sure. There are other islands in this chain."

Xander muttered something and turned side to side, peering into the darkness.

"Wouldn't that be the salt's crust on the hull." Lark spat over her shoulder into the woods. "We could be stuck on some uninhabited island—uninhabited apart from monsters, no doubt—and we have to make do with the academic's profound book learning to find our way."

"What's that supposed to mean?" the wizard shot back.

"You assured us that you had the capacity to cloak the ship and get us inside the sea gate, for one thing. Which maybe you could have done if you'd listened to your familiar and not bothered trying to unlock the gate on your own."

"And who let the boat drift right in front of the gate and get swamped?"

"I was trying to keep your cursed cloak aimed at the armada so we didn't end up flashing them our ass, if you'll excuse my French." Lark's right hand inched toward her holster—currently obscured by her glamour. "And how was I supposed to know that the gate would unleash a wave like that? This was *your* plan."

Fox's playing got a little louder, and now she hummed along with her tune.

"Yeah, and who saved the day by putting the helm crew to sleep, huh?" Jorvun's hand inched toward his wand pocket—also obscured by the glamour.

"Saved the day?" Lark came up on one knee. "You don't think I could have taken care of them? Or Xander for that matter? Or maybe even Elric?"

"Maybe even?" Elric made a wounded face.

"Stop." I flapped over to land in the middle of the group. "Please, cut it out. This isn't helping anything. We all messed up to some extent. Most of you packed far too much, for starters. I didn't do a great job of scouting. My boss didn't have enough power left for the cloak. The wind blew us in front of the gate. You all got the Frostvalen accent wrong. I'm apparently incapable of lying, which it turns out is a detriment to diplomacy. Oh and most of your costumes were ridiculous. Yeah, we're all to blame, but we banded together and got the frost off that dreadhull. Together. Right? Right. And all those creatures too. So let's celebrate our escape and make a plan. Maybe we're on Fangcover Island. Maybe we're not. We can figure that out tomorrow. For now, we should set up camp and brainstorm ideas for finding some dinner. Okay? Okay??"

"Little guy's got a point." Lark eased herself back down onto the mossy ground.

Jorvun scowled and crossed his arms but said nothing.

"So you really think there's monsters on this island?" Xander asked with a quaver in his throat.

"Of course there are monsters," Aneko said. "There are monsters in every forest. Aren't there?"

"I just thought..." Xander picked up a fist-sized rock and held it cocked. "I mean, I thought it was the armada following us back there. And it could have been, but it could have been something else."

"I covered our retreat." The flickerkit padded over to the paladin and put a paw on his arm. "Just relax, big guy. If something had been following us, I would have seen it."

"And I scouted ahead," I added. "I saw nothing. Promise."

"But what if... what if... Maybe it's a monster with a cloak spell. Or illusion magic, like our glamour. What if this ledge—"

"Xander." Fox stopped playing. "You drank a vial of Alpha Power, didn't you? Back on the ship?"

"That's got nothing to do with—"

"It has everything to do with it," Fox said. "And you know it. Remember the time we fought that battalion down in the Baja Reach? When I single-handedly defeated that ogre?"

"I don't think that actually happened," Xander said.

"That's because you took two vials of AP and were squirrelly for days."

"What did you mean by *maybe even Elric?*" Elric asked.

"Okay, everyone, please." I thumped my tail on the ground to get their attention. "Let's not get distracted again. I'm aware that we might be going to bed without any food, but I'd like to do something about that if we can. Now, any ideas?"

"There's a stream in the gully," Aneko said. "Do people in Valorica eat fish?"

"Brilliant!" I almost blurted something about the

fish I'd stolen from the gulls when I'd botched my scouting mission, but I didn't want to steer the conversation back to our failures. "Fish would be amazing. Any other... forest things we could eat?"

"I used to be a survivalist," Fox said. "I learned about wild plants and all sorts of woodcraft skills, but, ah, that was a different ecosystem."

"Sure," Lark said. "Well, I only know fishing and buying provisions in markets, so I can't help."

"I think I've got..." Elric patted around in his pockets, which, of course, were still hidden beneath the glamour. "Oh, here it is. My Spicer 3000." He pulled out what looked to be a salt shaker with a small dial on the side—and an askew EMG logo. "So if there are fish down there, we can make a marinade of some kind."

"Maybe..." Xander was still casting suspicious glances into the dark forest around us. "Maybe there are some bird nests out there? We could find some eggs?"

"That's going to be difficult in the dark," I said. "But great idea. We'll hang on to that one for tomorrow. What about you, Boss? Any herbcraft that could help us out?"

He just glared. Oh boy. I guess we were back to him being sore at me for overstepping my role as familiar. I would have thought that defusing conflict and taking initiative on dinner would be welcome, but this wizard's ego was as unpredictable, apparently, as Xander's supplements. Well, his ego could get frosted. I was hungry.

"Okay, I guess not." I motioned for Aneko to join me. "We can go check the stream. Maybe the rest of you could gather some firewood? Or even pile up some moss and ferns to make our sleep a bit more comfortable?"

"I don't think a fire is a good idea." Xander hugged his knees to his chest. "It could attract—you know..."

"A monster?" Lark said. "We will set up a watch, obviously. If the forests here are anything like those around Ravenna, my blasters can sort us out. Though it would be a shame to shed blood so far from the salt."

"What about the Shaelun?" Elric asked.

"The armada will have a schedule to keep," Fox said, "if I know anything from my time in the Merchant—"

"Teeth on a toastie," Jorvun cut in with a tone that was at once venomous but also begrudgingly cooperative. "It's fine. I can cast an illusion around us tonight. And I know a spell for smokeless fire."

Perfect. With a bit of coaxing, patience, and luck, the party just might tolerate each other long enough to overthrow this ice-bitten King of the North. I really was earning my place in dragon college, one paw at a time.

Lark announced that she would take up firewood duty, and Fox volunteered to help, claiming that she'd been an elite deadfall collector back in her survivalist days. Elric tried to get Xander to help him gather moss and ferns, but the paladin was too scared to venture off the ledge, so the inventor set off on his own. Jorvun, meanwhile, took up a rigid cross-legged pose, closed his eyes, and began a deep-breathing exercise that helped him stoke his umbrix for a more complicated spell—something I would have to learn how to do at some point. I wanted to hang back and listen, but I also didn't want to make it obvious that I'd started paying much closer attention to the arcane, so I linked arms with Aneko, and we set off down toward the burbling stream.

And guess what—there were salmon! Big ones too, slowly swimming upstream or resting in shallow bends of the creek. The arduous journey back to their spawning grounds.

"Wait a minute," I said, "I thought they spawned in the autumn."

"Most do," Aneko explained, "but these are spring salmon."

This flickerkit really knew her stuff. Considering the fish were tired from their long fight upstream, it was pretty easy to catch one—and honestly, it didn't feel very fair. But whatever. It was one thing to have empathy for creatures and humans and even monsters. But food animals? I would say it's still important to have respect and not be cruel to them. But a dragon has to eat.

We found a smaller salmon that had become stuck behind a fallen log. I blasted it with frostfire, and together we hauled it onto the bank.

"They won't expect us to catch anything so quickly," I said. "Let's eat this one here."

"Because you prefer it raw?" Aneko set to carving the fish up with her impressively sharp claws.

"No. I mean, I do. But I don't want my boss to know how much I've had to eat."

"That's a strange thing to say." Aneko efficiently gutted the salmon and carved one flank into a perfect fillet. Clearly she'd done this before. "Why would he care?"

"I'm not sure," I said. "He says that I might get sick if I overeat, but food has never made me feel sick. Quite the opposite. Yet he is always very strict about my meals. Probably it's just so he can threaten to take away my dinner if I do something wrong."

"Really? But you're a *familiar*."

"I don't like it," I said, "but I think it's a normal part of employment."

"I don't know, Glimm." She finished carving the other flank and handed me a huge fillet. "Most pets are treated better than that."

"It's not that bad." I sank my teeth into the salmon and—holy sleet—was it ever delicious. For the next several chews, I was able to ignore Aneko's concerns. But when I finally swallowed, the doubt was still there. It did seem cruel that Jorvun would take away my meals sometimes, even if I'd done something wrong. I always wanted to learn and to do better. I would make that effort without punishment. But the wizard was strict with himself too. Maybe, in his severity, he was teaching me a lesson that I still hadn't fully grasped. "Anyway," I said after another big swallow, "I love being a familiar, and we do get along very well. Most of the time. I think you're not seeing his best side right now. This trip has been hard on him."

"Maybe you're right." She gave me a little shrug that suggested she didn't actually think I was right. "It's just a shame that, for someone who hates lying so much, you are forced to deceive your boss about something as essential as sustenance."

Ouch. Did having a sneaky meal count as deception? I hadn't really considered that before. I'd always thought of lying as specifically saying something that wasn't true. But then again, when Jorvun commanded me to keep his father and his Frostvalen identity secret, it did feel like we were both doing something wrong. So as we finished our meal, then returned to the stream, I considered the difference between a lie and a deception. What else was I keeping from my boss? That I had discovered my arcane abilities. But that was different, wasn't it? When it came to food, I was deceiving him so that I could have more. In that sense, it was for selfish reasons. But with magic, I didn't want to tell him, at least not yet, because I thought it would make him mad. His ego had taken enough of an assault on this trip. So was it different if a deception was for someone else's benefit? It had to be, right?

But hold on, was a deception about food really just about me? There was definitely a selfish component. I wanted to eat a lot more than my daily meals allowed, though I was pretty used to my limited diet. But when I did get extra snacks, my boss seemed annoyed, like I was getting paid for work I hadn't actually done. So in that respect, not telling him about sneaky meals was also a favour to him. If he didn't know about it, he couldn't get mad, which meant that I was keeping him in a happier mindset. And wasn't that my job, after all?

Anyway, I had a lot to think about as we dragged three more salmon out of the water—two big ones and another medium-sized. They were all too heavy for us to carry individually, but working together we managed to fly them one at a time up to camp. When we returned to the stream for the last one, a rustle of branches on the other bank caught our attention.

"Pssst," came a quiet voice through the darkness.

Xander's paranoia about monsters had seemed unfounded, but the idea was in both of our heads, so Aneko and I both fluttered into the air to put some distance between ourselves and whatever was crawling out of the bushes.

"Pssst," the voice said again. And then a small figure stepped into a patch of moonlight.

The creature bowed to us in a way that was so disarming, we both immediately glided back to the ground. He stood upright, almost with the posture of a human, then folded his arms neatly behind his back, watching us with a quiet, almost scholarly calm.

He was small but sturdy—slightly taller than Aneko

and far more compact. His body was built for climbing, all wiry limbs and nimble fingers. A loose membrane of leathery skin stretched between his arms and legs, and as he shifted his weight, it caught the light in a pale sheen. I guessed that he could probably fly, or at least glide. His back and tail, by contrast, were covered in dense, dark quills that bristled slightly when he moved. I hadn't seen anything like him during the escape, though perhaps in the chaos I'd simply missed him.

What struck me most, however, wasn't his appearance. It was his presence. He held himself with poise, like he was part military commander and part university lecturer. When he finally spoke, his voice was low and deliberate.

"You dropped your fish." He gestured to the salmon that had landed near the water's edge.

I blinked. "Right. Uh. Thanks."

"I'm glad to see you're safe," he said and then turned his gaze to Aneko. "Both of you."

I turned to whisper, "What *is* he?"

"A bristlegriff," she said. "Rare. From the eastern glades of Zulha."

The creature gave another small bow. "And my name is Minzo."

"Nice to meet you." I returned his bow. "I'm Glimm, and this is—"

"Aneko, yes. We met at the docks in Longfen."

"Good to see you again," Aneko said with a flick and spark of her tail. "Have you set out on your own or...?"

"No, I'm with the others." Minzo motioned vaguely behind him. "Once we regrouped, we followed your trail, though we weren't certain if it was safe to approach. I'm sure the high alert of the day has left your humans feeling anxious."

"Some more than others," I said. "Is there anything we can, ah, do to help?"

"Might we travel with you?" Minzo asked. "None of us know these lands, and though we are happy to have our freedom, most see the benefit of finding our way to a city."

Hmmm. On one paw, I loved the idea of helping these creatures find their way out of the wilds, not to mention the possibility of making some new friends. But on the other paw, they had all seen me do magic, and that might find its way back to my boss. Yet... was that really such a big deal? I couldn't be sure, but something twisting in my guts made me feel like I needed to find the right time and place to let him know about my magical discovery. Jorvun was definitely prone to jealousy. Not that I could outdo him at magic, but still. He took so much pride in his intellect and power. So maybe I could ask these creatures to not mention the magic thing? But that was like asking them all to lie. If an omission of information did in fact count as lying, as Aneko seemed to suggest.

But what about the creatures themselves? Would the wizard be okay with them all joining us, even just to follow us into town? It was really hard to predict how he'd react to unexpected developments. Would the fact that I'd set these creatures free somehow deprive him of the pride he felt about being instrumental in our own escape? Or could that pride translate—like, if he'd helped us escape, he'd helped them too? Okay, so this was getting a bit convoluted, and as I stood there thinking, Minzo had started to frown at me like he was wondering why I was taking so long to answer.

"My boss is temperamental," I said at last. "He

might be okay with you joining our party, but he might not. And as his familiar, it's kind of my job to keep him happy. But at the same time, I definitely want to help you find your way out of these woods."

"Okay," Minzo said, "that's fine. So what do you propose instead?"

"Keep following us at a distance. You tracked our trail this far, right? When we set out tomorrow, we'll get Aneko to take point, and I'll take up the rear. If we ever get to lighter terrain where our path might be harder to discern, I'll mark our direction with frostfire. Would that work?"

"That will work wonderfully." Rather than bowing for a third time, which is what I expected, Minzo saluted me, like I had just given him orders to take back to the troops. What an odd creature. "We will follow at a distance, as you ask. And I will seek you out again when the time is right. Thank you, Glimm, for your leadership on the journey ahead and behind."

"Oh, okay, of course," I said with no small amount of awkwardness. Leadership? I wasn't sure about that. But if that was how any of the creatures felt, I was glad they would be keeping their distance. If Jorvun thought in any way that I'd taken a leadership role with many tens of creatures, I was pretty sure he would be annoyed. "Have a good night."

And with that, Minzo disappeared back into the bushes. I gave Aneko a shrug as we lifted the final salmon into the air and started our slow flap toward camp.

When we were halfway back, she asked, "Something else to keep from your boss, eh?"

"I know," I said. "I'm not thrilled about it. But if part of my job is keeping my boss happy, I'm not sure what else to do."

"And what happens when he finds out?"

"Good question." I shrugged and almost let go of my half of the fish. "But if all goes well, maybe he won't. Right?"

"Sure, maybe he won't," Aneko said with a hint of amusement. "Anyway, your secrets are safe with me."

CHAPTER ELEVEN

Crime and Embellishment

After dinner, we agreed on the watch rotation, then curled up on the softest bits of moss and fern we could find. Having one person awake at a time all night meant that the fire never went out, so we managed to stay warm, and that meant everyone slept pretty well. My watch was last. I did a quick aerial survey to make sure nothing was sneaking up on us, as best as I could assess in the dark, then I gathered more wood and got the flames nice and crackling. Jorvun was dream-whimpering, and I hoped for the sake of his reputation that no one in the party was awake to hear him. Fortunately, he didn't moan anything about his Daddy this time.

I luxuriated in the heat of the fire for a while, which made me wonder what the difference would be between damp nighttime cold and icy winter cold. Surely, as a frost dragon, the snow and ice would warm me up in some other way. I was certain I would love it. But I had to admit, heat was nice too.

Once I'd soaked in my fill of the flames, I flapped up to a high branch directly over the camp. Jorvun's illusion spell was still in effect, although I could feel the power bleeding away into the wilderness. From my perch, the ledge looked like it had when we'd first arrived: just rocks and moss. And yet, since I knew there was a camp down there, I could see through the magic. But if I was just a random dragon or flickerkit or whatever flying overhead, I wouldn't think twice about it. Mossy ledge and nothing else. It wasn't a perfect concealment, like the failed boat-cloaking spell should have been, but the simpler illusion required much less strength from Jorvun. He could even keep it going while he slept. Magic really had some amaz-ing applications. I wondered if that was something they would teach at dragon college. I supposed that would de-pend on how many dragons were magical. Maybe I was a rarity. If it wasn't normal for a dragon to have an umbrix, then they probably wouldn't. Assuming, once Jorvun was king, we would be rich, I could always get an arcane tu-tor. Of course, this was also assuming Jorvun wouldn't teach me himself. He'd be busy with king stuff at that point anyway. But what if I confessed my secret before then? Would he be willing to share his knowledge with me? It seemed absurd that he wouldn't, and yet... I had an unshakable hesitation to talk to him about it.

The world was still pretty black when I took up my perch, a thick and breathless dark where the only motion came from the sway of tree limbs far below. The moon had set some time earlier. My watch passed in slow drips, the sky shifting so gradually that I kept thinking I'd imagined it. But then the stars began to thin. A wash of pale ink spread behind the ridgeline to the east, turning the treetops to charcoal smudges. Gradually, the edges of things came back. The faint outline of barkvine tracing the branches around me. The wet gleam of dew on murk-pine needles. And then, after what felt like an hour of al-most-light, a bloom of pink on the horizon. It deepened to orange, and then to the full warmth of sunlight spilling between the trees. Far overhead, the dome of the barrier wall shimmered faintly, nowhere near as visible as it had been from the Maelreach. Maybe because it was so dis-tant, or maybe they'd made it thinner on top to let in maximum sunshine.

The forest awoke with a scattering of birdsong: whistles, caws, chirps, and the high-pitched gossip of branch-hoppers waking to complain about the dew. My mouth watered before I could stop it. I couldn't help pic-turing all the birds I might catch if I was lucky—plump from rest, slow from sleep. Not that I was particularly good at catching birds. They most often outflew me, feathers whipping around corners with smug little tail flicks. Salmon, now—that was a different story. The stream in the gully still held plenty. Oh, to think of that cold, buttery flesh.

No. Stop it. I pulled my wings tight and forced my-self to scan the tree line again. *Focus.* This was my watch. The others were counting on me. Beyond the ledge, the forest sloped downward to the north, where I caught a glint of water. The ocean, dark and endless, just visible between breaks in the trees. South and southeast, the land climbed into the stony humps and snowy peaks of the island's central range. But it was east that held my eye. The horizon had cleared just enough to reveal thin plumes of smoke, drifting steadily upward. Maybe a town. And was that—? A winding silver line caught the rising light. A river? Maybe. Or possibly a road, snaking toward the smoke. I was about to launch into the air for a higher vantage when I was distracted by Elric's voice drifting up from below—quiet, companionable, and oddly playful. He was talking to himself again, or rather, to the pocket mirror balanced carefully in his lap.

"We've made landfall on an island called Fangcover," he said. "Now I don't know if your mom has told you about the trade war that's going on right now. Has she? Oh, okay, great. Yes, that's what we're up here for. We're going to put an end to it. Eggy toast, tree sap candies, snowglow charms—that's right. You'll be able to have all those things again, and all because your Pops—"

He paused, and it seemed like a little voice spoke back to him—from *within* the mirror. At first I thought I'd imagined it, that maybe it was just a bird chirping somewhere in the bushes below, but when I flapped to an adjacent branch for a better look, I could see a child's *face* in the mirror.

"Okay, yes, sure," Elric said. "Choir practice, nice. Sounds like fun. I'll try to call again soon. I'm sure you'll want to hear all about everything your Pops is—"

With that, the mirror shimmered, flashed, and the child's face was gone. Elric's shoulders slumped as he stared at his own reflection for a moment, then he sighed, shook his head, and flipped the mirror closed.

"Who were you talking to?" Fox asked through a yawn.

"Oh, that was my son Jimmy." The inventor's lips formed a smile of sorts, but it was a forced smile. He also tried to sound upbeat, but it was clear that something in his interaction had left him dejected.

"And how in the name of our great King Dummkopf

are you able to talk to your son?" Fox edged closer. "Isn't that a pocket mirror?"

"It's a whisperglass—an enchanted pocket mirror," Elric said. "New prototype. I hope to have an entire line of them one day. I'm sure they will be a bestseller."

Xander groaned, rolled onto his stomach, and wrapped both arms around his head.

"Then Jimmy has one as well?"

"No, this is the only one I've come across—I mean, that I've been able to have manufactured."

"So the other person... what are they talking to?"

"Good question," Elric said. "I've never been on the receiving end. The enchantment is called Scrollr, so maybe my face appears on the nearest scroll? Or maybe it just appears in the air somewhere near the person I'm calling. Next time I'm on with one of my kids, I should ask them."

"How many kids do you have?" Lark asked as she rubbed sleep from her eyes.

"Fourteen—and counting." The inventor beamed, although I could still detect a trace of sadness in his expression.

"Brine and Keel," the pirate said. "How did you find a woman willing to push out that many otters for you?"

"Oh, well." Elric shoved the hand mirror into his pocket and glanced away. "A number of mothers, to be honest. I've never been very good at convincing them to stick around."

"Still, a devoted father," Jorvun mumbled as though speaking to no one in particular. He sniffed, and I wondered if his eyes had become a bit glassy. "That's really something..."

Next it was Aneko's turn to stir. She yawned, sat up, then started washing her face by licking her paws.

"Can I see it?" Fox blurted. "The mirror, I mean. Or actually—can I use it?"

"Sure." Elric pulled it back out and handed it to the bard. "If you promise to be careful."

"Of course. Of course." Fox took the hand mirror, and a gleam of—something—spread across her face. She looked a bit like I imagine I do when I've been offered an unexpected treat. No, actually, even more enthusiastic. "So how does it work?"

"You just imagine the person who you want to talk to, say the trigger word—*scry-fi*—and then the person's name," he said. "They will have the opportunity to accept your invitation to speak. I suppose in case they are on the toilet or something. And that's it. If they accept your call, you get to talk to them."

My boss grunted as he got to his feet and stretched, then muttered a word that sounded like *nullivar*. The quiet magical buzz of the illusion concealing our camp ceased.

"If we're all up, we might as well get moving," he said. "Where's Glimm?"

"Up here!" I waved down at him. "And I know what direction we need to go. It looks like there's a town to the east. And maybe a road to the southeast."

"Fantastic," the wizard said. "Well done."

It seemed my boss had woken up in a good mood! I'd been worried about how much rest he would get on a rocky ledge. But clearly he had been exhausted enough to sleep—even with a spell tugging at his umbrix all night. Well, if he was in a good mood, then I was too.

"Looks like it will be a long way," I said. "Most of the day, I would guess. So... breakfast?"

"Yes, I suppose so," Jorvun grumbled. "But I'd rather not start the day with the same thing I ate last night."

"I could eat fish three meals a day," Lark said, "and often do."

"Same," said Aneko.

"Same," I chimed in.

"How did you like that spice rub last night?" Elric asked. "I could do the same, but if you'd prefer a different flavour, my Spicer 3000 has a number of options."

"Something different," Jorvun said.

"How about a baharat or tandoori blend?"

Aneko and I hurried to the stream while they discussed the marinade. Honestly, I didn't know what was wrong with them. This was some of the best fish I'd ever had, and I couldn't imagine wanting to disguise the flavour with spicy powders that had, in all likelihood, been derived from vegetables. As on the night before, we caught a small fish and ate our fill at the streambank, then brought bigger fare to the humans. Once they had spoiled the meat with spices and fire, we were able to get the day started.

The woods grew less steep after the first hour, but the trail was still a challenge for our humans, especially Xander, who seemed to have a residual headache from his Alpha Power potion. Aneko and I flitted ahead through branches thick with murkpine and sporebark, scanning for the best routes, and of course for any sign of danger. Of that, there was none. It was possible there were monsters out there, but five humans are a force to be reckoned with, so we were probably sending the denizens of the wood into hiding with our noisy approach.

Fox, in particular, was almost shouting into Elric's hand mirror. She'd spent the first hour of our hike trying to get through to someone at MaxNews, her dream network, but for whatever reason they refused to answer the call. Finally she reached a reporter at Bratburn News, which, according to the happy dance she performed, must have been a reasonable second choice. She fell to the back of the group, in part because both her hands were occupied—one with her lute case and the other holding the mirror—so she was a bit slower climbing over logs and around boulders. And also, perhaps, because her version of events was somewhat different than what we had gone through over the last couple days.

First of all, she made it sound like she had assembled the party in Ravenna herself. As soon as I heard this, I glided back to stay within earshot. Fox really was a fascinating individual. More and more, I found myself doubting the claims she made about her past. She didn't seem that old. I'm terrible at assessing human age, but I would guess she wasn't too far out of late adolescence. So a newish adult? I'm not sure how many years that equates to. Yet her personal and professional history made it sound like she was as old as my boss.

"It's a crack team that I was able to pull together," she said. "Not another journalist among them. They are all elite warriors, plus a mage with a powerful dragon familiar. My goal in breaking through the barrier wall was to find out what's really going on in the North. Like how are the Frostvalenites faring under Trudera's oppressive regime? In the end, all that matters to me is the truth, so I decided it was worthwhile to recruit a party interested in regime change. Of course, I will remain neutral in whatever lies ahead, but I figure it only makes sense to surround myself with people who are going to take me to the heart of this political dungstorm..."

A powerful dragon familiar? This was some good storytelling. Yet she spoke with such self-assuredness and confidence that I had to wonder: Was she spinning a tale that she thought would be more newsworthy? Or did she actually believe this version of events?

"To get through the barrier wall, I had the Saltborn captain bring us to the sea gate, which I anticipated would open with a wave big enough to capsize our storm-leaf. This was timed perfectly, just as a Shaelun armada approached. I then sent the dragon to arrange for our *rescue*. Ha—what a ruse! And it worked perfectly. The Shaelun brought us inside the wall, and when they least expected it, we set loose a horde of creatures from their hold, crashed the ship into Fangcover Island, and slipped away into the woods. Exactly as planned."

Wow. What a fantasy. I'd much rather be a participant in Fox's version of events than what we had actually been through. She was giving me quite a new perspective on the complexities of human fabrication. Lying for the sake of lying? Was that a thing? But anyway, I couldn't spend too much time listening to her spin wild tales. I had a job to do, so I fluttered ahead to check on the rest of the party. They didn't seem to be aware of Fox's news-report-in-progress.

"They really say *oot* instead of *out*?" Xander asked as he stepped over a rotting log.

"That's what I heard," Elric replied.

"Not quite *oot*," Lark said. "I think you're overdoing it a bit."

"I'm the expert on languages here," Jorvun cut in. "It's definitely *oot*."

"The great academic has spoken." Lark shook her head. "I'm just going to avoid both words until I can hear them pronounced a few more times."

Wherever the terrain grew rockier or the trail

forked, I doubled to the back of the troop and left a quick spray of frostfire to indicate our direction. The day was warming up, so my ice wouldn't last forever, but I hoped it was enough to give the creatures following us a clear sign.

The party kept bickering about vowel sounds and regional slang as we made our way southeastward. As the sun rose higher, the woods thinned. Cedaris gave way to broom scrub, then a rise of dry hill covered in scrabble moss and scattered ratgrass. From the top, we spotted the road: a packed gravel artery running northeast to southwest through a lowland grove. The moment the party saw it, Xander dropped to one knee in gratitude.

"Civilization!" he cried. "Praise the High Matron of Nutriment!"

We followed the road due east. The gravel crunched pleasantly underfoot—well, under *their* feet. Pleasantly because there was much less moaning about bushwhacking. Just an easy path forward and the smell of distant smoke, which grew stronger as we descended back toward the coast. By late afternoon, the shadows stretched out long across the road. The trees thinned even more, replaced by fields—some wild, others cleared and cut. Horses penned in by cruel fences with iron barbs. And another animal—similar to a horse, but goofier looking, chewing grass with an odd circular motion to its jaw.

I flapped over to Aneko. "What the heck is that?"

"A cow." She laughed at me and did a little somersault in the air. "Have you never seen a cow before?"

"No, I grew up in the city." It was my turn to laugh. "But what's crazy is I've eaten cow. And they're pretty tasty. I had no idea they were so big!"

A few distant rooftops came into view. And then,

as we rounded a bend in the road, a sign appeared: *Welcome to Scoomb*.

Amazing! Scouting and guiding mission? Accomplished. As the party hurried ahead, excitement clearly invigorating their feet, I flapped a bit higher to see if I could spot where we'd started the day. To be honest, I was thinking about all the juicy salmon we'd left behind. I couldn't actually tell where our camp was across the canopy of leaf and needle, but I did spy some movement in the bushes back down the road. I almost shouted a warning that there was a monster coming at the party from behind, but then I realized it was Minzo the bristlegriff. He waved at me from the shallow ditch at the edge of the gravel, then gave me a little salute. What a relief! My trail markers had done the job. I returned his wave—not the salute though, which seemed a bit awkward somehow—then soared back down to my party as they reached the edge of town.

"Before we get any farther—" Aneko fluttered to the front and cleared her throat. "—I think it's time to change your clothing."

Frost's mercy, the flickerkit was right. I'd gotten so used to seeing them all in their Shaelun uniforms that I'd almost forgotten it was a disguise.

"I was just going to say the same thing," Fox said.

"Actually, I've been contemplating this for some time." Jorvun kept walking, whereas the others had stopped to consider. "The last time we donned Frostvalen attire, we went a bit overboard—if you'll excuse the pun."

Xander was the only one who laughed, though it took him a moment.

"I propose that we get a bit closer to the town," my boss went on. "Keeping out of sight, of course, until we can see exactly what the locals are wearing."

"That's a decent plan," Lark said. "All right, let's say we give this academic another chance. Once we have our new glamours... what's next?"

"Dinner, for a start," Jorvun said. "And not fish this time."

"Makes sense." Lark shrugged off the anti-fish sentiment. "But how, exactly, are we going to pay for it?"

"I have a few clinks." Xander dug into his pockets.

"In Frostvalen currency?" Jorvun asked.

"Oh." Xander stopped digging. "Right. No, it's not."

"Exactly." Jorvun locked onto Elric. "Now all of you know our dear inventor here is something of an entrepreneur—"

"Something of an—?" Elric looked like he had just been backhanded.

"—but in his youth, he was quite a swindler."

"Oh, well..." Elric laughed as if to cover his initial reaction, then puffed up his chest, screwed up his mouth, and nodded immodestly. "Yes, it's true. I was quite the— wait a minute, are you saying...? Are we going to...?"

"Yes indeed," Jorvun said. "We're going to rob a bank."

CHAPTER TWELVE

The Tweens' Gambit

The party waited at the *Welcome to Scoomb* sign while Aneko and I flew into town for some reconnaissance. We had a few orders of business: first, we needed to assess the local attire; second, we had to locate a bank and tavern; third, we were to take note of anyone in uniform, whether the police, the military, or even the Shaelun.

Attire: check. The people here dressed more or less the same as the people in Ravenna, although there was a small-town vibe—not a huge surprise. But no one looked anything like the costumes the party had assumed after the shipwreck.

Bank and tavern: check. The town of Scoomb stretched across a low ridge, its main road curving past more than ten squat buildings with cedaris-plank siding and mismatched paint. Near the centre stood the Old Country Tavern (Aneko read the sign for me), which seemed like a fun place to visit, with a sod-covered roof and a trio of goats munching peacefully up top. Yes, goats on the roof! How strange. Across from it was the Scoomb Emporium (again, thanks, Aneko), a long, barnlike structure with a wide courtyard cluttered with many tens of wooden and stone statues—gnomes, elk, sun gods, a massive turnip, and what might've been a screaming monk or a surprised fishmonger. The bank was modest, with a narrow brick facade and a brass-plated sign that read, apparently, *Vankitty Credit Union*. Down the road, a post office with a purple awning leaned slightly to the left, and beyond that, on the far side of town, an open-air market bustled with many crowded stalls under canvas awnings, packed with townsfolk. Northward, fields and pasture sloped gently toward the glittering sea.

Police: check. Five officers lounged around a picnic table in front of a shop selling sweet fried bread—puffed spirals of dough with crystallized sugar crackling on top. I caught the scent on the wind and nearly lost focus. It didn't smell like there was any meat involved, but honestly, I didn't care. The officers looked relaxed, chatting and sipping something from clay mugs. Their uniforms were stiff-looking red coats with brass buttons, high collars, and black boots polished to a shine. One of them had a tasty little pigeon sitting on her shoulder. Police pigeon? How cute. And their mounts—rotund and slightly bored-looking quarter horses—stood nearby, tails twitching.

We flew back to the party and explained the score. First things first, they all turned off the glamour spells— and, frost's mercy, they were filthy.

"Okay, so you don't need to don a costume," I said, "but I recommend turning the glamours back on. Can you make yourselves... slightly cleaner versions of your current attire? Also—Boss, Xander, Elric—keep your facial hair in mind. You're all looking a bit scruffy."

"It would be nice if we could get some rooms for the night," Lark said. "An actual bed would be amazing, not to mention a bath."

I didn't want to press the point, but she was right. They had definitely taken on an odour.

"That's going to depend on how well this robbery goes," Jorvun said. "If we can get in and out without being seen, then there's no reason we can't. But we should also have a backup plan."

"There's a hitching post on the other side of the market," Aneko said. "Single horses as well as parked wagons. If we have to get out of town in a hurry, I think that's the place to head."

"Great," Jorvun said. "But I expect our plan will go off flawlessly. I mean, with my magical prowess and Elric's burglary experience, what could go wrong?"

"Don't say that," Lark said. "Don't tempt the storm."

"I used to do a bit of burglary myself," Fox said.

"Here's what I'm thinking," Jorvun said without acknowledging Lark or Fox. "Elric and I will head over to this bank. They should be closing soon, if they haven't already. Not that I think it's necessary, but we'll take Glimm and Aneko to keep watch. The rest of you, head over to that tavern and order us a bunch of food. I'm keen to sample the local fare, so a bunch of shared dishes would be fantastic. We will do the deed, then come and meet you."

"But we don't have any money," Xander said.

"Restaurants charge *after* the meal," Jorvun said. "So no problem. We'll be along shortly."

"I agree," Elric said, "a bath would be really nice."

Lark and Jorvun both frowned at his delay.

"Are you paying attention?" Jorvun asked.

"What? Yes, of course," Elric said. "Magical burglary. Let's do this."

So a pirate, paladin, and bard walked into the bar. Aneko took position in a tree in front of the bank. I found a perch on the roof of the Scoomb Emporium that gave me a clear line of sight to the bank's rear entrance. That was where Jorvun and Elric were going to make their attempt. But they still had to walk across town, find a sneaky spot where the wizard could raise his cloaking spell around them both, and then make their way to the alley behind the bank. In other words, I had time to look around.

On the other side of the Emporium, in the front courtyard, there was a bit of a commotion. Two groups of people had assembled, and it seemed like there was something of an argument taking place. The one group had set up on the stairs of the Emporium—which, like the bank, had closed for the evening. They were holding signs and marching around in a little circle, chanting something that sounded like *funk new era*. How odd. One of them also waved a flag that I recognized from a little pin that Jorvun used to wear before the trade war began. It was two vertical bands of red on either side of a band of white, and in the very middle was a coiled-up red dragon. Pretty sure that was Frostvale's national flag. The second group was at the bottom of the steps, and they didn't seem to be organized in the same way. At least, they didn't have signs, a flag, or a chant. Instead, they were mostly just shaking their heads or fists.

Okay, might as well take a quick peek.

When I flapped over and landed on the back of a

bench at the edge of the courtyard, I realized the chant wasn't *funk new era* but *fuck Trudera*. Holy sleet. They were political dissidents! Now this was very interesting. It seemed like many of the locals didn't agree with them, or at least there were slightly more people in the second group who were shouting things at the protestors. Like *go back to the Prairies* and *no one here voted for him anyway* and *if you're so smart, why don't you run for office*.

I wasn't sure what it meant to *run for office*, or where the Prairies were, but I was glad that so many people were willing to stand up for the King of the North. If my boss was going to replace him, it would definitely help if at least half the people were happy about his rule. Either way, it was also good to know some people were disgruntled. Maybe I could learn a bit more about whatever Trudera had done to annoy them, and that way my boss could take it into consideration and become a more popular leader. How fortunate that I'd happened upon this spectacle. It was really going to help me in my job as Jorvun's advisor.

Anyway, I had to get back to my post, so I took one last look around the square and—hold on a second, what was that? A poster with a dragon on it? I couldn't yet feel any magic in the area, which meant that Jorvun hadn't started his cloaking spell, so I flapped over to investigate. The poster had curled a little at the corners, but the image was still crisp: a majestic blue dragon soaring over a mountain range, his wings tipped with sunlight and a long purple scarf trailing dramatically behind. He looked so strong and elegant. Plus he was a frost dragon, just like me, though the image made it seem like he was much bigger.

WE'VE COME FOR YOUR EGGS

I landed on the ground in front of the poster to better study the shape of the dragon's horns, the confident arc of his neck, the tiny splash of frostfire curling from his mouth. A line of symbols curved across the top in thick gold letters. More lines below, probably explaining something important. Though of course I couldn't read them. But just then a lady came around the corner. It seemed like she was in a hurry, the way she was thumping along in her brown leather hiking boots and athleisure doublet and hose, but I just had to know what the poster said.

"Excuse me!" I held up a paw and stepped into her path. "Could I bother you for a moment?"

"Hey there, cutie." She stopped and gave me a huge full-tooth grin. (I tried not to visibly cringe.) "What's up?"

"Up? Oh, I was just..." I pointed at the poster. "Can you tell me what this says?"

"Can't you read it yourself?" She frowned like I'd just ask her the strangest question she'd ever heard.

"Nope, I can't read."

"How odd." She put her hands on her hips and looked me up and down. "I guess you're still pretty small, eh. Well anyway, sure, I'd be happy to. It's an advertisement for the Aerie."

"The Aerie?"

"Wow, were you hatched last week?" She laughed as if this was a great joke. "The renowned dragon college, silly."

Snowshards and permafrost. Actually? How amazing! In my excitement, I let go of her insults about my age and literacy.

"No way," I said. "Is it here in Scoomb??"

"Gosh no. It's in the East—out in Ontareth, some-where up in the Palachenn Peaks."

"Oh." That meant I'd have to part from my boss to attend. Boarding school wasn't what I had pictured, but that wasn't so bad. I was sure I'd make lots of friends.

"Don't worry your little head," she said. "Plenty of time for you to grow up before you need to start thinking about college."

"Right. Okay." How old did she think I was? I as-sumed *hatched last week* was a gross exaggeration. Maybe she just didn't know very much about dragons. "Hey, one other question while I have you here."

"Oh, you're such a darling." She stooped over a bit, and for a second, I thought she might pet me or some-thing. "Shoot."

"Shoot what?"

"No, I mean, um, go ahead," she said. "Ask me your question."

"How do I get to Fangcover City from here?"

"Well, I suppose one day you will be strong enough to fly there, but otherwise you'd need to travel over the Badahat Pass to Gorptoria, which is about a day's travel, then take the ferry," she said. "But you must have a par-ent or guardian who knows all of this. You're... you're not a runaway, are you?"

How awkward. She had been nice enough to stop, but I was getting a bit annoyed with her assumptions about my age and capabilities. Plus, I had a job to do. I'd let Trudera protestors and dragon posters distract me long enough. It wouldn't be wise to repeat my scouting fail from the sea gate episode.

"Nope, not a runaway," I blurted. "Thanks for all your help."

WE'VE COME FOR YOUR EGGS

And with that, I flew off, out of the square and back to my perch on the Emporium roof. Just in time, too. Jorvun and Elric were huddled under a tree at the end of the alley, and I felt the first shimmers of magic as he began his invocation.

The alley was quiet, so my job was looking pretty easy. From her tree on the other side of the bank, Aneko waved her paw at me, so I gathered that all was well over there too. That meant I could concentrate on Jorvun's spell. Not that I could hear the words, but I quite enjoyed the swirl of magic, especially when he was working something more complex than a single utterance. This was one of those. Four pulses corresponding to four words of power. No, wait, there was a fifth pulse, though it was smaller, like a little knot tied at the end.

Pretty sure he was cloaking them, which probably meant this was a variation of the spell he'd attempted to wrap around the *Brine Whisperer*. If my memory could be trusted, the words of power had been *fadere, obscure, mantella, sneekum*. The four pulses that were rolling up to me, kind of like concentric circles on a pond, felt very similar. I closed my eyes for a moment to let the magic wash over my skin. No, not similar. They were the same. Definitely. This was the same spell. And yet it felt more contained, which must have been the little knot. An affix of some kind. Last time, he'd been attempting to cast big, a globe of cloaking that hid an entire ship. This time, he just needed to cloak himself and Elric. When he'd put those Shaelun to sleep on the boat, he had added a containment affix so it only applied to the two of them. *Duad.*

Yes! That was it for sure. When he'd cast the floaty feather spell on all of us, he'd used the affix *omnis*. But he hadn't used that on the stormleaf because... well, probably because it wasn't just individuals he was cloaking, but an entire large space. So containment wouldn't have worked? I wasn't totally certain about my conclusions, but they felt right. Regardless, it was pretty exciting to be working out the mechanics of the wizard's invocation just by proximity and a bit of context.

By the time Jorvun had repeated the spell seven times, the power had really wrapped itself around them. And sure enough, he stopped chanting and the two of them walked out from their hiding place and started up the alley toward the bank's back door. Not that I could see them. I mean, I could and I couldn't. It was a bit like the illusion spell he'd cast over our camp. The arcane signature was undeniable, like there were two blobs of power floating toward me, but the wizard and ex-burglar/inventor were otherwise invisible.

Their voices, however, were not disguised. When they got to the rear entrance, the bickering started.

"One quick spell should do the trick," Jorvun said. "Now, let's see..."

"Actually, I have a new lockpick kit with me."

"Speed is essential. The longer we stand here, the more likely—"

"Trust me, I'll be quick," Elric insisted. "Besides, you should save your power in case anything goes wrong."

"Excuse me? You're starting to sound like my condescending familiar. I have loads more power available."

Condescending familiar? My boss could be such a frostwit sometimes. The most annoying part is that I was close enough to hear him and he knew it. So it was like he was talking about me behind my back and insulting me to my face at the same time. Honestly, in that moment, I almost flapped off back to the tavern. What a complete jerk. And to think of all the things I had done on this adventure to help. It was like he had no idea what a fantastic employee I was.

Anyway, while Jorvun was insulting me, Elric had apparently gotten his lockpicks out and done the job. The door clicked open.

"There we go," he said. "See, I told you I'd be quick."

At this point the two of them disappeared into the back of the bank. I mean, they had already disappeared since they were invisible, but now it was also difficult to follow their banter. So I waved at Aneko to let her know that everything was okay. We'd agreed in advance on a simple code—a single-paw wave was good, two paws bad. Then I dropped off the roof and glided into the alley to land on a barrel next to the door. Unfortunately, it turned out this was a garbage barrel, so it smelled horrendous, but at least it got me close enough to hear what was going on inside. Evidently, they had come to another locked door.

"Now this one is definitely going to require lockpicks," Elric said, "though it will take me a bit longer."

"You've already proven yourself," my boss hissed. "And a surplus of time is something we don't have. Stand aside."

"No, you don't understand. That symbol right there? It's from a company I once worked for. I got on with them just so I could learn more about their security systems. They specialize in subtle anti-magic locks and alarm triggers."

"I *don't understand?* Excuse me? They may be subtle to you, but you need to trust me. I've been doing this for *decades*. If there was anti-magic anything, I'd be able to feel it. They probably just bought a sticker from this company to make thieves *think* it's anti-magic. Like when people get one of those vicious-looking *Beware of hellhound* signs, when in fact they only have a chihuahua."

Have you met any chihuahuas? I get that they are tiny, but they can be pretty vicious. Anyway, this conversation was concerning for two reasons. First of all, and most importantly, I could definitely sense something weirdly magical within the bank. It was similar to the power that flowed out of Jorvun when he was casting, only it was going in the opposite direction. Like inverted magic? Not a huge arcane signature, but it was undeniable. Was that anti-magic? It was certainly subtle, so I had to conclude, for safety's sake at least, that Elric was right. Second of all, this was concerning because *my boss couldn't sense it*, and he was standing inside, much closer to the source. What did it mean that I could feel the anti-magic from out here and meanwhile he was willing to swear that the door in front of them was entirely mundane?

Jorvun wasn't going to be happy, but it was time for me to act. I had to go in there after him and tell him, yet again, that he was wrong about something. Would it get me a scolding? Yes. Would it put him in a foul mood for at least another day? Yup. Would it cost me a nice dinner at the tavern—a sampling of local fare? Maybe. But if this robbery didn't work out, we wouldn't have any money to pay for dinner, and that would put the party in a new spot of trouble. And!! If my boss was about to set off an alarm, not being able to pay for dinner might end up being a much smaller problem.

"*Aperi sesame!*"

Frosted fishfoot. My hesitation was going to cost us.

A light flashed from the back of the bank. Elric and Jorvun both screamed. I'm not sure what launched out of the door first, the failed burglars or the scent of burnt hair. But there they were, smoking and coughing and clawing at their eyes. The invisibility spell had definitely been cancelled. At the same time, a very obnoxious alarm split the air.

"What in nine hells..." Jorvun said as he staggered across the alley.

"I tried to warn you." Elric blinked furiously while gingerly patting his singed hair.

Had they both been blinded? It seemed so. Maybe temporarily, but with the alarm calling all nearby law enforcement, even a short delay was going to be trouble. I flapped up above the bank to wave Aneko over, but just as I got up to the roof, she came soaring over the edge.

"Anti-magic wards?" she asked.

"How did you know?"

"Pretty typical security system for a bank," she said as she fluttered past me. Then she shouted, "I'll swing back to the fried bread shop and see how far away those cops are."

"Great," I shouted back. "I'll lead them toward the park next to the market."

"Glimm!" Jorvun shouted at me from below. "Where—?"

"I'm right here." I swooped down and hover-flapped a few feet away from them. "I'm going to get you out of here. First things first, your glamours. The anti-magic blast shut them off. You need to look like something other than charred bank robbers. I'm thinking... children. But not the super small kind that need a parent with them. But too small to be able to rob a bank. Which ones are those?"

"Tweens?" Elric suggested. "I have a few kids around that age. They love me to pieces, honestly."

"Okay, sure. Tweens," I said. (*To pieces?* What an odd expression.) "And Jorvun, if I'm sitting on your shoulder when you activate the enchantment, will I also be concealed?"

"Oh, um, maybe," he said. "According to my research in—"

"No time," I interrupted him.

He set his teeth and tilted his head in a way that was normally accompanied by a sharp glare. Yikes. At least I was spared that part. Well, whatever. I had a job to do.

I alighted on his shoulder. "Just activate the glamour, and we'll see what happens."

"*Illume*," they both intoned.

The magic twisted out of their rings and wrapped about them—or us, rather. Jorvun was a short and chubby boy whereas Elric had transformed into a scrawny girl. As for me, I'd thought I might just be invisible, concealed by the glamour in the same way Lark's blasters had been. However, it seemed that I'd just shrunk. A dragon the size of a pigeon. Hmm. I wasn't sure how I felt about that.

"Did it work?" Elric was still blinking furiously.

"I think so?" Jorvun squinted and rubbed at his eyes.

"Yes, you both look great," I said. "Now—Elric, come over here so that you're standing shoulder to shoulder... Almost. Okay, perfect. Just stay side by side like that so I don't have to steer both of you."

"Steer?" Jorvun asked with disdain.

"Oh, are your eyes better now?" I didn't give him a

chance to answer. "Walk—straight ahead. Actually, a little to the left... there you go. Just keep going like this. But faster. Don't worry, I won't let you run into anything."

I'd gotten them out of the alley and halfway up the next street when Aneko appeared above us.

"Two officers are just ahead of you," she said, "about to turn the corner."

"Okay, hard left. Hard *left*," I said. "Elric, get over here. Shoulder to shoulder. Now stop. There we go. You're standing before a wall with a big mural on it. Just look up like you're checking it out."

The mural, at first glance, seemed to be a map of some kind, but it took me a second to consider everything I was seeing. It was fresh, perhaps painted in the last few months—the colours bright, the lines crisp. It showed the landmass of Frostvale curled like a sleeping animal, surrounded by a shimmering wall of white and silver strokes. The barrier wall! It looked like ice but also flame, a kind of magical shimmer that pulsed outward in jagged beams. At either edge of the mural—one to the west, one to the east—stood two enormous dragons, one pink and one blue, each breathing the wall into existence. Their wings were curled protectively around the North, their mouths wide open in blue-white flame.

Inside the wall, the northern land was painted in rich, saturated colours: blue fields, shining cities, and proud people with square shoulders and immaculate tools. One woman carried a child on her back while swinging a basketful of eggs. A teacher stood before a chalkboard beneath the sigil of a snowflake. Everyone in the North looked sturdy. Resilient. Maybe a little smug. Definitely not hungry.

But south of the wall? Frost's mercy. It was a mess

of reds and oranges, and the people there were all frowning or howling or just kind of slumped over. One man, shirtless and wild-eyed, was firing a blaster that looked a lot like Lark's into the air. Another held a torch to a pile of books. Several others just stood around, sneering and scratching their stomachs. It was hard not to feel judged by proxy. I wasn't from Valorica, technically—but I'd spent most of my life there, and seeing it portrayed this way made something twist inside me.

"Wow," I said. "I guess subtlety isn't really a Frostvalen thing."

"What do you mean?" Elric asked.

"Ah, never mind," I said.

"If we have to stand here," Jorvun said, "you might as well describe it to us. All I can make out is a blur of colours."

The two officers Aneko had warned us about came around the corner at a half jog, bellies and belts bouncing. We had to stay put for a bit longer.

"It's a map, of sorts," I said. "Of Frostvale and Valorica. But here's the weird part. There are two dragons, one in each corner, and it seems like they are creating the barrier wall. Any idea what that's about?"

"Nope," Elric said. "Maybe some kind of symbolism? Dragons are pretty emblematic of the North."

"Artistic licence," Jorvun said. "I'm sure that's all it is."

"Quiet now," I said. "The officers are about to jog past us, and neither of you *sound* like tweens."

Getting them to glamour into children was, it turned out, a great idea. Not that I was likely to receive any extra snacks for coming up with a plan like that in a hurry. But whatever. The police came and went, and soon we were continuing up the street. Aneko kept tabs on us, but from there to the market, all was clear. Finally, we arrived in the shade of a little park next to the bustling stalls.

"My vision is finally coming back," Jorvun said. "At least, much better out of the sun—Elric, are you a girl?"

"Introducing: Jenny. My third daughter," he said with a curtsy. "Who are you supposed to be?"

"Oh, just me, I guess." Jorvun looked down and patted his soft stomach. "I suppose I was a bit of a husky boy once upon a time."

"I'm glad you're not permanently blinded," I said. "That would have made the rest of our quest even more difficult."

"Even more difficult?" Jorvun glared vaguely in my direction. "What's that supposed to mean?"

"It certainly hasn't been easy so far, has it?" I had some worse words in mind, but I decided to keep them to myself. This wizard could really get on my nerves sometimes. "Aneko, will you stay with them? I'll fly back to the tavern and get the others. I suppose since they won't be able to pay for the meal they've ordered, they are also going to need to escape."

That was really turning into the theme of our adventure, wasn't it? Escape from the ocean post-shipwreck. Escape from the Shaelun. Escape from the failed burglary. If we ever got to the point of needing to escape Frostvale, I thought, I would let them take care of that on their own. My hopes of getting to dragon college wavered in possibility. The Aerie! So cool that I had learned its name. In a way, that made it into more of a reality, but I couldn't shake everything Jorvun had told me over the years about how competitive their admissions process was, or how expensive the tuition. I was in Frostvale now, the land of my ancestors. But that alone wasn't enough. If my dreams were to come true, I had to find a way to get my increasingly disappointing boss onto a throne. Seeing him flop down on a park bench next to skinny Jenny-Elric (Jelric?), still smelling like he'd burnt off his eyebrows and half his hair and rubbing his dazzled eyes, all because he was too proud to listen to the advice of others...? Yeah, I was getting pretty worried about our prospects.

One flap at a time, though. We weren't out of Scoomb just yet.

As soon as I left Jorvun's shoulder, I was back to my full size. I flew at a moderate pace—fast enough to hurry, but not so fast as to draw attention. As I got to the tavern, I spotted three other police officers coming up the street. They weren't jogging, but their heads were swinging side to side, so it seemed they were on the prowl for any bank-robber-ish types. I swooped low around some cherry trees, which, from what I could tell, were ornamental like the ones in Ravenna. Why would anyone plant a fruit tree that doesn't bear fruit? Pretty stupid, if you ask me. Anyway, I didn't see our party on the patio outside the tavern, so I landed and hopped politely inside.

"Hey there, little girl," the hostess said to me just inside the door. "How cute! Table for one?"

"Boy," I blurted. "And no, I'm meeting some friends."

"Oh." She looked positively baffled for a moment, then shook her head. "Whatever suits your fancy. Come right on in and have a look around."

Whatever suits my fancy? What a strange thing to say. But I had more important matters to concern myself with. I hopped on past her. Probably not good etiquette to fly around inside a tavern. I think Jorvun had said something like that once, but then again, when I was with him I could just ride on his shoulder or in his big front pocket.

I found the party at a back table, where I chanced a quick flap to land on the seatback of an empty chair. Xander and Lark were stuffing their faces with all manner of delicious snacks. Breaded chicken fingers? One of my favourites! And smoked squid rings? Piggle bites? Mini burgers? Plus a dish of deep-fried potatoes loaded up with cheese curds and smothered in gravy? Oh, and Xander had a bowl of pickled eggs in front of him, but it seemed like he was going to be eating those all by himself. Meanwhile, Fox was casually chewing on a potato wedge while chatting with Elric's pocket mirror.

"Hey, you!" Lark lit up when she noticed me. "How's the caper going?"

Xander gave me a wave and indicated his mouth was too full of egg to talk.

"Yeah," I said. "About that..."

"The people of Frostvale are, I would say—" Fox looked down and made a face as if she was checking some notes, although her scriptlet was closed on the table next to a mug of ale. "—a sad and quite unfortunate lot. It's clear the trade war is having a devastating..."

"Long story short," I went on, "we need to go."

"Brine-fucking-dammit." Lark dropped her head into her hands. "If you'll excuse my French."

"Thass too bad," Xander managed to say. "How wo we pay fo oh food?"

"We have no way to pay," I said. "So we need to get you out of here. I was thinking you could slip out one by one, but that compounds the number of times the staff might notice that something is going on, and it also gives them more opportunities to react. Probably better if we all just get up and walk out like nothing is the matter. It's pretty busy in here, so maybe they won't even notice."

"That complete fraud of an academic," Lark said. "This is his fault, isn't it."

"I'm not sure that laying blame is going to help the situation." Might as well try some diplomacy, right? Well, that was my goal, but then Lark narrowed her eyes at me, so I added, "Yes, totally the wizard's fault. But many things could have gone wrong. It was a hasty plan."

Xander made an effortful swallow and picked up another egg. "Do we need to go right now?"

"Not just yet, I think. There were some police coming up the street. Best to wait for them to pass. So you have time for at least one more egg."

"Oh good," he said. "These are amazing."

No doubt. It all looked pretty amazing. And yeah, we had a minute or two, right? So I grabbed a chicken finger and started munching.

"...the streets are lined with children begging for a mouthful, unfortunate little buggers. Skinny limbs, distended bellies, all of that." Fox sighed dramatically. "We've been able to help many of them, and though I don't condone thievery in normal situations, we've had the opportunity to do some, well, stealing from the rich and giving to the poor, so to speak. I mean, I'm here for the story, first and foremost, but if I can do some good along the way, then I'll do my best to..."

Fox really was a strange case. I supposed it was an interesting tale that she was spinning, but wasn't journalism supposed to involve reporting on actual events, with as much accuracy as a subjective human could muster? Well, what did I know. I was just a small dragon, and I never really paid much attention to the news.

WE'VE COME FOR YOUR EGGS

On bite three of my chicken finger, which honestly was one of the best I'd ever had, a deep rumbling voice back at the entrance made me glance over my shoulder. And... ice me sideways, it was the police. Not only that, when I turned to look, I locked eyes with one of the officers. Not only that, he pointed at me, and the trio immediately made for our table.

"We've got trouble," I whispered.

Lark's hand went to her blaster. Xander almost choked, then spat pickled egg all over the floor next to him. Fox went on blathering for a few more seconds, but then she too noticed the law approaching.

"Sorry," she said. "We've got company. If we survive this, I'll get back to you soon." Then she flipped the mirror closed and slipped it into her pocket.

"Well well well," the biggest of the three officers said. She was a bit taller than even Xander, and almost as wide as him in the shoulders. The other two took up position on either side of her, hands on hips. All three of them had stun batons and shackles dangling from their belts. "It just so happens that we received a report about five Valorican spies escaped from a Shaelun vessel, along with their little blue dragon. And here we have three strangers in town and, let's see—" She squinted at me for effect. "—yup, a little blue dragon. Meanwhile, two other strangers were picked up on a magi-eye trying to break into the back of the bank. I'm going to jump to a wild conclusion that you know these two individuals."

Lark turned slowly and looked each officer up and down, as if assessing the number of blaster shots she would need to end the threat against us. I really hoped it wouldn't come to violence, but I couldn't see how else we were going to get out of this situation. Meanwhile,

Xander slipped a small red vial out of his pocket and quickly dumped the contents into his mouth.

"Well, actually," Fox said, "you are quite mistaken. We are missionaries with the Church of the Holy Moon—from a parish in Eastern Frostvale. Maybe you've heard of us, eh? We've come oot West in the hopes of establishing a new order."

"Oot?" The officer shook her head. "Nice try covering up your accent. No way, no how. You four are coming with us."

At that moment, just as Lark dropped her head and started to spin around, a blaster in each hand, Xander bellowed like an enraged beast, and in one smooth motion, lifted our table above his head and threw it at the three officers. Food and ale went absolutely everywhere, and the cops were knocked backward onto the floor.

As Lark jumped clear of the debris, she frowned in disappointment but kept her blasters at the ready. Xander hunched over like a bear about to take down an impertinent hiker. I was momentarily distracted by all the glorious food that would go to waste. Out of the three of us, somewhat surprisingly, Fox took charge.

"Move!" she shouted while hefting her lute case. "Run, run, run!"

So run we did. Well, not me. I dove for a fat chicken finger, because why not, then flapped off after them.

CHAPTER THIRTEEN

Wagon Theft Auto

My three fugitives stampeded out of the tavern and into the street, but without a plan or a clear sense of the town, they started to run in different directions. While I supposed that would help them individually evade capture, it wasn't that helpful in terms of getting them safely to the park beside the market.

"This way," I shouted. Fox and Lark immediately turned in my direction, but Xander looked like a rampaging bull. I had to fly in front of him and wave my chicken finger in his face. "No. Stop. Follow me!"

I darted across the street and up a path that led toward the Emporium. My hope was that I could get them out of sight before the police came charging out of the tavern, but... nope. There they were, and they saw exactly where we were headed.

"Faster. Don't look back, but the police are in pursuit." I took one last look before we got around the corner. All three officers were limping somewhat. I didn't blame them. Xander had thrown our table at them with the force of... well, of a rampaging bull. An apt metaphor *and* a vibe. His nostrils were flared, and he was breathing like he had already run ten blocks instead of just across the street.

As we reached the end of the walking path, the officers came into view again. Snowshards! We had gained on them a bit, but it was going to be hard to lose them. Unless... oh right. Glamour time.

"There are a bunch of statues to the right." I flapped above their heads, speaking as quietly as I could. I didn't want to shout and give away the plan. "Get behind them and use your rings. I want you all to turn into tweens."

"Tweens?" Lark asked. "Excuse my French, but what the fuck is a tween?"

"It's a stage of human adolescence," I said. "Elric has one of them. Or more than one? Anyway, he says they are endearing."

"I think it means pre-teen," Fox said.

"Brine and Keel." Lark shook her head. "Okay, fine. Tweens it is."

Xander grunted and gasped for air. But at least he was sticking with the pack. I just hoped he had enough wherewithal after that Alpha Power or whatever he drank to understand the assignment.

And... barely. The others spoke the trigger word and transformed, but we had to collectively yell at the paladin to break through his delirium.

Perfect. Three more tweens. Now it was time for me to lead the cops astray. I gave Lark and Fox directions to the park. I mean, I gave directions to all three of them, but let's be real. Then I flew low behind the strange

Emporium statues, including a cluster of Shaelun luck gods next to a few of naked human women bent over in some sort of carnal bum display (did people actually buy these things?), and came out on the other side. I waited until the cops spotted me and disappeared into a store selling tie-dyed tunics. Sure enough, they headed my way, so I slipped out a side door, looped around the back of the building, and then took a circuitous route across town before doubling back toward the market, munching on my chicken finger as I went. If the police asked anyone where a small cobalt dragon had flown off to, they would head in exactly the wrong direction.

I got back to the park at the same time as the three new tweens, each of whom had transformed into a smaller version of themselves—like Jorvun, but bearing a bit more resemblance to their actual adult appearance. If the police took a good look at them, they might make the connection, but whatever. The ruse had worked.

"I think I lost the officers," I said. "But we should probably get out of town as soon as possible."

"Agreed," Jorvun said with an authoritative tone— we were back to him trying to act like he hadn't frosted the entire day for us.

"Why do you smell like burnt hair?" Lark asked.

As if she couldn't guess. The pirate was trying to pester my boss. And sure, he deserved some pestering. But now wasn't the time for it.

"An accident at the bank," I said. "We can discuss all of that later." When Jorvun scowled at me, I added, "Or we can just let it go."

"There was something in those eggs," Xander said.

"What are you talking about?" Elric asked. "What eggs?"

"Again, now isn't the time," I said.

"There's a wagon parkade on the other side of the market." Aneko's antennae twitched to the right to indicate the direction. "I've picked up a couple targets for us at the far edge. Minimal security. I think people in this town are pretty trusting. Shouldn't be too much trouble to commandeer one of them."

The tweens set out and crossed through the market, with Aneko fluttering overhead to keep them on track. We didn't want the group to attract any attention, just in case, so Jorvun, Elric, and Fox wandered off individually, but of course Xander needed a babysitter, so Lark took him by the arm and followed the flickerkit on the most direct route. Meanwhile, I went in the opposite direction, doing a quick check of the streets leading to the market from the tavern. The other two cops were a few blocks away, but walking slowly, on the prowl. They had the little police pigeon with them, which was flying in a lazy circle above their heads. Their lack of urgency suggested that they hadn't run into the three that Xander had tabled. And that also meant they probably didn't know about a connection between the would-be bank robbers and the bulletin for Valorican spies. Still, it wasn't great that they were heading toward the market. We had to be quick.

No point in letting them catch sight of me, so I dove back into the trees, then stayed low until I was around the corner and headed up an alley, then followed a couple residential blocks until I came out on the southeast side of the market. Aneko had been right. The parkade was full of wagons and devoid of any significant security personnel—just a skinny old man helping to direct traffic at the entrance. We didn't even need to get past him to leave. Between the parkade and the road was a relatively flat field of grass. Heading in that direction was likely to alert someone to our theft, but that was less of a surety than a bunch of tweens taking a wagon out the parkade entrance. Of course, they could always transform again.

But here was the trickier part: the wagons weren't parked with their horses still attached. A long hitching bar ran up the centre of the parkade. The wagons, horseless, were parked along the perimeter. So it seemed that people pulled into a spot, unhitched their horses from their wagon, then tied the steeds off in the middle. I supposed that made sense. If one of the horses got spooked while still attached to a wagon, they could cause all sorts of damage without a human nearby to guide them or calm them down.

I landed on a wagon canopy at the edge of the parkade and tried to work out how we were going to choose the right horses for the right wagon, and how we were going to get them hooked up. Did anyone in the party have enough horse experience? But right at that moment, the tweens appeared at the edge of the market and wandered over to me. I flapped three times and landed on Jorvun's shoulder. When I did, he grunted as if I had unbalanced him or something. Odd. Maybe he was weaker when disguised as a tween? But no, that didn't make sense. The glamour was just an illusion.

"Hair on a hoagie. You didn't mention that the horses were all unhitched," Jorvun said. "How in nine hells are we going to do this?"

It seemed my boss was not a horseman. I hadn't thought so.

"Don't look at me," Lark said. "I'm only familiar with seahorses."

"Shhhh, you guys," Xander hissed. "Keep your voices down. I think these animals are listening to us."

"I was a pretty accomplished equestrian back in high school," Fox said. "Jumping and barrel racing. But I'm not familiar with this kind of tack."

Elric just shrugged.

Aneko, who had flown ahead of the group and landed on a wagon at the far corner, waved us over. It was crafted with dark, shining wood, and unlike most of the other vehicles, it didn't have a tongue and crossbars sticking out of the front.

"All aboard." The flickerkit gave us all a bow.

"You must have missed our discussion," Jorvun said. "Getting a horse attached is going to be—"

"Sorry," Aneko interrupted with a raised paw. "This is an auto-wagon. Fully enchanted. No steeds necessary."

"A what-wagon?" Lark asked.

"A wagon that doesn't need a horse," Aneko said. "Simple as that. Super popular in Shaelun. They occasionally need to refill on magical energy, but fortunately we have a wizard for that."

"An auto-wagon..." The would-be inventor's eyes were wide, and his mouth hung open. In fact, he looked something like my boss might if he just found a new spellbook, or maybe how I look when a stranger offers me an unexpected snack. "This is amazing... this is... this is exactly what EMG needs to be selling. Yes, I can see it now—an entire fleet of auto-wagons with my logo, and the world thinking that I am somehow responsible for all the wonderful innovations they contain. Can you imagine? Think about how proud my children would be, and—"

"Elric," I said. "Get in the wagon."

"Right." He took in the vehicle for one last moment, then sighed. "Yes, let's get out of here."

Lark mumbled something about heresy as she climbed onto the driver's bench at the front, which had a small wheel similar to the helm on a ship. No one protested her decision to take that role. Aneko settled in next to her. The rest of the tweens climbed into the passenger compartment, while I perched at the back.

"This should do it," Aneko said.

I couldn't see what she was talking about, but something clicked up front, and then we were moving. Lark took us straight across the field, and it wasn't until we reached the road on the other side that the parkade attendant stood, shielded his eyes from the sun, and squinted at us. I was expecting him to shout or scream or blow a horn of some kind to alert everyone nearby of the theft, but apparently he decided nothing was amiss apart from our decision to cut across the field. He sat back down on his stool at the entrance, and that was that.

Once we got onto the road, Lark increased the wagon's speed. Scoomb was quickly disappearing behind us. Just as we passed the last of the residential housing, the landscape giving way to farms, ranches, and forest as we had seen on the other side of the town, I caught a bit of movement at the side of the road. A little creature bounded out of the brush, landed with a flourish, then gave me a formal salute. It was Minzo the bristlegriff! To be honest, in all the excitement, I'd forgotten about the freed creatures. I waved back at him. I'd led them to a town like they'd asked. It wasn't a very big town for the many tens of them, but it was a start. I hoped they would be able to find whatever happiness they sought. I mean, there wasn't anything else I could do for them, was there?

After a while, we left the farmland behind and were surrounded by massive trees on all sides. I noticed that just below my perch there was a lockbox attached to the back of the wagon. That got me wondering about snacks. While I'd had some nice fish for breakfast and an entire chicken finger plus a few bites of another (rudely interrupted by the arrival of the police), I could always eat more. I swung down into the wagon's passenger compartment to let them know, and, maybe because I had my brain set on search-for-snacks mode, I also noticed that there were two more compartments underneath the benches. These weren't locked, so when I pointed them out, Jorvun, Elric, and Fox—who had all turned off their glamours—flipped them open and started digging through the contents. I hopped up onto the rear-facing bench next to Xander, who, still in tween form, sat sideways with his knees hugged to his chest. With wide, fearful eyes, he stared into the woods while whispering something about *frogs in the darkness*. I was getting the impression that his Alpha Power formulation wasn't as wonderful as he made it out to be.

Anyway, here was what we found under the benches: a book labelled *Feather Journal* that included a number of sketches and descriptions of tasty-looking local birds, a pair of binoculars with an auto-focus enchantment that got Elric quite excited, a portable kettle and collapsible teacups, wagon-patch scrolls for quick magical fixes should the vehicle break down (it seemed the owner had at least some capacity for the arcane— sorry, make that *previous* owner), a monogrammed silk blanket embroidered with *W&F Kippenfold 30th Anniversary* (how cute), and a snuff box containing some kind of raverleaf stimulant (which Jorvun immediately hid from Xander). Most importantly, there was a map of the southern half of Fangcover Island, with a number of pencilled-in notes about ideal bird-watching locations. We were able to confirm the road we had followed into Scoomb and the route we were on now. There was a crossroad up ahead: one path led straight through the island's interior, then doubled back toward Gorptoria (a much longer route, and one the Kippenfolds had marked as *bumpy and occasionally washed out*), and a second path offering a more direct route via the Badahat Pass.

"That's where a lady told me to go," I said.

"What lady?" Jorvun asked.

"Oh, I forgot to tell you. When you were on your way to the bank, I checked out some Trudera protestors outside the Emporium, and I also saw a poster for the dragon college," I said. "It's called the Aerie, by the way. This lady helped me read it, and then I asked her for directions to Fangcover City. She said to go over the Badahat Pass, then take a ferry from Gorptoria."

"Are you telling me that you told a complete stranger our destination?" Jorvun's expression, which had been fairly neutral since our escape from Scoomb, maybe even slightly relaxed, was once again frosted right over.

"Um... well, I think I made it sound like I was going there on my own." I cringed and sunk back into the seat. "And anyway, at least I learned that we need to take the Badahat Pass?"

"That's pretty obvious from the map," he spat back at me.

"But we didn't have the map yet," Fox cut in. "So I think it was a good call."

(Thanks, Fox. Much appreciated.)

"A good call??" The wizard's face turned scarlet, and

his voice rose in volume. "Word is going to get around town that a group of Valorican spies tried to rob the bank, attacked some police officers, and then stole a wagon—with a little blue dragon in their company. Do you think this lady isn't going to come forward and tell them exactly where we're headed, and by which route??"

"You have a good point, Boss," I said with a bit of attitude. At this point, I should have gone into de-escalation mode, but my own anger was flaring up. "Keep in mind that when I asked her, we hadn't yet *failed* at the bank robbery. And no cops had yet been attacked. My fault for assuming that our plan to obtain some Frostvalen gilds and book into an inn would work out."

"Failed??" His face got redder. His voice raspier. "How dare you..."

Frost's mercy. He was definitely seething now. Elric and Fox were giving each other a look like, *oh shit, now what?* Now what indeed! *Okay, Glimm. Think. You went a step too far. Time for some diplomacy.*

"Sorry, Boss." I held my paws up in surrender. "You're right. I chose my words badly. And I should never have talked to that lady. I should have trusted in you to know the route. I can only hope my error won't cause us any more trouble, because we've certainly had a tough run. Haven't we? We slept in the wild last night, so probably none of us had the best sleep. We had to have two meals in a row of salmon, and yeah, not everyone likes to eat the same thing twice. And on top of that, some of us haven't had any dinner. That's a lot, right?"

Jorvun just stared at me, nostrils flaring. It seemed like my diplomacy was working? He wasn't yelling at me anymore, so... I decided to press on. The food angle seemed like a good one.

"Speaking of dinner," I continued, "the reason I left my lookout perch was that I noticed a lockbox at the back of the wagon. I was thinking… if there aren't any snacks in these compartments, maybe there are back there? Not sure if it's worth stopping to check, because it's a fancy-looking lock, so I assume we'll need your high-level magical skills to get it open."

Elric opened his mouth to say something while also reaching for the pocket where he kept his lockpick kit, but I quickly bared my teeth at him (see that, humans—not a smile, but a clear warning), and he shut his mouth and gave me a little nod. Message received.

Jorvun sat there in silence for a time, slowly getting over himself. My words were having the desired effect. I was about to conclude that diplomacy didn't actually require deception, but then I thought about what Aneko would say. My final statement, now that I considered it, was very nearly a lie. In suggesting the lockbox couldn't be opened without the wizard's magic, I had played to his ego, because of course Elric could also get in there, and I also continued the concealment of my own arcane abilities. Had I engaged in this much deception back in Ravenna? I didn't think that I had, but that was mostly because our life was simpler. There were fewer unknowns to ruin Jorvun's mood or threaten his fragile self-confidence. That was really what it came down to. In order to do my job—to keep my boss happy and me adequately fed—I had learned the terrible human art of deceit. And worse still, I was getting better at it.

"Fine," Jorvun said at last. His tone was resigned, though he shot me a final glare. "Let's check this damned lockbox. Elric is starving, no doubt, and I'm feeling a bit weak myself. I mean, I ought to keep my strength up in case I need to draw on more of my power." He leaned out of the passenger compartment and shouted at Lark, "Pull over, will you? Just a quick stop."

While Jorvun dealt with the lock, everyone took the opportunity to pee at the side of the road. This was especially important for the three who had been drinking ale at the tavern, though Xander took some encouragement. After a quick *aperi sesame*, Jorvun hooted in delight. In addition to some camping equipment, the lockbox contained a number of granola bricks, a satchel of preserved cloudfruit, and a tin of roasted nuts, dried cheese, and smoked bacon. Jackpot!

Just as I was considering the best way to get my hands on some bacon, what with Jorvun's recent indignation, Aneko shouted from the driver's bench.

"Incoming!" She waved both paws at us, then pointed into the sky back down the road. "I repeat, we've got incoming!"

CHAPTER FOURTEEN

You've Gotta Be Trolling Me

Aneko and I must have sharper eyesight, because the humans couldn't yet see the small flock of birds that were flying over the road, coming from the direction of Scoomb.

"What is it?" Lark stood in front of the driver's bench and squinted into the sky.

"Quick. Get that binocular thing," I said. "Might just be birds, but... Aneko, are you thinking what I'm thinking?"

"Yes, indeed," she said.

Then at the exact same time, we both said, "Police pigeons."

"Pigeons?" Elric scoffed. "I mean... I don't think they are much of a—"

"Spies," Jorvun said. "They will tell the authorities

exactly where we are, and then they'll be able to send word ahead to Gorptoria to set up a checkpoint."

"Probably not even real birds," Xander said.

Fox dashed to the passenger compartment and got out the binoculars. After a moment she said, "Oh yeah. There they are. Definitely little police pigeons."

"Fuck," Lark said. "Mind my French, but what are we going to do? Hide in the woods?"

"Everyone back in the wagon," Jorvun said. "We don't have much time, but I have an idea."

We all crowded into the passenger compartment, except for Jorvun, who sat up front with Lark.

Illusion magic was one of Jorvun's specialties. Indeed, back at the sea gate, if he'd had a better night's sleep, and if he hadn't first attempted an ambitious unlocking spell, he should have been able to cloak the *Brine Whisperer*. Fortunately, this wagon was a lot smaller, and when he started his spell with *obscure visum*, I guessed that he was altering our appearance rather than hiding us from sight. And that made sense, since if Aneko and I could see the pigeons without binoculars, they had already spotted us.

I paid close attention to see what I could learn from his casting. It went like this:

"Obscure visum, mantella haycartus, creakorum rusticus, unis agricolae senex."

He got to the end of that line and repeated it, and with each repetition, the burbling of power made my skin tingle more and more. This was a pretty big spell, and he was reaching deep into his umbrix for enough power to cast it. Probably he could have used less power, or at least used his power more efficiently, if there had been a reasonable amount of time to prepare.

"Obscure visum, mantella haycartus, creakorum rusticus, unis agricolae senex."

But did he have enough power? Could he pull this off in time? We had mere seconds before the pigeons would be close enough to see the illusion take shape. How smart was a police pigeon anyway? Were they enchanted in some way so that a police officer back in Scoomb was seeing exactly what they were seeing? Or were they equipped with homing tranq darts? From my ignorant perspective, the possibilities seemed endless. And again—we had seconds. Meanwhile, I could feel Jorvun scraping the bottom of his umbrix. A change was coming over the wagon, but was it enough? Would it be in time? And was there anything I could do to help?

I supposed I could join him in casting the spell, whispering the same words and contributing my own well of power to the casting. But then everyone would know I could work magic. And I had no idea if two people casting the same spell was even a good thing. What if it made the opposite happen or canceled the magic out? Or what if it just made us all explode? But I had to do something. My frosted college education was at stake here!

Or... what if I could just feed some of my own power into his flow of energy? Like top up his umbrix somehow? I don't know how the idea occurred to me. It's not like I had any training in these sorts of things. But anyway, the notion appeared in my head like icy inspiration. Couldn't hurt to give it a try, I figured. So I tapped into my umbrix, and power rose up into my chest. With careful and precise effort, I sent a stream of magic forward toward Jorvun. I couldn't see him from where I was sitting in the passenger compartment, but the energetic blaze of his magic lit him up for me clearly. And just like that, my power connected with his, just a bit, and just enough to keep him from using up his entire reserve. I had a flash of fear that he might feel my magic coming in and know in that instant about my secret. But if so, well, I'd have to deal with it. And he was bound to find out sooner or later.

The illusion spell coalesced around us. We were no longer a fancy, shiny auto-wagon with five human and two creature passengers. Instead, we were a creaking, rustic old hay cart with two sway-backed horses driven by a crusty old farmer. A moment later, Jorvun stopped casting...

...and the illusion held!

I peeked outside as the pigeons made their final approach, swooped low, and slowed to take a good look at us. Tasty little morsels. Maybe it would have been better for Jorvun just to have cast a sleep spell at them, then I could have had a wonderful snack. Well, me and Aneko. I doubt any of the others would want to join us. But then again, there was that possibility of enchanted vision, so perhaps this illusion approach was for the best. Still, it seemed a shame not to be able to taste even one of them.

After they checked us out, they continued up the road. We all stayed quiet, and Jorvun kept feeding a trickle of power into the illusion spell to maintain it. Ahead of us, the road bent up into thickly forested hills, which meant if the pigeons turned around and came back, we wouldn't have the same amount of time to cast a new illusion. And, to be honest, there was no way Jorvun had enough strength left to repeat the effort. He was going to need a good long sleep for sure.

As it turned out, this consideration—how much effort my boss had expended—was something that I should have heeded a bit more. Once the spell was in place, I'd stopped sharing my power. I guess I just assumed that he would be fine to keep it going. Back at our camp in the woods, he'd maintained our cover all night, but then again, that had been a much simpler working—easier to see through, for one thing, and also he hadn't set it up in a mad rush. But I didn't. Instead, I watched the forest roll by, chatted with Aneko and Fox about what sort of programs might be offered at the Aerie, and munched through a few pieces of the Kippenfolds' very delicious bacon. Eventually, the pigeons returned, slowed again to take another look at us, then headed back toward Scoomb.

"We're good," Lark said from the front. "They're finally out of sight—to my eyes, at least."

That was when our illusion released with an energetic pop. A second later, Jorvun collapsed and almost fell off the side of the driver's bench.

Lark stopped the wagon so we could lay my boss out in the passenger compartment. Despite being exhausted by his arcane effort, he was pretty happy with himself. He kept mumbling things like "...really showed them, didn't I..." and "...don't mess with a wizard..." And fortunately, he didn't give any indication that he knew I'd helped him with the spell. To give him space to lie down, Elric sat with Xander, and Fox went up front with Lark. Aneko and I took up position on the roof. Might as well keep an eye out for more pigeons, though if they showed up, I wasn't sure what we could do about it. Well, maybe I would have to reveal my secret and attempt the illusion myself, but if the working took such a toll on an experienced wizard like Jorvun, I probably wouldn't stand a chance.

Evening came on quickly. The trees were so tall that the sun hadn't been in view for a while. We went from bright sky to twilight in what seemed a few minutes. That started a new debate. We had the Kippenfolds' camping gear in the back, so Lark, Elric, and Fox thought we should pull off the road and rest for the night. That idea terrified Xander, who was still muttering about birds not being real, and Jorvun thought we should put more distance between ourselves and the wagon theft (no mention of the failed bank robbery). Personally, I thought camping made the most sense since it would allow Jorvun to regain his spent power, but I decided to stay out of it.

As darkness gathered around us, it seemed Lark's argument to camp would win out since it was getting harder to see the road, but then Fox found a button set into the side of the driver's bench that turned on two magical headlights. Problem solved. So on we went.

We came to a sleepy little town called Dunk, but nothing was going on, and the party decided that we'd had enough burglary attempts for one day, so we just kept going. Eventually we arrived at the crossroad, as predicted by our handy map. Right into the island's interior or straight ahead to the Badahat Pass. Easy choice, right? Except there was a sign to warn travellers of trolls in the pass. Trolls! Of course, I couldn't read the sign, but from what I gathered, the warning said something about not travelling alone. Well, we weren't alone. We were a mighty party of adventurers. But it was also dark out, and humans' vision at night is terrible, so Jorvun and Xander finally gave in and agreed to set up camp. It wasn't easy setting up in the dark (well, it was for me and Aneko since we just watched from the top of the wagon), and the ground in the ditch was lumpy, but they got the tent together, built a small fire, pulled watches, and then took turns getting some sleep.

No one got a great rest, and based on the moaning and complaining, Jorvun slept least of all. When he dragged himself out of the tent at first light, he looked about ten years older than when we left Ravenna, and he had deep, dark circles under his eyes. That told me he still had a long way to go in restoring his umbrix. Not a wonderful reality to follow us into troll country, but at least we still had Lark's blasters. Oh, and it didn't look like we could rely on Xander for much either. He was so ill from his Alpha Power hangover that he had to spread out on the floor of the passenger compartment with his head over the edge for periodic spurts of vomit. Lovely.

Okay, so we had Lark's blasters. They would be enough against some trolls, right? Otherwise... maybe Fox could convince them not to eat the party by playing them a nice song.

Speaking of Fox, as soon as the wagon was rolling, she got out Elric's pocket mirror and called up whoever it was back in Valorica to let them know she was still alive and to give them another ridiculous update. Aneko and I glanced at each other, then agreed it was probably time for a scouting mission. The flickerkit backtracked to see if anyone (or anything) was following us, while I flapped off ahead to look for any signs of trolls. As I left, Fox was telling her contact about the pack of ten harpies that the Scoomb police had sent after us, most of which she'd handily dispatched on her own.

The air grew cooler as I climbed. Below me, the wagon rolled southward through misty gullies and groves of murkpine and cedaris. With a bit more height, the road faded to a pale ribbon etched into the hillside. Soon enough I couldn't see them at all, and that suited me fine. I needed a break from Fox's tall tales and Xander's retching. Honestly, it was just nice to have some alone time to stretch my wings.

The pass wound upward in tight curves, then straightened into a shelf road that clung to the mountain's edge. On one side: the steep slope of a forested ridge. On the other: an open plunge down to the coast, where the land spilled out in layers of green and darker green. I caught a flicker of white from a waterfall tumbling into a misty basin, then beyond that, the glassy stretch of ocean cut with small islands. I didn't know the names of these places, but I hoped to one day. Maybe the dragon college would have a course on coastal geography.

But I was supposed to be scouting, not sightseeing, so I dove back down to where I'd have a better view of the path ahead. Sporebark grew thick along the right side of the road, interspersed with barkvine and some trees I didn't recognize—maybe a kind of fireleaf or even scrubtop ash. Much of the landscape reminded me of the forests around Ravenna, but it was thicker here, wilder. The farther I followed the road up into the pass, the more the scent of salt air faded, replaced by damp moss, cold stone, and the peppery bite of a breeze from higher peaks. The looming cliffs were beautiful. They also made perfect ambush points.

It wasn't long before I spotted a cluster of smashed wagons near the side of the road—busted wheels, cracked frames, and shredded canvas. No signs of life, but clearly something had torn these apart. A little way along I came upon a ledge strewn with bones, bleached to ivory. Human or animal? I couldn't be sure. I flapped higher, careful to keep my shadow tight to the cliff as I passed, but I didn't see anyone—or anything.

Beyond that, though, the road evened out. It dipped once into a wooded gully, then climbed again to the top of the pass. And from there, frost's mercy, what a view. On this side, the mountains rose farther inland like the ridged spine of a sleeping beast, but to the north, the entire peninsula stretched out—dark green ridges and mist-threaded inlets that glimmered in the morning light. On the northern end of the peninsula was a half-moon bay and what looked like another small town curled into it, fishing boats like toothpicks on the water. And on the southernmost end, in the far, far distance, a glittering city hugged a rocky headland.

Gorptoria. Had to be.

I hovered there for a moment, caught in a mix of awe and purpose. It was good news, really. We were close. And the worst of the pass seemed to be behind me. No more busted wagons. No more bone piles. If I was right, then the trolls must be somewhere back the way I came.

So I turned and began my descent, winging with greater speed now that I had some idea of the stretch of the pass that would require the most vigilance. I came gliding around one of the last bends—just past that wide ledge with the sun-bleached bones—and that's when I saw them.

Two hulking forms crouched in the undergrowth below the cliffs, half-hidden beneath a thick overhang of drooping cedaris. They hadn't been there when I passed over before. Or maybe they had. Maybe I just hadn't noticed them. They were immobile, silent, and they blended pretty perfectly into the gloom of the trees. But then... one turned its head and fixed its small, glinting eyes on me. The other reached for something—a rock the size of Xander's head.

Well. This was bad.

Wait a minute. Were they laughing? I'd never heard a troll laugh before, but that's what it sounded like. An ugly, guttural laughter, like, *hey, look at the little dragon. Wouldn't it be hilarious if I could knock it out of the air??* Monsters can definitely be bullies. Well, that and worse. So I flapped higher to make sure I was out of the troll's range. But how far can a troll throw? No idea, so I just kept flapping. At first, when the monster's muscled arm whipped around, I thought it had dropped the rock. A split second later, I realized that, no, it was coming right for me—so fast that I lost sight of it for a moment. Wow. I pulled my wings in tight and rolled sideways just as the gust of air following the projectile washed over my scales. Holy sleet.

Staying in line of sight was clearly not a good idea. These frostnuts could throw! I kept my wings tucked and let myself fall straight down. When I was a couple seconds from the treetops on the other side of the road from the trolls, I unfurled and banked hard in a long arc just above the canopy. Out of sight.

Now what? Back to the wagon? After following the road a ways from the cover of the forest, I spotted them. Still a few minutes off. At the edge of a large outcropping of mossy granite, I alighted upon the uppermost branch of an ancient arbuth tree with smooth red bark and long waxy leaves. *Think, Glimm, think.* What did I know about trolls? They are big, horrible, and strong. And... they can regenerate? Maybe. Jorvun had told me something like that once. Or was he talking about chimeras? No, I was pretty sure he'd been telling me about trolls. A family of them had once taken up residence in the woods east of Ravenna and were eating the occasional traveller.

Lark had her blasters. That should be enough to stop them, right? Assuming she could hit them in the head or something. Gross. But that rock they'd thrown at me was big, and it flew far and with great accuracy. So what were the chances of Lark getting off a shot before the trolls smashed the wagon to pieces with projectiles of their own? Pukey Xander was useless. I couldn't imagine a combat scenario in which Fox or Elric would be super helpful. And my boss was seriously depleted. Aneko might have some ideas, but honestly... maybe I was their best bet.

Worth a try. Wings and magic gave me a pretty decent advantage, right? So I crossed the road and flew back toward the trolls' hiding spot, flapping as quietly as possible and staying hidden within the canopy. And... yup, there it was—the thick boughs of cedaris next to the road. I landed on a branch a good distance away and watched for a moment. These ugly monsters were great at blending in, but then one of them scratched its butt. Okay, I could see them. I flapped over, a couple trees closer, then a couple more. They didn't move, so I had to assume they hadn't heard me. One more flap and I was right behind them. And frosted fishlegs, did they ever smell terrible. I held my breath, coaxed the flow of power up and out of my umbrix, and pointed my paw at them.

"*Somno, duad.*"

Slump and topple: both trolls hit the dirt. I waited for a moment, then chanced a closer look. Brilliant. Very nice job, Glimm, if I didn't say so myself. The two ugly frostnuts were snoring hard.

Back to the wagon! I landed on the roof next to Aneko, who had apparently just returned from her back-track scouting mission.

"Trolls ahead," I announced. Then I had to catch my breath before I could tell them anything else. "A few minutes out."

Lark was driving, and Elric was again sitting next to her. Fox and Jorvun popped their heads out of the back. Xander groaned something incomprehensible and then gagged.

"How many of them?" Lark asked.

"Two," I said. "But here's the thing..."

Oh no. How was I going to explain the situation without revealing that I'd used magic? I hadn't thought this through. Aneko gave me a little frown, like she already knew what I was wrestling with. Frost's mercy, was this flickerkit ever astute. We locked eyes and... well, I just had to do my best.

"...the trolls are asleep," I said. That was true, wasn't it? I didn't need to bore them with the particulars. "Snoring pretty hard. But they are right by the side of the road, so I'm hoping that if we are really quiet, we can just roll past them. Still, best to have blasters ready, and maybe a lightning bolt from Jorvun, assuming you got enough sleep for something like that?"

"Excuse me?" Jorvun scowled. What else was new. "I certainly have enough power for a lightning bolt or three."

"Fire," Aneko said. "Trolls have very fast regeneration. The only way to kill them is with fire. If you don't put them down, they'll just get angry—and an angry troll is not to be messed with."

"Right, of course." Jorvun gave his head a little shake and sat up straight. "Lightning bolt, fireball, whatever."

"I'm just hoping they don't wake up," I said.

"Wouldn't that be grand? We could just slip right past them and carry on with our day."

"Trolls are indeed a dangerous threat," Jorvun said. "Glimm is right." (What!! Did you hear that??) "If we don't have to engage them, then we might as well count ourselves lucky."

"Are you sure?" Elric said in something approaching a whine. "Think of the glory!"

"What?" Lark leaned slightly away from the ex-burglar/inventor and shot him an are-you-contagious kind of look.

"I just mean, if we stopped these trolls from bothering the locals? We'd be heroes, of a sort. I could tell my kids—"

"Wow." Lark shook her head. "Didn't expect that from the merchant."

It seemed I'd misinterpreted the look she'd given him. Not are-you-contagious but instead: are-you-courageous. Because normally? Not a word I would have chosen to describe Elric.

"Frostvale is the enemy," Xander groaned from the floor of the passenger compartment. "Think of the eggs..."

"You're just grouchy because of your hangover," Fox said. "I think it's a great idea. Let's kill these damned trolls! It will make a fantastic story."

Yeah, and I was pretty sure who would be named the hero of the story, at least to her Valorican news contact—and who wouldn't actually participate in the fight.

"I always say, if you fulfill your obligations every day," Jorvun said, "you don't need to worry about the future. However, our obligation is first and foremost to this mission. Frostvale is not going to be conquered if the five of us end up dead. No, I'm sorry. Trolls are too dangerous, even for my powerful magic. I could certainly throw some fireballs at them, but in the time it takes them to die, one or more of you could get killed, and I don't want that on my conscience."

In other words: he didn't have enough magical power to fight them. This blatant lie made me feel a little tiny bit better about my much, much, much smaller deception.

"An academic with a conscience?" Lark laughed at her own joke. "All right, then. It's the wizard's fire we need to stop them, so it's the wizard's call. Still, let's be ready, because I don't see how they aren't going to wake up if they are right beside the road."

"Don't worry about that," Jorvun said. "I can cast a noise concealment on the wheels."

Lark pulled the wagon over for a quick seating change. Elric took the helm. (Is it called a helm on a wagon?) Lark slid over into his seat with both blasters at the ready. Then Jorvun sat cross-legged on the rear bench with a clear view of the south ditch.

"Tacitae, rotalis, quad."

Spellwords: noted. Also noted: the burble from Jorvun's umbrix was very thin. No wonder he didn't want to fight the trolls. But I wasn't worried. The wagon now rolled on in almost perfect silence. And besides, I had put the monsters into a deep magical sleep.

A couple minutes later, the overhanging cedaris boughs marking the trolls' hiding spot came into view. I flew ahead to check on the monsters. Both were still snoring away, so I hover-flapped in the middle of the road and beckoned the wagon forward. Just as they rolled up next to the trolls, I heard Jorvun whisper.

"Magical sleep. How unusual. Trolls are supposed to be resistant to cognitive impairment spells, on account of their tiny brains. Whoever accomplished this was a powerful wizard indeed."

"Magical sleep?" Lark asked from the front, with more volume to her voice. "Fantastic. Let's get out of here."

I almost fell onto the road as I froze mid hover-flap. There were two reasons for this. First, because of what my boss had just said. A powerful wizard was needed to pull off a spell like this against trolls? Was he serious? That didn't seem possible. But then... *resistance to sleep spells* sounded like a very bad thing, even if the spell had worked in the first place.

And that brings me to reason number two: as soon as Lark finished speaking, one of the trolls snorted awake.

CHAPTER FIFTEEN

Ferry Important Information

Everything happened very quickly. The troll snorted and roared. Fox shrieked. The other troll lurched awake. Xander heaved a mouthful of vomit on the road. Lark fired off six blasts in a couple seconds—and since we were right beside the monsters, her accuracy was fantastic. The trolls were riddled with whatever little projectiles shoot out of the end of a blaster.

And yet... the trolls didn't seem to even notice the blaster shots. Or maybe they did, because they both leapt out of the ditch next to the wagon, flexed, rumbled out the most terrifying roar-growl combo I've ever heard, and bared their teeth in something that—take note, dear party—was definitely not a smile. Like Aneko had said: making them angry was a bad idea.

"*Pyra volatis,*" Jorvun shouted.

But no fireball issued. I felt the pathetic fizzle of power inside him. If I'd known he was going to cast at that moment, I could have sent him some of my own magic to help, but this was a scene of pure chaos. It almost occurred to me that I could try the spell he'd just failed to cast, or I could try the sleep spell again, but I was completely flustered. I'd honestly expected these two smelly brutes to stay unconscious. If I'd anticipated that something like this might happen, I could have been more prepared. I could have had a spell ready, the words lingering on my lips, my umbrix primed and ready to fuel my intent, but in my shock at what was unfolding, all I had to offer was my basest instinct.

I flapped closer, just over the wagon, and spewed frostfire, as much and as quickly as I could muster, all over the two trolls. I'm not sure what I was thinking. Well, I wasn't thinking. I was just reacting. Even as the bluish-white liquid enveloped them and crystallized into a thin shell, I didn't believe for a second that it would be enough to freeze them in place. These trolls were just too strong. Meanwhile, Jorvun was scrambling to get his wand out of his jacket pocket, which seemed to be stuck, but it gave me the faintest bit of hope that he'd be able to pull it out in time and save us, because clearly the pathetic sheen of ice I'd sprayed on the monsters wasn't going to be sufficient.

But then, somewhere next to me, Aneko muttered something like, "Great thinking, Glimm," as she fluttered closer to the trolls.

I was about to scream at her to get back—the brutes would smash free of my ice any second. In a flash, I imagined the dear little flickerkit taking the brunt of a troll fist and hurtling across the road to smash into a tree. But what actually happened was quite remarkable. She swooped in, cracked her little tail at the monsters, and shot out a spray of sparks right into their frostfire-covered faces.

Whoomp.

A moment later, I was picking myself up out of the ditch on the other side of the road. What in the power of permafrost had just happened?

The wagon was on its side. Elric and Lark were sprawled in the middle of the road. I couldn't see Fox, Xander, or my boss, but someone inside the passenger compartment was groaning. Poor little Aneko was tangled around a branch in the trees behind me. And the trolls were... gone.

In place of the two monsters was a single smoking crater about as deep as I am tall. So—a small crater, but a crater nonetheless. Around the rim and also all over the trees behind where the trolls had been standing was a nasty splatter of black and green goo. Our enemy was no more.

Again: what had just happened? I was completely confused. And very much still stunned by the blast.

As the dust settled and smoke dissipated, Lark and Elric sat up and rubbed their heads. Fox was the first to climb out of the overturned wagon, hefting her lute case. Then came Jorvun, who looked as perplexed as I felt. Then Xander pulled himself free, dropped onto the ground, and dry heaved a few times. Finally, Aneko fluttered down from the trees.

"Excuse my French," Lark said, "but what in the holy fuck was that?"

I shrugged. Jorvun opened his mouth to say something, then shut it and just shook his head instead. Xander sputtered.

"This reminds me of the time—" Fox started.

"Frostfire," Aneko blurted, like that was a perfectly reasonable explanation.

"But... it's just frost," I said.

"I'm surprised that you're surprised," she said. "If it was just frost, why do you think they call it frost*fire*?"

"I guess... because I fire it out of my mouth?"

"Well, as you saw, that's not the case." She gave me a big smile—without teeth, of course—as if to console me on not knowing the basics of my own physiology. "Frost dragons have a gland that produces and stores cryoplasma, which is a bit like a combination of nitroglycerin and thermite. As you get bigger, and I imagine with the right training, you'll be better able to refine it to be even more flammable and explosive."

"I have to say—" Lark shook her head in amazement. "—we're damn lucky to have you with us, Aneko. You are one clever little thing, aren't you."

The flickerkit gave Lark a bow.

"He's not getting any bigger," Jorvun muttered. (And out of nowhere, I might add. Was he not even going to acknowledge this amazing discovery about my frostfire??) "He's a miniature blue."

"Ah... okay." Aneko shrugged while also shooting me a doubtful look.

"Actually, I was going to say—" Elric cocked his head at me, like this somehow gave him a sharper assessment of my physical self. "—you actually do seem a bit bigger than when we set out."

"He's just putting on weight," Jorvun spat. "Too many extra snacks lately."

After that, no one said or did anything for a long, awkward moment—apart from Xander, who gagged a couple more times. Yes, my boss had just insinuated that I was getting fat. Was that why he was always so restrictive of my diet? He wanted me to keep a slim figure? In that moment, I wasn't sure what was more shocking—the blast we had just endured, this revelation about my frostfire, or the wizard's veiled threat that I was about to be put on a diet.

Okay, it was the frostfire. I could blow things up! Including monsters!

And then that got me thinking about the trolls and how I was responsible for their deaths. I mean, they were going to kill and eat us, so it's not that I felt terrible about it, and obviously I kill and eat food creatures if I get the chance, but it still left me with an uneasy knot in my stomach that I had contributed to the obliteration of these two beings who were just trying to survive. But then I remembered how they had laughed as they threw a rock at me. What jerks! And just like that, I was over it.

Once everyone had recovered sufficiently from the blast, the humans (minus Xander) worked together to get the wagon right side up while Aneko and I searched the area. She said that a troll's primary motivation was to eat people, but they also liked to collect shiny things. And sure enough, on the ledge above the road, near those sun-bleached bones, we found a pile of clinks and gilds hidden under a heap of shredded clothing. At last, the party had some Frostvalen currency! We could all finally have a lovely night's sleep on a proper mattress. We used an unfortunate someone's torn-up shirt as a sling and together carried our spoils down to the road. Meanwhile, they had the wagon righted, and with the application of one of the Kippenfolds' magical patches, our vehicle rolled onward with only a few slight complaints from the enchanted engine.

The climb to the summit was slow and winding. Even with the patch, the wagon no longer rode as smoothly as it had. But all the same, on we went. Trees pressed close on both sides, their trunks dark with dew and needles clumped thick with moss. Murkpine and cedaris formed a jagged green canopy that cast the road in shadow, pierced only now and then by narrow shafts of light. Whenever the trees broke, I caught glimpses of what I'd seen earlier from the air: the glittering sea far below, dotted with rocky islets, and farther to the north, the dark emerald mounds of a beautiful island chain.

As we crested the rocky summit, the trees thinned, and the land opened before us. Up front, Lark and Elric gasped. The pirate stopped the wagon for a few minutes so Jorvun, Fox, and Xander could climb out of the back and take a look. A lush green peninsula stretched southward, thick with patchwork fields and winding roads that glinted in the light. Beyond it all lay Gorptoria, a soft sprawl of domes, turrets, and distant spires tucked along the ocean's curve. White buildings gleamed under the sun, clustered around a narrow inlet and bay at the island's southernmost tip. Perhaps inspired by the view, the humans used their glamour rings to change into cleaner and slightly more glamorous versions of themselves: Jorvun's oilskin took on a fresh sheen, the gold trim on Fox's doublet seemed twice as thick, Xander's simple leather-and-linen combo now resembled suede and silk, Elric's trench coat was now embroidered with a fine nightshade paisley, and the many pearls that studded Lark's leather tunic seemed larger and more... pearlescent?

And then—on we went.

The road curved down in slow switchbacks. We

passed flowering bushes with yellow trumpet blossoms and moss-covered roadside shrines—some to the High Matron, others to forgotten river spirits and wild gods. As we descended, the trees gave way to tidy orchards and sleepy farms with high fences, barns painted in bright colours, and happy cows chewing cud like they had no idea a trade war was happening. At the edge of the city, the houses grew closer together, the fences lower and more decorative. Everything was blooming. Even the ditches were overflowing with ivy bells and crownroot lilies. Aneko and I scouted ahead, flitting from chimney to chimney, until the first proper neighbourhood gave way to cobbled streets and a neat little sign that said: *Welcome to Historic Gorptoria—Where Flowers Come to Thrive.*

We waited atop the sign for the wagon to catch up, just taking in the sunshine and all the splendour. I thought back to the mural we'd seen in Scoomb, with everyone in the North happy and industrious, whereas those south of the border were painted angry and weird. Gorptoria was providing some insight into where that sentiment might have come from. They did seem to have it pretty good, at least here on Fangcover Island. Was the rest of the country like this? Back in Ravenna, people talked about Frostvale like it was a place of ice and snow, with strange inhabitants who only ate potatoes covered in cheese and gravy. Of course, I'd always dismissed the more negative opinions of my homeland, even if I'd never visited. But wow, this city was defying my lofty expectations. I tried to imagine Jorvun as the king of all this wonder. To be honest, he didn't quite seem to have the right vibe. He was so grouchy all the time, but maybe I was just focused on that more recently. He wasn't always rude and moody. Perhaps travelling just has that effect on some people. Surely, if we were living here and presiding over these flower-obsessed humans, he would have to cheer up a bit. Or maybe a lot. Maybe all his moodiness stemmed from his feeling of disconnection, from not knowing his father, from being denied a place in his own family, and from being cut out of such an impressive inheritance. He was my boss, after all, and Trudera's sole heir, so yeah, I probably needed to start thinking more positively about his reign.

"You're pretty quiet," Aneko said after a while. "You doing okay?"

"Yeah, I'm fine. Just a crazy day, you know?"

"You are definitely learning a lot about yourself on this trip."

"That's true," I said. "Although it seems like everything I learn just brings up more questions."

"You know you can always come to me with those questions." She gave me a little nudge, hip to hip. "I'm not an expert in dragons by any means, but... well, neither, it seems, is your wizard."

"I'm seeing that, yeah. More and more every day." I took a deep breath and let it out in a big sigh. "Yes, I do want to know more, but I guess I'm also nervous somehow."

"Nervous?"

"I've been thinking more about deception. Like how you said concealing things is a form of lying. And I can see what you mean, for sure. But I always prided myself in truthfulness, like it was something that maybe set dragons apart from humans. They really do make up a lot, don't they?"

"They certainly do," she said. "But if you're

surrounded by them, if you're learning from them, I think it's pretty natural to pick up on their habits, good and bad."

"I suppose." For a while I sat there in silence, just watching our enchanted wagon rolling closer and closer. Soon we'd need to flap onward and figure out where the frosted ferry terminal was. "I guess what makes me nervous is... I'm not sure how much Jorvun doesn't know and how much he has chosen not to tell me. Does that make sense?"

"Absolutely. Come here, Glimm." She slid a paw around my back and pulled me in for a hug, wings and all. Then, with her little flickerkit mouth next to my ear, she whispered, "If you observe someone being dishonest all the time with other people, it's totally fair to wonder how truthful they are being with you."

"Hey, speaking of dishonesty," I said when we disentangled from our hug, "there's something you should know about our mission here in Frostvale."

"Are we not assassinating the king?"

"How did you guess?"

"You're a good creature, Glimm." Aneko gave me a sly shrug. "If that was the actual mission, I figured you wouldn't be so eager for it to succeed."

"Well, I'm eager because I want to get into dragon college. Means to an end, as my boss says. But you're right, I wouldn't be comfortable with assassination. No, Jorvun made me swear not to tell anyone, and I've kept my word with the humans, but I don't want to deceive you—ever. The truth is, he is the bastard son of King Trudera. So he wants to prove his relation and claim his inheritance, ideally as the next king, since Trudera has begun the process of succession."

"Interesting..." Aneko paused for a minute as she watched our wagon bumping and lurching up the road. "Do you think it will work?"

"I have no idea."

"Your boss doesn't seem to be particularly good at planning. Or research. For one thing, he has a dragon familiar and he doesn't seem to know the first thing about dragons. So the question is—does his overconfidence extend to what he thinks he knows about the Frostvalen political situation? For example, is the king obliged to accept him as an heir? And is an heir even guaranteed the throne? I don't know enough about the politics of this country to say. I suppose we'll just have to wait and see how it goes."

Wait and see, yes indeed. And in the meantime, I had a lot to think about. But was I ever glad to have a friend like Aneko to be able to talk to about all this stuff. I really wanted to ask her more about dragons she had met, and anything else she thought I might not know about my kind. Yet there was this lingering hesitation deep inside me, somewhere down near my umbrix maybe, about what it would mean to know the whole truth about myself, my life, and my boss.

For now, however, I had a job to do. The wagon had caught up to us and was rattling past the Gorptoria sign. Ah, yes, Gorptoria. That was something easier to think about. What a crazy place we had found ourselves. I had another look around, and maybe it was my conversation with Aneko, but something about the locale had shifted in my perception.

The city felt... well, smug. Gardens manicured with magical precision. Elderly couples out for strolls, dressed in linen and wide-brimmed hats. A trio of children played croquet on an actual lawn. We passed bakeries and tea-houses with charming awnings and chalkboard menus, all wafting steam and smugness in equal measure. Tourists were everywhere—snapping sketch-crystal souvenirs of statues and fountains, licking thornberry gelato, and riding around on rental ponies. Aneko and I paused on a lamppost to reconfirm our route. Below us, a street performer was balancing atop a unicycle, juggling four bright pears while a squibbit collected clinks in a painted teacup.

Smug, and maybe a bit boring somehow, but undeniably pretty.

We followed the coastward boulevard through blocks of boutiques and dainty museums, then finally came upon the Inner Quay. What a sight! On the other side of the bay was a magnificent palace made of scarlet stone, with at least three tens of spires, and each spire was capped with a copper dome that had turned a wonderful creamy green in the salt air. To our left, at the head of the bay, was another regal building called the Parlour Hotel (Aneko read the sign for me), a grand edifice dripping with vines and flower baskets, with a covered patio full of people drinking tea and nibbling on layered desserts like they were attending some daily ceremony of self-satisfaction. And there, occupying the centre of the harbour, was the ferry terminal—an ornate building of glass and pale green stone. Along the docks that spread out over the sheltered bay, ferries loaded passengers beside private yachts, sailing sloops, and small cargo barges.

We circled back to the party and led them along a wharfside path that joined the main road near the ferry terminal.

"That's it," I called down. "Straight ahead."

Lark squinted, nodded once, and steered the wagon toward the crowd of tourists swarming the open plaza. Most didn't give us a second glance. Just another rustic-looking party arriving from who knows where—probably on vacation. What a ridiculous assumption. Vacation? We were here to conquer a government.

Once we'd parked alongside the quay, we lined up for tickets to Fangcover City. We didn't even need to attempt a heist first. The money from the trolls would be more than enough to cover it, or so Elric announced after reading the sign and doing some math in his head. What an impressive skill! And to think, my chance to study literacy and numeracy was so close at hand!

Jorvun took the lead, of course, with me riding on his shoulder, and when we arrived at the front of the line, he proclaimed to the clerk with undeniable enthusiasm that we needed, "Seven tickets to the capital, please. Five humans, two creatures."

The clerk, a human even younger than Fox, so probably late adolescent, wore a hat with a forward-facing brim that covered her eyes. In response to the wizard's request, she pulled the brim up and looked him square in the face, and her expression very clearly communicated: *are you a complete frostwit?*

"What?" Jorvun asked in the awkward silence that followed.

"Um," the clerk said, still projecting astonished confusion, "where do you think you are?"

"Gorptoria, obviously," Jorvun said with no small amount of annoyance. "And we want seven tickets to Fangcover City."

"But you said *to the capital.*"

"Yes, exactly." The wizard shook his head so vigorously that he almost knocked me off his shoulder. "I don't know what the issue is. Fangcover City, *the capital*. Seven tickets, if you don't mind."

"I guess you're from out east or something." The clerk pulled her cap back down over her eyes. "I'll sell you seven tickets to Fangcover City if you want, but you're already in the capital." She pointed at the palace over on the south side of the bay. "What the heck do you think that is?"

Jorvun froze. He didn't turn to look at the palace. He didn't respond to the clerk. He just stood there, locked in place and trembling slightly. Yes indeed, my boss, our leader, expert on all things Frostvalen, supposedly, hadn't even known what the nation's capital city was. Wow. For someone who prided himself on being smart, he must have been feeling pretty damn stupid in this moment.

"Great," Elric said. "Pretty convenient, if you ask me."

"I actually had a premonition that Gorptoria was the capital," Fox said.

"Are those gulls looking at us?" Xander asked.

"Goddam motherfucking academics," Lark said. "If you'll excuse my French."

CHAPTER SIXTEEN

Failing to Plan or Planning to Fail

Following the Gorptoria-is-actually-the-capital surprise, Jorvun didn't say a word. He just marched across the road to the Parlour Hotel—with the entirety of the troll loot in his pocket—and booked us two rooms. The party trailed him at a distance. Fair to say that everyone had learned to be wary of his mood. No one made any requests. No one questioned whether our collectively earned cash (let's be real—Aneko and I earned it) ought to be spent on such fancy lodgings. We simply followed in his wake, let him finalize the arrangements, and then trudged upstairs.

The rooms were smaller than I'd expected for such a luxurious hotel, maybe because the place was so old. I heard once that humans from many tens of years ago used to be a lot smaller on account of not understanding nutrition. So maybe they hadn't needed as much space? But even though our rooms each had two beds, and the one room had an extra cot, they were barely bigger than the single room Jorvun and I had stayed in across from the marina back in Ravenna. So yeah, a bit cramped, but at least there were two rooms—oh, and they were connected by a door in between, so it opened up into what felt like one bigger room. Lavish, though, for sure.

The floor was covered in plush cream carpet with dark-wood baseboards. Up near the ceiling, gilded crown moulding shimmered faintly in the lamplight. One wall was papered in a floral print of silver thistle and blue broom, faded in spots but clearly expensive once. The beds were carved mahogany with heavy brocade coverlets and far too many pillows, along with a mirrored wardrobe and a narrow writing desk tucked beside the hearth. Even the little folding cot, which the party decided immediately would go to Fox, was antique and ornate, with a dark oak frame and burnished iron legs. The bathrooms were tiled in a checker of white and jade-green porcelain, with clawfoot tubs that gleamed like polished shell and taps shaped like lion mouths. But the best part by far were the balconies: wrought-iron railed and barely big enough for two, but overlooking the inner harbour, the ferry terminal, and the glittering bay.

The awkward silence continued, with no one yet willing to address Jorvun's epic fail, while one by one the party took turns having much-needed baths. Aneko and I perched out on the balcony and watched the tourists march up and down the street. At one point I noticed that there was quite a lot of foot traffic in and out of the palace. I'd been thinking that we'd need a plan to break in, or to get past guards, but it seemed even the palace was a tourist attraction. Like Elric had noted, there was a certain amount of convenience to Jorvun's fail. Our travels had come to an end earlier than expected. And the palace was a place we could just walk right inside. My boss, perhaps as soon as tomorrow, could claim his hereditary right and become the country's new king. A prince at the very least. Perhaps that was why he'd checked us into the Parlour Hotel, no matter if the price took most of our clinks and gilds. We were on the threshold of his ascension. We would have money. He would have power. And I would finally get the education I'd dreamed of for so long.

And yet, something told me it wasn't going to be that simple. Nothing about this quest had been simple. From the sea gate fail to the armada fail to the heist fail to the troll fail to the capital fail—I had pretty good reason to be worried. But then again, we had managed to overcome each failure. We had managed to arrive here, such that I was sitting on this balcony railing, watching the tourists wander in and out of the grand building that was going to decide our ultimate fate. And not to get braggy here or anything, but at every episode of failure, I had been indispensable. Between Aneko and me, we had gotten the party out of every single defeat. Without us, they would still be... well, they would have drowned in the ocean outside the sea gate. Simple as that. Or if they had managed to get the attention of the Shaelun, they would have landed themselves in prison. And if they hadn't messed up their accents and had actually managed to trick the Shaelun, they would have been caught and imprisoned for bank robbery. And no need to imagine what death by trolls would have looked like. Gross.

On one paw, this line of thinking was making me feel

pretty decent about myself and my contributions to the quest. But on the other paw, the thought of what would happen inside that frosted palace was clenching up my guts.

Or maybe I was just getting hungry? Yes, definitely. Well, probably both were contributing factors.

Back inside the room, Elric was yammering at his mirror, trying with some desperation to get a hold of his offspring, presumably to let them know that we were about to make history—if we were. However, from what I could gather, none of his kids wanted to speak to him. Three refused to take the call, another said she was on her way to a strikeball tournament, and another said he was too busy washing the kitchen floor. Elric finally gave up and handed the mirror to Fox, who had been sitting nearby the whole time, clearly waiting for him to give her a turn on the device.

But just as she whispered the trigger, *scry-fi*, and invoked her network contact, Jorvun came out of the bathroom, hair wet and tousled, and announced that it was time for a team meeting.

"First of all," he said, "I'd like to thank you all for joining me on this quest. We've run into more challenges than I expected, but together, we have persevered."

Aneko shot me a knowing side-eye glance that called the wizard's *we* into question.

"And now," he went on, "our adventure is nearly at its end. Tomorrow we will case the palace to get a sense of the security, find our way into the legislative chamber, at which point I will, ah, fireball Trudera, and then we will all escape."

"That's it?" Lark asked.

"Yes." My boss gave the pirate a solemn nod. "That is indeed it."

"Oh." Elric frowned and rubbed at his chin—which he had taken the opportunity to shave with supplies provided by the hotel. "I guess, well, I wonder if anyone else was expecting something a bit more elaborate than that?"

"I'm excited to write a song about this saga," Fox said, "not to mention land a major network deal. But what about during? How are we meant to help?"

"Oh, I'm sure there are many ways you can help," Jorvun said, "if Plan A doesn't work out, I mean. Didn't you say that you studied the arcane in bard college?" (Fox nodded emphatically.) "And Elric, you must have a weapon of some kind in one of your pockets?" (Elric stuck out his bottom lip, cocked his head, slipped a hand inside his trench coat, then beamed like he'd just remembered something exciting.) "Of course, Lark has her blasters." (Lark sat motionless, staring the wizard down with an undeniable challenge in her expression.) "And if need be, Xander can quaff a supplement and throw some tables around." (Xander looked panicked for a moment, then patted around his pockets; when he evidently found another vial, he gave an anxious sigh.)

"Sure," Lark cut in at last. "We bust into the chamber, you launch a fireball, and Trudera dies. Let's imagine for a second that this Plan A goes off without a hitch, which, given everything leading up to this point, seems unlikely. But no, I'll cut the pessimism, and yet I'm still looking for realism. So say you manage to assassinate Trudera. Then what? How will that end the trade war? How does his death bring down the barrier wall? What if the next King of Frostvale is even more of a formidable opponent? I know I've talked a lot of shit about academics, if you'll excuse my French, but I honestly thought you had more of a plan than this. Not just for the assassination, but for the entire quest. And… really? Just walk into the legislature and fireball him? I don't know. This seems like a plan Xander could have come up with while high on Alpha Power."

"I have an informant," Jorvun blurted before Xander could protest the insult to his inebriated planning skills. "And my informant has informants. There is much, ah, internal strife in Frostvale. It may seem like everything is perfect here in Gorptoria, but under the surface, dissent is festering. There are many who resent being deprived of the great products of Valorica—our bourbon in particular. And these dissidents are lying in wait for the day their great King Trudera falls. They are ready to pounce. Ready to set the people free. Ready to embrace the South and everything Dummkopf stands for."

He was really committing to this story of his. Lie after lie after lie. My boss had no friendly feelings toward Dummkopf. Perhaps the only thing he respected about him was that the man projected a kind of feeble bravado, willing to say whatever popped into his head and insult whomever he wanted. But as a leader, Jorvun thought he was a complete idiot. He'd ranted about the man on a number of occasions over the years, and yet here he was, pretending to be a supporter—and to have a network of Frostvalen Dummkopf supporters who were willing to betray their country at a moment's notice. None of it was very plausible, and that's because he was making it all up as he went.

"I don't know," Lark said. "I feel like we're just going to end up in a dungeon, fancy though a Gorptorian dungeon may be."

"At this point," Jorvun shot back, "do you have much

of a choice? We're trapped inside the barrier wall now. It's only a matter of time before they track down the party of so-called Valorican spies who escaped from the Shaelun."

Ugh. I couldn't handle another minute of it. My boss could be pompous to begin with, but arguing his point like this with so much fake confidence? It was gross. Not only was he deepening his lie, he was being completely rude. Maybe Elric was a bit of a sycophant, and maybe Xander was a bit slow, even before he addled his brain with Alpha Power. And maybe Fox was living in a dream world. But they weren't terrible people. Just misguided, at least from my perspective. And Lark? She might have some bloodthirsty tendencies, but she was consistently nice to me. No, time to bail on this argument. Let the humans settle their differences. I didn't need to sit through the entire excruciating event.

So I gave Aneko a nudge. She knew exactly what I was thinking. We hopped out onto the balcony and swooped down to the streets below, then out and over the bay. We followed the inlet out to open ocean, where a stone breakwater blocked whitecap waves to keep the inlet and harbour calm. Farther out, partway across the strait, the barrier wall shimmered and danced. Above us, too, but the barrier that stretched over us seemed a lot thinner, probably so that it didn't obstruct sunlight. To think, just a few days ago, we'd been sailing along on the other side of that pulsing magical wall, and with no idea of the strange and dark directions our adventure would take. The wind across the strait was formidable, which made flying difficult for Aneko's delicate wings, so we circled back around, returned to the Inner Quay, and flapped up to the rooftop peak of the Parlour Hotel.

There we sat, with the sun sitting low in the sky, reflecting on the wild day we'd had. Camping at the side of the road, scouting the pass, fighting trolls, discovering that frostfire is even more fire than it is frost, arriving in Gorptoria, not having to travel to Fangcover City like we'd expected, and then checking into such a fancy hotel. Wild, right? It was really a lot.

And then, as if to give the day a shiny and extra unexpected conclusion, just as we were discussing the creature horde that I'd set free from the Shaelun dreadhull, wondering what they might be up to and whether they'd found interesting jobs in Scoomb, a familiar face appeared at the edge of the roof.

It was Minzo!

Aneko and I were both shocked. It was one of those funny moments when you're thinking or talking about someone and then they just appear. Coincidences like that, even if they are actually random, can feel like a message from the universe. Or something like that. As soon as I realized it was really the little bristlegriff climbing up to join us, a kind of calm reassurance went all through my body in a way that made me realize how much anxiety I'd been holding on to. I mean, we were about to attempt a government overthrow the next day. And with a wizard in the lead who was proving himself to be a pretty terrible strategist.

"It's so good to see you!" Aneko waved furiously as Minzo saluted, then bowed, then leaned over the edge and waved to someone down below.

"Good to see you too," Minzo said as he came over to sit with us on the tarred cedaris planks.

"What are you doing in Gorptoria?" I asked. "Are any of the other creatures with you?"

WE'VE COME FOR YOUR EGGS

No sooner had the words come out of my mouth than two cloud weasels climbed up over the edge. Then came a jungleroo and a squibbit. They all waved and then climbed to a lower peak, where they sat and watched us from, almost like they wanted to show their respect by keeping a bit of distance. How strange. It was true that I'd set them free, but I had just done what any reasonable creature would.

"Indeed," Minzo said, "as you can see, it's not just me. A few found jobs or families to live with in Scoomb, but most felt like it was too small of a town for so many creatures to compete for roles. But more than that, many of us were compelled to keep following you—to see where you might lead us. And not just those of us you see here. There are more throughout the city, setting up dens in various parks and thickets. All eager to join your cause."

"I didn't know I was leading anyone," I said. "I mean, I'm happy to help, but I don't know if I should be given that kind of responsibility. I'm just—"

"A dragon," Minzo cut in. "Small still though you are. You can speak to the arcane world, and you did so to set us free. Some might say we are in your debt, but we have followed you here not out of a need to balance the scales, but because we are inspired by your strength, skill, and determination."

"Frosted fishbutt." I took a deep breath—I needed to because suddenly I felt all wiggly and strange. On one paw, I was happy that I'd helped them escape, and I was glad to have the chance to make more creature friends. But on the other paw, this seemed like a lot of responsibility. Who did they think I was? And why did my being a dragon impress them so much? Surely I was just another creature like the rest of them, even if I could do a bit of magic. "Okay, wow. I really appreciate all those nice words. But at the same time, I'm afraid you might not be able to follow me much farther. I mean, I hope you can, and I'd be grateful to get to know you all better, but we're about to undertake a dangerous mission with our humans, and if it doesn't work out, we might all end up in a dungeon tomorrow."

"That sounds exactly like the kind of adventure we'd like to support you on," Minzo said.

"Oh, no." I held up both paws in protest. "You've all got your freedom now. And you already helped by creating the diversion that allowed us to escape from the dreadhull. I couldn't ask any more of you."

Aneko cleared her throat in her flickerkit way, which was the cutest little "hem." Then she said, "Given how prone our party is to failure, Glimm, maybe it would be good to have a Plan B of our own."

Of course the flickerkit was right, but I still didn't want any of them to risk anything for me. Once upon a time, I'd been excited for my boss to claim the Frostvalen throne, and not just because it would provide a path to my education. But over the last few days, I had to admit that I'd been souring on the idea of Jorvun as a king. He could be quite mean when he was in a bad mood. If he was willing to take that out on me, what would it mean for an entire nation? But then again, the biggest issue was a lack of sleep. He had never done well without a good night's rest. We'd had a pretty great time together over the years, even if he was strict with my meals. No, I should do my best to maintain faith in him—and in his plan. And if it was my job to support him as his familiar, then arranging for assistance from an army of creatures was one of my many duties.

WE'VE COME FOR YOUR EGGS

"Okay," I said at last. "Sure. I mean, thanks. It would be amazing if you could all help. But here's the thing. I don't really know what to expect, which means I don't know how or when your assistance might become necessary. Let's start with an overview..."

I explained everything, from the beginning. My life with Jorvun back in Ravenna. The truth of his parentage. His lifelong dream of announcing himself to his father, in part because I think, deep down, he really craved that connection, but also as a fulfillment of a wizard's natural desire for power and prestige. I told them all about the challenges we'd faced in our journey, Jorvun's often myopic approaches and dodgy moods, and then I explained how, in maintaining his lie to the party about why we were actually here, I didn't know exactly what his plan was. But presumably we would case the palace, break into the throne room, and at that point he would have to tell the party the truth. Killing Trudera didn't wash, and I knew he was still carrying around the Seed Sense kit he'd bought from Elric. So it only stood to reason that he was going to force the king to submit to a paternity test.

And what would happen after that? Maybe Trudera would weep with joy for his long-lost son. Or maybe he would deny the whole thing, claim the Seed Sense was giving a false positive, and throw us all in a dungeon. It was this sort of outcome that would necessitate help from the creatures.

But what would that help look like? And how would we let them know?

We had much to discuss, and so discuss we did. The sun dropped behind the edge of the world, casting Gorptoria in twilight as we considered strategies and counterstrategies. As darkness gathered, the streets came alive with lanterns, torches, and mostly mild tourist nightlife. This wasn't a city, apparently, where people went too wild. As we wrapped up our planning session, a string of many, many tens of magical lights flared all over the palace, illuminating every curve and spire. The city, it occurred to me in that moment, was so pretty it was almost gross.

With that, we bade each other goodnight. The creatures scampered down the walls of the Parlour Hotel as Aneko and I swooped back to our balcony. The humans were already in bed, all snoring apart from Jorvun, who it seemed had waited up for me. See—he's not all bad, right? They had apparently ordered food up to the room. Wow, in all the excitement I hadn't realized how hungry I was. Aneko and I ransacked the leftovers of cheesy flatbread and chicken wings. Okay, mostly just the chicken wings. I was crunching through my third when Jorvun cleared his throat and patted the bed as if to say I'd had enough. I could have eaten ten more, but what was I to do. Protesting would just wake everyone up. So with one flap I alighted on the bed and snuggled down next to the wizard's feet. Aneko curled up next to Fox and gave me a little wink.

Whatever awaited us on the morrow, we would face it together. Me, my human party, my best flickerkit friend, and an army of creatures ready to jump in and help in case anything went wrong. With that reassurance in mind, I fell quickly into a deep sleep.

CHAPTER SEVENTEEN

State of Delusion

The next morning, the party got themselves ready in silence. There was a quiet excitement running through all of us, I think, but also some uneasy glances. I managed to get through five of the leftover chicken wings, and my boss didn't say a thing—such was his state of nervous enthusiasm. And then we descended the Parlour Hotel's regal central staircase, through the lobby, and out into the morning light. The Inner Quay was already packed with tourists.

We crossed the street to the marina boardwalk and then over to the palace. The manicured flowerbeds and lawn were framed by ornate black-iron fencing and hedges trimmed perfectly square. The path to the main entrance ran straight up the centre, a grand flagstone promenade flanked by red-gold foxrose and teacup hydrangea. Ahead of us, the palace loomed—in height and in anticipation. Up close, the scarlet stone had more texture than I'd expected, rough-hewn and veined, like it had been quarried directly from some royal volcano. The copper domes atop the spires caught the morning light and in places glinted through the burnished green.

Tourists clustered around directional signs, plaques, and a life-sized bronze statue of some famous Frostvalenite (or so I assumed—what a dream it would be to finally learn to read). A group of schoolchildren were herded past us toward the east entrance by a tour guide in a felted tricorn hat. Jorvun marched without hesitation or any interest in the milling crowds toward the wide front steps. And up we went, following the throng toward two massive doors beneath an arch of carved stone—frost lilies, mountain peaks, and stylized flames woven into a heraldic crest. Guards in formal red uniforms milled around the edge of the grounds, though none seemed particularly alert. One leaned against a railing, a cup of steaming something in hand. Another was laughing with a pair of ferry workers. It looked less like the seat of power and more like a spectacular museum.

Just like that, we were inside. Easy. No siege. No grappling hooks. No disguises apart from the humans' light Gorptorian glamour and an added concealment for Lark's pistols. As we passed through the great front doors, the chill morning gave way to heated marble floors and warm filtered light. The entrance hall opened into a soaring rotunda, capped by a stained glass dome that shimmered with soft blues and greens, the light catching on the veins in the red stone walls. A great ring of columns held the space aloft, each carved with intricate vinework and crowned with stone griffins. Wide staircases swept upward on our left and right, while ahead of us, the Hall of Honour stretched onward, a gallery full of paintings and tapestries, from famous people to historical scenes.

WE'VE COME FOR YOUR EGGS

The tourists were gathering to appreciate a massive mural above the eastern staircase, its colours soft and somewhat faded. At the centre stood a lone figure on a winding mountain path—one leg flesh, the other an arcane prosthetic, sculpted from bronze and bound with glowing runes. He leaned forward into the climb, a staff of blue fire in one hand, the other raised in quiet salute. His cloak snapped behind him in the wind, casting its shadow upon the slope. Below him, scattered across the foothills, stood townsfolk and children, all watching in silence. Some clutched bundles of flowers. Others raised banners marked with a single frost lily. The path ahead vanished into the clouds, but above them all, etched into the sky in lines of gold leaf, were the words: *One step, then another.*

I rode on Jorvun's shoulder as he drifted from plaque to plaque, reading names under his breath like they were ancient incantations. Lark stuck close to the velvet ropes that guided the tourist flow, eyes darting in a way that could have seemed suspicious, assessing the guards and exits, but the security officers barely glanced at the crowd, no doubt used to gawking out-of-towners. Aneko fluttered behind Xander, Fox, and Elric, who were as spellbound as the rest. On either side of the hall, stained glass windows cast jewel-toned patches across the floor.

Eventually, Jorvun gestured for the party to follow and veered off down a quieter corridor. The bustle of the rotunda fell away behind us. This hall was darker, the windows smaller, and the foot traffic nonexistent. Richly patterned carpets muffled footsteps, and sconces on the walls burned with a gentle magical glow. At the end of the corridor stood two thick oak doors banded in iron and set with heavy handles shaped like dragon heads. Two guards stood on either side, their Frostvalen uniforms crisp and formal, each gripping an intimidating halberd.

Jorvun stopped about ten paces from the guards and turned back to the group. "Balls on a biscuit," he said, voice hushed and certain. "This is it. The seat of power."

"Okay, so... plan?" Lark asked.

"Let's just do this," the wizard said.

"Right now?" Elric asked. "I thought this was just reconnaissance."

Behind Jorvun, one of the guards cleared his throat.

"Why not right now?" Jorvun's shoulders tensed, and power burbled up from his umbrix. He was definitely ready to make his move. "Just follow my lead. And if anything goes wrong, glamour into security guards, get into the crowd, then glamour into tourists. We will meet back at the wagon."

"Brine and Keel, watch over us." Lark raised a hand to petition her gods.

"Excuse me," one of the guards said. "This is a restricted area. Can we help you with something?"

"Elric, can I have the mirror?" Fox hissed. "I want to live-stream this."

"Oh, yes," Jorvun said as he approached the guards. "We had a question about the, um... *somno, duad.*"

As the guards collapsed into unconsciousness, Jorvun jumped forward to grab both of their halberds and keep them from crashing to the floor. As he took the weapons to the edge of the hallway, Lark and Xander pulled the sleeping guards behind a cabinet so anyone passing at the end of the hall wouldn't see them. Meanwhile Fox was calling up her contact and Elric was digging for something in one of his pockets.

"Ready?" Jorvun asked.

"There's a war on for your mind," Xander said, as if that made any sense, "and I don't want to go to war without a halberd."

"No, just leave it," the wizard hissed. "There will be more guards inside the chamber. We don't want to immediately alarm them."

The paladin was about to protest, but Lark linked arms with him and said, "The academic is right. But if you need a weapon, you'll know where to find one, right?"

"Fine." Xander pulled out a vial of Alpha Power. "Okay, I'm ready."

With that, Jorvun threw open the large oak doors.

The legislative chamber was a vaulted, circular hall walled in panels of dark redwood and trimmed with gilt. Arched windows high above filtered in soft light through stained glass depictions of what were presumably historical scenes—dragons in flight, magical harvests, warriors clasping hands in victory. Around the perimeter, concentric rows of curved seating formed a ring of desks, each occupied by a suited councillor or robed minister, murmuring among themselves or leafing through vellum dossiers.

The centre of the chamber was sunken slightly, like a miniature arena, with a single circular stone embedded in the floor. It bore the sigil of Frostvale—a coiled red dragon—and presumably marked the place where petitioners were expected to stand. Beyond that, up a short flight of marble steps, was a more elaborate seating section with an impressive ashwood throne cushioned in dark velvet and set with small blue gems along the arms. Seated upon the throne was a tall, lean man with the long-limbed stillness of a lizard sunning on a rock. His robes, midnight blue and trimmed in iron-grey, hung too perfectly to be made of natural cloth—enchanted, I guessed, to resist wrinkles and stains. He had a sharp jaw, high cheekbones, and eyes like wet slate, cold but reflective, watching everything and offering nothing. On four smaller thrones next to his, two on each side, sat his advisors, presumably, but I couldn't tell you what they looked like because I couldn't take my eyes off the man I presumed to be King Trudera.

His hair, thick and dark, was combed straight back and held in place with some kind of magical pomade. He didn't move. He didn't even blink—though he did glance at *me* a couple times, which made me a bit nervous. And when he finally did speak, his voice was crisp and low, the kind of tone that turned questions into footnotes and accusations into scheduling conflicts. You got the sense he could destroy a political rival not with scandal or spellcraft, but with a four-minute rebuttal.

"And what," he said, "is the meaning of this interruption?"

Jorvun bowed slightly, but without taking his eyes off the man, and then he did something I would never have expected. He turned to the party and cast a spell at them.

"*Rigidus, clampo, quad.*"

And just like that, the four Valorican party members were frozen in place, unable to attack, unable to speak, unable to run. They had become four lifelike statues: Lark with her hand upon a currently invisible blaster; Fox holding the whisperglass pointed outward to transmit the goings-on to her contact in the South; Elric still with his hand in one pocket; Xander hunched over, eyes wild, vial of Alpha Power halfway to his mouth. Wow. I mean, I guess it made sense. Jorvun didn't want them messing up his negotiation. Somewhere behind me, Aneko gasped, so I swooped off Jorvun's shoulder and landed beside her—perched on the polished oak banister at the edge of the petitioner circle.

At the sound of the wizard's incantation, the room erupted in alarmed murmurs. Guards I hadn't even noticed came running forward from behind the dais and around the sides of the half-moon seating area, but then the leader held up a hand for them to wait, so they stopped just outside the circle.

As the murmuring calmed down, Jorvun took a step forward.

"I have come to claim my right of ascendancy," he boomed as he shook a fist at the throne. No, wait—it wasn't just a fist. He had the Seed Sense in his hand. "Perhaps succession has already taken place, since you are not the man I expected to meet here today. But I, Jorvun Prattlethorn, demand to speak with Justice Trudera. Though I may be his bastard son, my claims upon his name are not without legitimacy."

The leader, who I'd incorrectly assumed was Trudera, had kept a straight face throughout Jorvun's short speech, but now his lips cracked into a condescending smirk, and he gave a little snort of amusement.

"I'm not sure how you got past the guards, but we don't have time for this lunacy," he said once he'd regained his composure. "We had a security bulletin about some Valorican spies who crashed and escaped a Shaelun ship. I have to assume that's who you—"

"But I can prove it!" Jorvun held the box of Seed Sense a bit higher. "I can prove my paternity!!"

"Sure you can." The man shook his head. All traces of amusement were replaced by pity. "The real mystery of the day is how you ended up with that dragon. But regardless, I'm not sure if you're dealing with some mental health issues right now or if your delusion is simply born of the unfortunate state of the Valorican education system. So let me give you a quick lesson in geography and international politics. My name is Dravo Eby. I am the premier of Cascadriel, the westernmost *province* of Frostvale. In other words, Gorptoria is a *provincial* capital. Trudera presides over the country from the *nation's* capital, which is more than seven hundred leagues to the east in a city called Awtava."

For a moment I was stuck on *how you ended up with that dragon.* Like... what was that supposed to mean? But just as I was pondering this, the rest of Eby's words came rushing through and made me set this consideration aside.

"Oh dear," Aneko whispered.

Oh dear and then some. How? Why? This was Jorvun's lifelong ambition. And he wasn't illiterate like me. He had so many books, most of which were now at the bottom of the ocean, and most of which were about magic, but still. This seemed like a pretty huge detail to get wrong. Didn't he have contacts in Frostvale? Who had sent him that letter about Trudera's succession? How in the world had he not put more effort into preparing for this mission? Arrogant overconfidence was the only answer I could come up with. He had some notions about Frostvale, and clearly there was some widespread ignorance about Valorica's neighbour to the north, so he must have just taken those popular misconceptions as fact. Like: Fangcover is a big port city, so it must be the capital.

Or maybe that was just the only Frostvalen city people in Ravenna were familiar with? I couldn't quite grasp the immensity of this complete and utter disaster.

"Next time you plan on invading a country," Eby went on, "make sure you do a bit of research first."

No doubt. Ice me sideways. This was bad. This was very bad. Lying to the party all this time was frosted to begin with, but now they were locked in an immobilization spell. We were surrounded by guards. And the authorities knew we had broken into the country from Valorica. They also knew we'd crashed a Shaelun dreadhull into the coast, which probably was a punishable offence on its own. Even if Jorvun was Trudera's bastard son, I couldn't see how we were going to get out of this situation. We needed to act fast, but the party couldn't act at all, and Jorvun was just standing there, staring up at Eby with his mouth hanging open.

One of the guards who had come around the dais stepped closer, and that was when I realized he was holding something in both hands—a net of some kind, and there was a tingle of familiar energy or non-energy emanating from it. The guard looked over his shoulder at Eby, who gave him a nod, and then he threw the net at my boss while muttering a trigger word of some kind. I knew it was a trigger word because the buzz of non-energy was suddenly more palpable, the net increased in size, and as it came down over Jorvun, it also grew some heavy-looking anvil-type things at each of its four corners. The next thing I knew, the wizard was on the ground, cursing, spitting out some spellwords, each of which fizzled into the anti-magic of the net.

"And by the way—" Eby stood and squinted down at my boss. "—Trudera has more bastards than you could shake a flail at. I can promise that he won't give any claim you might have, legitimate or otherwise, a second thought."

Jorvun moaned and covered his face with both hands.

More guards were closing in. If I was going to do something, it had to be now. But what? The anvils that had appeared at the corners of the net clamped Jorvun into place. I didn't think there was anything I could do about that. But the party—did they really deserve to be thrown into a dungeon for Jorvun's incompetence? Well, maybe. They had been willing participants in the assassination of a king, even if the plan was all wrong. But still, I felt like they had been tricked into this and then doubly betrayed at the last second. And while they were all a bit wacky, they had been so nice to me. Every single one of them had snuck me a treat when Jorvun wasn't looking. For that, at least, I owed them something. Didn't I? The alternative was that Aneko and I fly away on our own, but that seemed pretty cowardly.

I pointed my paw at the spell-locked four, tugged at my umbrix, and said, "*Nullivar*." Just like that, Jorvun's spell came undone. And just like that, the party sprang into action.

Lark pulled out her blasters, now very much visible in her hands, and spun around to face the approaching guards, all of whom jumped back a step. Fox shook her head, and when she realized she was still broadcasting, she started a slow pan of the room. Elric pulled what looked like a large black beetle out of his pocket and threw it on the ground between the party and the nearest guards. Xander quaffed his vial and roared.

"Gonna frostfire," I said to Aneko. "Don't explode them, please."

"No worries," she said as I launched off the banister.

As I iced the guard who had thrown the net, Elric's beetle thing spewed a thick column of black smoke that gave the party a second of cover and maybe another second of reaction time. Xander ripped off a length of the banister and swung it at two more guards who were coming around the other side of the dais. Lark fired a warning shot that shattered one of the arched windows near the roof. Eby, his advisors, and most of the ministers dove for cover. Fox kept recording. I flapped higher so I could see over the smoke. Most of the guards were behind us, and more were coming through the entrance, these ones with batons that crackled with blue energy. Stun sticks, most likely. Not good. But there was another door behind the dais, and only three guards stood between the party and that exit.

"Creatures, come to our aid!!" I projected my voice up at the shattered window, as loud as I possibly could. But it wasn't very loud, so I followed that with possibly the best roar of my life.

A moment later, several ropes came tumbling down through the rent, then Minzo swung into the chamber, followed by three jungleroos. Another window smashed open, and another. More ropes. More creatures. There were a couple snuffalos, three velvetaurs, a snorchin, a tusslemonk, all climbing down the ropes, jumping into the fray, and charging about the room. Two pebblecrakes flew in and flung clawfuls of stones at Dravo Eby. The guards looked around in horror. The ministers howled in fear.

"This way," I shouted between gouts of frostfire.

Lark led the retreat, firing a couple more warning shots—at least I hoped they were warning shots. She had a bloodthirsty look on her face, eyes narrowed and teeth bared (not a smile, correct). I really needed to get them out of there before the situation got any worse. Fox grabbed Xander by the back of his leather jerkin and pulled him toward the door as he swung his banister back and forth. And as they ran, Elric dropped a couple more smoke beetles.

Of course the door was locked, but my magical secret was a secret no more, so with a quick *aperi sesame* I had us out and through. On the other side, I paused for a second to consider how I might delay our pursuers. Frostfire around the edges? That would take too long. What if, instead, I could concoct a spell using a combination of Jorvun's spellwords? Worth a try. Once Fox slammed the door shut behind us, I leveled a paw.

"Rigidus, clampo, sesame."

My umbrix responded, and I felt the power flow out of me and into the heavy wood and brass knob. Had it worked? My instincts said that it was a success, but no time to stick around and find out. We found ourselves in a long, narrow hallway lit with magical sconces. We had done it. Well, we weren't out of danger completely, and we'd left my boss behind, but we were certainly in a better situation than we'd been a few moments earlier. I just hoped the creatures would all be able to escape back up their ropes before the guards recovered their wits.

We flapped (and ran) down the hall while the guards pounded on the door behind us. It seemed like my spell was holding! A service stairwell led us down to an emergency exit. The party glamoured into the same uniforms worn by the legislative guards, and then we slipped outside. We emerged at the southwest corner of the palace. Nearby, a crowd gathered around a massive fountain with multiple streams of water that rose and fell, almost like a clam opening and shutting its mouth. The humans were making their way through the crowd when the door we had exited through flew open and five actual guards ran out. Since Aneko and I were flapping above everyone's heads, they spotted us immediately. I swooped down to land on a lamppost next to Lark.

"Head for that grove of trees over there." I motioned with my nose toward the southeast edge of the grounds. "Glamour into tourist clothing, or even back into tweens. Then meet us at the hotel room. We'll lead the guards away from you."

Lark grunted and frowned in a strange way. For a brief moment, I wondered if she was mad at me. But no, it had to be that the plan had just gone very wrong and she was upset about that. And at Jorvun. But I had saved them and gotten them out of the building, and now I was going to help them escape the palace grounds, so no, she couldn't have been mad at me.

No time to ask or even wonder much about it though. I leapt off the lamppost and banked back toward the guards. Aneko followed me at first, but I signalled for her to fly due west while I made for the intersection of streets at the southwest corner of the palace grounds. We both stayed low, just over the milling crowds of tourists, and sure enough, the guards assumed we were with our humans, so they split into two groups and set off after us. Since I can fly a fair bit faster than Aneko, I doubled back for her once I was a block away from the palace, and together we turned north and flew out over the harbour. Once hidden by the tall inns on the other side of the water, we made our way back to the Inner Quay, moving from rooftop to rooftop and making sure there were no guards or police (or police pigeons) in sight. The humans would be well disguised, but a small blue dragon and flickerkit travelling across the skies together were more conspicuous.

Eventually we found our way around the north side of the Parlour Hotel, then up onto the roof, and when the coast was clear, we swooped down to our balcony. The party was already gathered in the first room: Lark and Xander on one bed, Elric and Fox on the cot. All staring at each other. And while it seemed like they had been discussing something, they fell silent when we appeared.

"Hey guys," I said. "I'm glad you all made it back here. Well, not all, I guess, but, um…"

Their faces were blank. Guarded. I let the silence linger between us, hoping that maybe one of them would say something to counteract the awkwardness, but they just kept staring. Then Aneko gave me a nudge.

"You have to expect that they are all feeling pretty betrayed," she said. "And you played a part in that betrayal."

"Oh." That was all I could think to say. Had I betrayed them? Jorvun was my boss, and he'd commanded me to keep his secret. I hadn't wanted to lie. Finally, I said, "I'm sorry. I guess you realize now that Jorvun lied about our mission from the start, and since I didn't say anything to contradict him, that means I also deceived you."

"Not just about the mission." Lark crossed her arms and glared a bit harder at me. "Why was it a secret that you can cast spells? Two godsdamn blasphemers in the party! And how about the fact that you had a creature army at your beck and call?"

"Oh." Frosted fishtits. I hadn't been keeping those secrets from *them*. I'd been keeping them from Jorvun.

But I guess in the end that worked out to be the same thing. This deception business was definitely not paying off. Would the wizard even have been mad about my magic? Maybe, but I didn't know for sure. And would he have been mad about the creatures? Again, my gut had told me that it was better left unsaid. But that brought us to the present situation. "I'm sorry, guys. I hope you can understand my reasoning. Jorvun didn't know about the magic. Actually, I didn't even know until we were on the dreadhull. And then I was nervous about telling him. The creatures too. I didn't know how he'd react."

"It could have been really helpful for us to know," Elric said. "Could have helped us plan better. Maybe."

"I can't believe," Xander said, "this whole time. A complete conspiracy."

"It's not a conspiracy," I insisted.

"I don't know," Fox said. "Normally I'd say that Xander is just being paranoid, but this feels pretty conspiratorial. You knew the wizard was Trudera's son. You knew we were walking into a trap."

"No!" I held up my paws in protest. "I had no idea he was going to freeze you or whatever that spell was. I didn't actually know what he was going to do. I mean, yeah, I knew that we weren't going to be assassinating the king, but I thought that was a good thing. I don't want to kill anyone."

"Tell that to the trolls," Lark said. "I don't know, Glimm. You had us fooled, for sure. And now I'm inclined to think that this is still an act. You and your wizard are both liars."

"What about Fox?" I almost shouted, such was the panic rising in me. "She lies about absolutely everything, and you're not mad at her."

Fox looked at me blankly like I'd just spoken in another language.

"That's different," Lark said. "That's pathological."

"Look, you guys have got to believe me. It's not an act. Please." I turned to Aneko. "I'm not sure what else to say."

"The flickerkit is part of the conspiracy," Xander shouted.

"I'm not sure that she is," Lark said. "What do you have to say for yourself, Aneko? Did Glimm tell you about the academic's actual plan?"

"Only yesterday," Aneko said. "But—"

"See!" Xander got to his feet and started pacing. "I'm not going to sit here and take it anymore!"

"Oh no you don't." Fox jumped up, grabbed the paladin by the sleeve, and pulled him back to the bed. "Don't forget that we're fugitives. That means no shouting and no doing anything crazy. Just... try to stay calm."

"In other words," Lark said to Aneko, "Glimm lied to you at first, and then for the better part of the day, you've been complicit in the plan to screw us over."

"Glimm and Jorvun have a problematic relationship," Aneko said, "to say the least. He's supposed to be a familiar, but the wizard treats him like a pet. No—worse than a pet. If you'd been paying attention, you'd have realized that Glimm is afraid of the wizard. That's why he didn't say anything about the magic, or the creatures, or the plan."

"Or so Glimm led you to believe," Elric said. "I knew the pair of them back in Ravenna, and I never had the sense that Glimm was scared of anything. He's a bold little guy. He stands up to Jorvun all the time."

"No, listen," I managed to cut in. "This is stupid.

Everyone is oversimplifying everything. Yes, back in Ravenna, Jorvun and I got along pretty well. But he also has some unpredictable moods, and I don't really know how to deal with him when he's angry. For one thing, he takes away my meals if I frost him off, and that's not very fun. But I'd like to think that we still have an understanding. Now I don't know what it's like for other familiars, or for pets for that matter, but I do know that he's my boss, and so I have a job to do, and sometimes that means keeping a secret if he tells me I have to keep it. But what I'm learning, or trying to learn, is that sometimes I need to tell him that his secret is dumb and I'm not going to keep it, because doing so isn't good for him, for me, or for anyone else. I could see that it was a problem. I knew pretty well that this whole adventure was going to end badly. And I could have done something about it, and I should have, but I didn't. And for that I'm sorry."

For a while no one said anything. A gentle wind blew in the open patio door. Two gulls shrieked at each other from a nearby rooftop—I did my best to suppress a memory of tasty stolen fish. From somewhere down on the sidewalk, a couple musicians launched into a quiet melody of harp and flute. Fox glanced over at her lute case and sniffed. Xander took a quivering breath and sank a bit deeper into the mattress. Elric flicked a bit of lint off his knee. Lark sighed and shook her head—but not necessarily in a rejection of what I'd said. More like an expression of lingering disappointment. And I couldn't blame her for that.

"So what do you think we should do now?" I asked when it seemed like the silence would go on forever.

"We're screwed," Lark said. "We're trapped here behind the barrier wall."

"Just a matter of time," Elric added, "before they catch up to us with police pigeons or sniff us out with police ferrets."

"I still don't think those pigeons are real," Xander said.

"I guess, until we get caught," Fox said, "I can still do a bit of hard-hitting journalism."

We fell back into silence. The street musicians played their way to the end of a ballad and then struck up a livelier number. There were many times on this journey when things had been going badly, and each time I'd been able to come up with a plan. Maybe that was needed again here. Well yes, that was definitely needed here. But would they listen? Or had their trust been too damaged? After Jorvun, I would have said that Lark was the leader, but it occurred to me in that moment that I had been leading them all along, in a way. A quiet way. But also trying not to lead them, because I hadn't wanted to upset my boss. And because I'm just a tiny blue dragon. Barely bigger than a flickerkit or a bristlegriff. But these humans really didn't know what to do. I'd helped get them trapped in this country. We'd committed crimes together, from illegally entering the sea gate to crashing a ship into Fangcover Island to attempted robbery to wagon theft to assaulting police officers *and* palace guards.

We were in a lot of trouble, now that I thought about it. And what did that mean for my chances at an education? The whole time, I'd been driven by this idea that if I could get Jorvun on the throne, my dreams would come true. But now the throne was all the way on the other side of the country, which might have been my homeland but was still a totally unknown realm to me, and Jorvun was locked in a dungeon. If I was going to get into dragon college, I needed an all-new strategy for achieving that. Or... maybe—a slightly new strategy.

What if we could still put Jorvun on the throne? But working together as a team, no lies or manipulations. Lark, Elric, Xander, and Fox all had reasons for coming on this quest. If they assisted Jorvun in becoming the next King of Frostvale, he'd have to help them achieve their goals. Especially if they all busted him out of prison. Right?

Aneko gave me a little nudge to the ribs. I looked up to find everyone staring at me. I think I might have been muttering to myself. Maybe. So I cleared my throat and sat up a bit straighter.

"I don't think we're, um, screwed," I said. A few seconds of silence passed. No one protested. Even Lark looked like she was going to at least listen to what I had to say. "If you'll hear me out... I have a plan."

CHAPTER EIGHTEEN

How to Free Wizards and Influence People

We finally got to see what the other side of the whisperglass looks like. Fox called Elric, even though we were still standing around in our hotel room together. The air in front of Elric wavered, fizzed, and then coalesced into a floating oval window centred on Fox's face.

"Hi!" She waved at us through the glass and also from across the room.

"Interesting," Elric said. "The reception is clearer than I expected, although maybe that's because you're broadcasting from nearby."

Lark helped secure the whisperglass to Fox's red doublet with some small, thin strips Elric referred to as *zip ties*, the likes of which none of us had ever seen. They were made out of a kind of shiny rubber that was at once hard and flexible. Attached in this way, we could no longer see Fox's face through the floating window but instead whatever she was facing. Next, she used her glamour ring to recreate her attire, slightly cleaner, with a few more embellishments of gold thread, and also concealing the whisperglass. Lastly, she handed her lute case to Xander with a stern expression.

"Take care of her for me," Fox said. "If my journalism career doesn't fly, I might need to fall back on busking."

"Of course." Xander took the case and hugged it close. "And you take care of yourself, what with all the fake birds and gay frogs out there. It's a dangerous world, and you're walking right into the maw."

"Dangerous, maybe," Fox said. "But just think of the story I'll be able to tell."

With that, Fox left us behind to venture down to the street. Two police officers, not sneaky at all, were keeping a close eye on our stolen wagon, evidently waiting for the thieves to return. We watched via the magic window as our bard strode across the street and walked right up to them.

"Hi," she said in her usual chipper tone. "I'm one of the Valorican spies you're looking for. I've been feeling tremendously guilty for my part in all of our crimes, including the theft of this here wagon, so I'd like to turn myself in."

The officers stared at her for a moment, mouths agape, before they were spurred into action.

"Well then," the shorter one said, then cleared her throat. "Good for you. That's what we like to hear. And you know what, we'll mention your change of heart in our report. Not that the courts will go easier on you, but you never know."

The taller, hairier one got out some manacles and locked Fox's hands behind her back. And off they went.

"That's my cue." Aneko gave me a tight-lipped smile and a cute little nod. Then she fluttered over the balcony and across the street to keep tabs on the newly arrested.

I'd wanted to go with her, but we decided that a blue dragon was a lot more conspicuous than a flickerkit, and certainly the two of us together would have been a giveaway. While we watched Fox's progress through the whisperglass window, Aneko would keep tabs on the bard and determine the fastest route from the hotel to whatever prison or dungeon they took new prisoners in Gorptoria.

The police marched Fox over to the edge of the palace grounds, where they had a wagon of their own drawn by two large steeds. One cop sat with the bard in the back while the other drove the team east, past the Parlour Hotel. Fox angled her torso slightly so the whisperglass was able to show her progress. Still, with the horses moving at a steady trot, it was hard to tell where they were headed. After a few blocks they turned—toward the north was our best guess. But the other issue was that the streets of Gorptoria were a bit random. Definitely not a grid. Good thing we had Aneko keeping tabs on them.

The whisperglass was still helpful, though. After one more turn (to the east again?), the wagon stopped in front of a large stone building with a sign above the front doors. Fox leaned back to give us a view of it. Honestly, she was turning out to be a decent videographer. Elric read the sign for me: *Gorptoria Courthouse*. Once the cops led Fox inside, Aneko's surveillance ended. They entered a lobby where many people waited on rows of benches and even more people worked on long scrolls at a series of desks. They stopped at one such desk, and the person (clerk? scribe?) took down Fox's name and particulars.

This lasted a few boring minutes, during which I kept watching the balcony for Aneko to return. The police wagon couldn't have travelled more than ten blocks, so she should have been able to fly back to us quite quickly. But no flickerkit. Maybe she'd spotted something else that she thought worthy of some recon. Finally the cops led Fox out of the lobby through two large locked doors. Then down a long corridor.

When they exited the building out the back, Fox paused to swing her torso side to side, giving us a full view of the scene before her—until one of the cops grunted and dragged her down the steps. It was a grassy area contained within two high walls and another building on the other side. Along the left wall were a series of benches, and along the right were a few picnic tables set in the shade of two large oak trees. A couple cops and other courthouse staff hung out on the benches, reveling in the warm sunshine.

On Fox went, up the path that bisected the grassy hangout area, and into the next building. Thanks to Elric once again for his literacy: this was the *Remand Bastion*. The jail, in other words.

The march continued: through a series of locked doors and gates; alongside an inner courtyard where a number of convicts lifted weights or sat smoking mirth-root around a central fountain; past two sections of holding cells to what appeared to be the back of the building, given that there were small barred windows set high in the wall. Here they turned left and walked past several cells, one of which Fox turned toward to allow us to see into.

It was Jorvun. For a moment I didn't even recognize him. He wore an unflattering hazard-orange jumpsuit—he has a winter skin tone, so not his colour at all. His hair was pointing in ten different directions. He had a painful-looking bruise under one eye. And his mouth was covered with a wide metal band that was etched in runes and clamped behind his head.

"What is that thing?" I whispered, though it wasn't like the guards could hear us through the whisperglass—Elric had set the device to one-way audio.

"A mage gag," Lark said. "So he can't cast."

"Hi, Jorvun." Fox's hand rose in our view as she waved at the wizard.

He grunted something in response, a sound that expressed shock, confusion, and maybe even dismay, before the guards shoved the bard onward.

They passed a few more cells before turning left, unlocking another door, and entering a dim room full of tall cabinets. The one cop said he'd wait outside. The other took Fox to a cabinet near the back and pulled out an orange jumpsuit, which honestly wouldn't look terrible on the bard. She's an autumn, after all.

"Strip," the cop told her. "Everything. Jewellery too." Then she flipped open a nearby cabinet. "Stuff it all into here."

Fox turned around and pulled off the glamour ring first, then quickly removed and folded her doublet to conceal the zip-tied whisperglass. Good thinking. But also, that was the end of our spy session. Elric motioned at a small X in the corner of the floating whisperglass window, and the projection vanished.

We waited for a moment, unsure what to do next. We had a general idea of how to get to the courthouse, but the plan had been for Aneko to lead us there. It didn't make sense that she hadn't returned yet. I was getting a bit worried about my smart little friend. We all were, which was obvious from the way no one said anything about it. Elric patted around in his pockets. Lark counted her remaining bullets. Xander rocked back and forth, chewing his thumbnail and clutching Fox's lute case.

Finally, a little creature appeared on the balcony—but it was Minzo, not Aneko.

"Glimm," he said in a sharp greeting, which he followed with a salute. "And humans."

"This is Minzo," I said. "He leads the creature army."

"Hi, Minzo." Lark saluted back, but with a little quirk in her lips, like she thought his formality was funny. Well, I guess it was a bit stiff, but bristlegriffs are just like that, from what I've heard.

Elric waved. Xander looked Minzo up and down as if assessing whether or not he was going to turn into a troll and eat everyone.

"I thank you for your vote of confidence," Minzo said, "but you, Glimm, lead the creature army. Though I have no formal rank, unless you wish to bestow one upon me, I would say that I am your general."

"Oh." I laughed awkwardly and shrugged at the party. They might have been on board with the plan to rescue Jorvun, but I wasn't sure if we'd fully moved past all the lying and sore feelings, part of which came down to me not telling them about the creatures who had decided to follow me. But also, it was just plain weird that they had chosen me as their leader. I mean, yes, I had helped them escape the ship, but they could go anywhere now, do anything. Their eager loyalty continued to surprise me. "Well then. Sure, let's make it official. General Minzo it is!"

"I am honoured, ma'am." Minzo bowed deeply.

"Sir," I said. "Not a ma'am. Or, well, you don't have to call me sir, I just meant that I'm—"

"Yessir!" Minzo straightened up and saluted again. "Beg your pardon."

"No pardon to beg," I said. "It's a common enough mistake."

"So where's Aneko?" Lark asked.

"Right." The bristlegriff gave her a sharp nod. "We ran into each other outside the courthouse. After the incident at the palace, we weren't clear on our orders, so we kept tabs on the wizard. As you now know, they transferred him to the temporary prison out back, where he is presumably awaiting trial."

"So Fox didn't need to get herself arrested," Xander blurted.

"Maybe not," I said, "but if she hadn't, we wouldn't know what part of the prison Jorvun is being kept in. That's still valuable information."

"Right." Xander took a quivering breath and gave the lute case a squeeze.

"I told Aneko where the creature squads are hiding out," Minzo went on. "She can round them up faster than me. By the time we make our way to the courthouse, many of them will be assembled nearby."

"Fantastic," I said. "Another diversion will really help our plan."

"Indeed." Minzo held up a thoughtful paw, one claw outstretched. "But I have one more bit of intel to share. In exploring Gorptoria, we found a series of ancient tunnels that run underneath the city streets. Many of the entrances are closed up, and they only connect the oldest buildings. So whereas there is a bricked-up entrance into the basement of the courthouse, which we weren't able to access, there is no entrance to the jail, though the tunnel runs clear underneath it, to the old boarding school and hospital one block to the east."

"How does that help us?" Elric asked.

"I'm not sure," Minzo said. "But Aneko thought it was interesting."

"It *is* interesting," I said. "And I'd like to have a look at those tunnels."

"Very well." The bristlegriff motioned over his shoulder toward the Inner Quay. "There's an outflow next to the wharf. Easiest way to get in. But your humans won't be able to get down there, I'm afraid. Not without attracting a lot of attention."

"That's fine." I turned to the party. "I want you three to proceed with the original plan. I mean, if that's all right with you."

Lark, Elric, and Xander all jumped to their feet in a way that felt... super weird. Again, I just wasn't used to people treating me like I was an actual leader. Honestly, it was a lot more comfortable to offer helpful suggestions and observations, and thereby lead the humans to a plan. But maybe there was deception in that? Even a little bit? Was me directly taking the lead a more honest approach? What an odd thought. I'd have to ask Aneko about that later.

"I think your tween glamour will be safest," I said. "Circle around to the back of the jail, or the perimeter wall behind the jail. We'll need to figure out a way to get over it."

"Aye, aye, Captain." Lark gave me a full-tooth grin (why??) and a wink.

Definitely a big improvement in her mood considering just an hour ago I thought she might shoot me.

"Hold on." We were just about to head out via the balcony when I had a final brain wave. "Elric, do you have any devices in your pockets that can make fire?"

"Devices? No," he said. "But I grabbed a pack of matches from the hotel lobby. Will that work?"

"Perfect." I flapped over and took the small box from him. "These might come in handy."

Minzo dove off the building, spread his strange membranous wings, and glided down to a weeping frost-willow at the northwestern edge of the hotel grounds. I swooped down after him. The tree had large limbs that draped over a small pond—and, oh my, the pond was filled with a bunch of bright orange fish. Damn, I wished I'd noticed that earlier. But now was not the time to get distracted. There were two new cops across the street keeping an eye on our wagon, but they were both turned toward the palace, so they hadn't seen us.

"Wait a minute, then follow me." Minzo glided down to the sidewalk, then crossed the road.

Half a block down from the cops, just before the tourist information tower, he hopped up onto the low brick wall that lined the edge of the wharf, looked in both directions, then disappeared over the edge. One of the cops turned toward the hotel, so I waited for a moment, but then a horse pulling a carriage past the palace whinnied loudly, and she turned back to see what the commotion was. That was my cue. I dove off my branch, burst through the feathery frostwillow leaves, and zipped out over the edge of the wharf. Sure enough, right below where Minzo had disappeared, there was a rainwater outflow, with a stolid bristlegriff waving me inside.

The pipe that ran about six feet under the street was large enough for a human to crawl through, and so quite spacious for the two of us. Not a lot of light, but not completely dark either—some sunshine poked through curb grates. About halfway under the road there was a junction of smaller pipes that ran north to south, toward the palace and into downtown, but Minzo led me past those to a darker section that extended under the grounds of the Parlour Hotel.

"Oh gross," I said when I caught a whiff of sewage. "Do I need to be careful where I step?"

"No, don't worry. This region is temperate rainforest. So the sewer we're in now is just for rainwater. The nastier sewer runs beneath us, and from what we can tell, it empties into a reservoir on the north coast, which then gets magically pumped down into the depths of the strait. But it's true, there is some unfortunate venting between the two systems."

"They pump raw sewage directly into the ocean?"

"I know, right?" Minzo clucked in dismay. "You'd expect such a garden-happy town would have a better method for waste management."

We hurried through the darkness for a quiet minute. Minzo had said there was a blocked entrance into the courthouse basement. My first idea had been to blast that open so the creatures could swarm the courts, ideally drawing some of the guards away from the prison. But as we hustled along, that plan was seeming less feasible. We had already used the creature chaos distraction in the palace. Would the guards fall for it again? Probably some would come to help, but I doubted they would leave the entire jail unprotected.

No, my plan was still missing something. Clearly we needed to rescue Fox, and yeah, Jorvun too, but it didn't make sense to rush in there and get the rest of the party captured, not to mention a bunch of the creatures.

"Here we are." Minzo had stopped a few paces ahead of me at a bricked-up archway. "We are ninety-nine percent sure this leads into the courthouse basement, but there are no gaps in the masonry for even a cloud weasel to slip through. We didn't want to draw any attention to our survey by opening a hole."

"I'm not very good at math," I said, "but ninety-nine sounds like a big percent."

"Yessir. Very big. Pretty much a certainty."

"Okay, great. So from here the tunnel leads under the jail?"

"Affirmative."

"Can we have a look?"

"Of course," Minzo said, "although when we were through here last, we found no other exits on this block."

So we continued on in the darkness. Since dragons have no pockets, I was gripping the matchbox in one paw and running my other paw along the wall, and I was snuffling like crazy to see if there was any scent evidence that could help us.

And, indeed, there was a scent that made me slow down—water. Not rainwater. Not old musty puddle water. But the bright, fresh, magically cleansed water that comes out of a tap. Minzo paused somewhere ahead of me.

"You smell that?" I asked.

"Yes," Minzo said. "Something is leaking into the tunnel from above. Broken pipes maybe."

Right at that moment, a droplet hit me on the nose.

I wiped it off and gave it a taste—yup, definitely from the city's water supply.

"Hold on." I fumbled with the matchbox, which turned out to be quite difficult. My paws aren't exactly made for manipulating objects in the same way that humans do. But then it occurred to me that bristlegriffs have monkey-like fingers. "Hey, can you strike one of these?"

Minzo took the box from me and struck a match. The little flame pushed back some of the inky darkness. The tunnel was more or less as my paws had described: large rough-cut stones and blackened wood supports. But there was something different in the ceiling directly above us. The roof leading up to and away from this point was all made of the same wooden crossbeams, laid tightly together. But from where the clean water was dripping, the beams ran lengthwise for about four feet, and there were gaps between them. It was hard to tell for sure with the match making the shadows dance all around us, so I climbed up the wall for a closer look. (No flapping—I didn't want to put the match out prematurely.) And sure enough, on the other side of these lengthwise beams, there was a metal grate of some kind. Interesting!

"If you had to guess," I said when I dropped down and landed beside Minzo, "where would you say we are in relation to the courthouse and jail?"

Minzo blew out the match, then mumbled some numbers to himself. "We must be below the jail," he said. "Yes, I think so. Right smack in the centre, I'd say."

"When they led Fox through, there was a courtyard in the middle of the structure. Prisoners hanging out, lifting weights, stuff like that. And right in the middle of the courtyard there was a fountain. Stands to reason, don't you think...?"

"That this water is leaking from the fountain? Makes sense to me."

"So with a little frostfire, maybe I can open up a hole right in the middle of the courtyard."

"I like where you're going with this," Minzo said. "Should we get some reinforcements?"

"Yes. But not everyone. I think... just the pugzips and cloud weasels."

"Sounds like you have a particular flavour of chaos in mind," Minzo said with undeniable excitement in his voice. "Okay, follow me."

I went over the particulars of my plan as we made our way to an alley a block away from the prison and slipped out of the curb grate. There was no one around, and the lane had been blocked off to traffic, presumably because of an old building that was halfway torn down. Two large piles of rubble awaited removal, and a sign bore a picture of a shiny new hotel, which I assume was what would go up in its place. Fortunately, there were no workers on site today and so no one to spy our escape route.

While the bristlegriff went to round up our squad, I found my tween humans in the accommodating limbs of a great oak tree across the street from the back wall of the prison.

"Hey, you're well hidden up here," I said. "Great spot."

"Not bad, huh." Lark was stretched out on a wide branch with her back resting against the trunk. "I mean, not bad, eh? It's almost comfortable."

"Speak for yourself." Xander straddled an even bigger branch, and he flinched as it creaked under his weight.

"Any updates?" Elric asked.

"We're going to try something, and I'm not yet sure it will work," I said. "But if you can just hang out here, I will come back to get you either way. Actually... Xander, since you're not loving the arboreal life, can I get you to check out a construction site back up this alley?" I pointed in the direction I had come. "See if you can find a ladder or something? We'll need to get you three over the prison wall when the time is right."

"Happy to!" Xander slid off his branch and swung down to the ground. "See any police pigeons or anything like that?"

"Nothing so far," I said.

He hurried away, and a couple minutes later, Minzo came around the corner with three cloud weasels and two pugzips following closely behind. I flew over and gave them all a wave, and soon we were back in the darkness below the city.

"I've explained the plan," Minzo said as we approached the spot in the tunnel with the drippy ceiling.

"Perfect," I said. "Of course, everything depends on this first part working. And for that, I'm going to need you pugzips and cloudlings to keep a safe distance."

"So once you've covered the ceiling in frostfire, I'll light it with a match?" Minzo asked.

"Not quite. The last time we tried this, the explosion was intense, so I don't want you to be too close. You could lose a hand."

"I don't mind making a sacrifice for the cause."

"No sacrifice necessary, Minzo. At least, I hope not. No, I was thinking... you can shoot those quills of yours, can't you?"

"Fling them more than shoot them, but yes."

"Do you think we can light one of them on fire? I mean, would that hurt?"

"Oh, I see what you're thinking. No sir, definitely won't hurt."

So that's what we did. Minzo lit a match for light, then I concentrated a bunch of frostfire in the middle of the dripping section of roof, getting some on two of the beams and some in between them to the grate beyond. And when I thought I'd done enough, I gouted out a bit more. But I didn't use up all of my reserves. There would be more than one cryo-plasma explosion needed today.

When I was done, I gave Minzo two claws up, then we backed down the tunnel to a safe distance. The bristlegriff struck a second match and then held the flame to the end of one of his tail quills. It took a little while for it to catch, and even then he let the flame build until half the quill was burning.

"Fire in the hole," Minzo shouted. Then, with a flick of his bum and a snap of his tail, the little burning projectile shot straight at the patch of frostfire.

We should have stood farther back.

A snap. A roar. A flash of light. The force of the explosion, channelled by the length of the tunnel, blew all of us backward and covered us in smoke and dust and wood chips. Then came the flood. We had definitely blown a hole in the roof, which as it turned out, had been bearing the weight of the large stone fountain. The bottom of the fountain gave out with a groan, a crack, and a crash, and the water all poured down into the tunnel in a silty rush. For a moment I was too stunned to move or think, but then I heard Minzo shouting commands, so that got me to my feet. The creature squad was climbing up the rent in the roof, brave as anything, and so I shook the mud from my wings and flapped over to join them.

WE'VE COME FOR YOUR EGGS

The prisoners in the courtyard were standing around in shock, just staring at the hole that had previously been a fountain. There were two guards at each door, and they too were slack-jawed and dumbfounded. Even as we burst into sight, they just blinked and shook their heads. Perfect. We had to make the most of their disorientation.

The cloud weasels immediately huffed out the thick smoky vapour they are named for. It swirled around the prisoners and spread out across the courtyard. The pugzips went for the guards, shooting little blasts of harmless and yet still painful zaps of electricity at them, which had them cowering and backing up. They were so overwhelmed that we managed to drive them into a panic. On both sides, they escaped through the two exits back into the prison, slamming the doors behind them.

That would give us a bit of time, but soon they would be back with reinforcements. Meanwhile, I was hovering in the middle of the courtyard above the hole, waving and blinking at the prisoners to convey as much friendliness as possible. Maybe some of them had heard about the attack on the palace involving a small blue dragon, or maybe they just knew a prison break when they saw it, because several of them looked eagerly curious and even smiled and waved back at me.

"Time to get out of here," I shouted once the guards were gone. "There is a tunnel underneath us, about an eight-foot drop through this hole. If you swing down over the edge, it shouldn't be too bad. But it's dark down there, so stay close and follow us."

A few of them shook their heads and backed away from the hole. Probably they had only committed minor offences and so weren't facing a significant jail sentence.

Escaping and getting caught would land them in a lot more trouble. But there were slightly more than ten prisoners who looked very happy to get out of there.

As they dropped down into the tunnel one and two at a time, the weasels managed to fill most of the courtyard with mist or fog or smoke or whatever it was that they produced. And they would keep producing it for as long as they could—they climbed up the courtyard walls and spewed more down from the roof. The pugzips joined them. When the guards came back with reinforcements, they would fill the foggy space with zaps to keep the guards out of the tunnel for as long as possible.

Once all the prisoners who wanted to escape had joined me in the passage, Minzo came scurrying to the front of the line. We hurried to the bricked-up entrance to the courthouse. This next part of the plan was a bit devious. I'm not sure if it counts as deception though. We could have sent the prisoners on to find other exits from the tunnels, and maybe that would have given them a better chance at escaping, but we needed them to help with the greater diversion. So with just tiny bits of frostfire, Minzo and I blasted a human-sized hole in the bricks.

"In exchange for helping you escape," I said, "I need your assistance. This leads into the courthouse basement. You will have to get past some guards, but they won't be expecting you. So once you get to the main floor, just run straight for the front door. They shouldn't be able to react in time, and hopefully most of them have already been called to the courtyard. Out front, there is a creature army stirring up more trouble and blocking traffic. They know you are coming, so they won't bother you. Head south toward the big park—there is a snuffalo that will lead you there. Lots of trees to hide out in. Once our operation is over, creatures will bring you clothes to change into, so stay hidden until then. Any questions? Actually, never mind. No time for questions."

Electricity crackled behind them in the dim light and fog that poured down through the hole. Somewhere above, humans were shouting, and the tunnel roof creaked and sprinkled dust on our heads from the commotion.

"Go, go, go!" I shouted.

The prisoners didn't need any more encouragement. They clambered through the gap in the bricks and in a few moments were gone, running up through the basement and into the courthouse.

"A brilliant plan," Minzo said. "It's an honour to serve beside you, Glimm."

"This is kind of fun, isn't it?" I had to laugh. The bristlegriff had started to salute me again, all solemn and respectful, but I interrupted him with a quick hug. I probably should have asked him if he minded a hug, but I was overcome with excitement. "Okay, time for stage two."

CHAPTER NINETEEN

Not Without My Whisperglass

Minzo headed for the street in front of the courthouse to check on the efforts of the creature army. No doubt they were having fun creating chaos and blocking up traffic. I wanted to go with him to see all the commotion, but duty called, so instead I made for the curb grate exit to the east of the compound.

My tweens were still hiding up in the tree. Xander hadn't managed to find a ladder, but he'd dragged a couple large boxes over from the construction site and stacked them in front of the wall at the back of the jail.

"Ready to rescue a bard and a wizard?" I asked.

"A bard, definitely," Lark said. "And an academic if we must."

All three of them dropped down from the branches. The ruckus from the other side of the courthouse compound echoed up the side street and around the corner: shouts, whistles, whinnying horses, bellowing golems, squealing snorchins, and the unmistakable (and maniacal) laughter of jungleroos. But our street was clear, so I flapped up onto the wall behind the jail as the humans hurried over to climb up the boxes. Xander got himself atop the wall first so he could help the others up, first Lark and then Elric.

Up at the front of the compound, the courthouse went right to the edge of the property, so the wall, which was about eight feet tall, connected directly to that building. But the jail had been built within the walls, with about three feet of clearance. In between grew a plant I recognized from Ravenna: thornberries. They produced tasty treats from mid to late summer, luscious black berries full of juice. And while I always preferred meat to fruit and vegetables, I was quite fond of the little morsels. But anyway, it was still too early in the year, and even if it wasn't, this was no time to be thinking about snacks. Yet the thornberry bush presented an annoying obstacle: thick, woody stems covered in sharp spines. Worse, the stuff dies off every winter, so underneath the current year's growth was all the dead (and still spiky) stems from previous seasons.

"Oh crap," Elric said.

"I bet those thorns are coated in a neurotoxin," Xander said.

"Why would they be covered in a neurotoxin?" Lark asked.

"Never mind," I cut in. "We can just blast into the prison from up here."

"That makes sense, actually," Elric said. "It would be hard to get back over this wall anyway. You know, without boxes stacked on this side."

"Well how are we going to get out of the blast hole if it's up this high?" Lark asked.

"Maybe we can find some boxes inside the jail." Xander pulled a vial of Alpha Power from his pocket. "Assuming they aren't booby-trapped."

"Do you actually need that stuff?" I asked. "It makes you go a bit crazy, if you hadn't noticed."

"This?" He held up the vial of red liquid. "But it makes me strong."

"You're already strong," I said. "I think you should save it. If we get in trouble, okay, go for it. But maybe this plan will work flawlessly. You never know."

"Okay." He stuffed the Alpha Power back in his pocket. "Where do you figure Jorvun and Fox's cells are?"

"Let me check," I said.

There were three little barred windows at the top of the jail, just under the eaves, which put them somewhat more than ten feet off the ground. With the three-foot gap between the perimeter wall and the back of the jail, Xander was almost tall enough to be able to lean across and peer inside, but not quite. So I started with the northernmost window: and there was Fox in the corner cell, pacing back and forth before the bars and muttering to herself. Bonus: no guards in sight. The second window gave me a view of three empty cells, and beyond the cells, across the corridor, was the door to the room where they had made Fox stash her clothes. And through the third window I saw... one empty cell and two to the left with prisoners I didn't recognize. No Jorvun. I almost panicked, because even if the wizard didn't deserve a rescue, the entire point of this mission was to bust him out so we could help him raise an army, march east, defeat Trudera, and then get the party back safely into Valorica and me into dragon college. No wizard meant failure. Frosted fishdick!!

"We've got a problem," I said. "Fox is there—" I pointed toward the north window. "—but Jorvun is missing."

"Of course he is." Lark shook her head in dismay. "Excuse my French, but this fucking academic messes up every single fucking plan every single fucking time."

"Why do you think the boxes will be booby-trapped?" Elric asked.

"So now what?" Lark shook her head, either at the situation or at Elric's delay.

"We rescue Fox," Xander said with finality. "Doesn't matter. We can't let her rot in there."

"Agreed," I said. "The cell below the middle window is the farthest from any prisoners. I think we should blast in through there—less chance of injury."

"Let's do this," Lark said. "The longer we sit around talking about it, the more time the police have to figure out what we're up to."

"If they haven't already," Xander said.

Back in the tunnel, Minzo and I had made a series of small explosions to create a hole in the brick for the prisoners to escape through. That might work again here, but I didn't want to draw any attention away from the chaos the creature army was making for us. However, I also needed to make sure the hole into the prison was big enough for them all to easily jump through. So with as fine a stream of frostfire as I could manage, I drew a big square onto the back of the structure right across from us.

"Snowshards," I said under my breath. "Elric, any chance you have more matches?"

"Nope, that was the only box I grabbed."

"What happened to the matches?" Lark asked.

"Minzo had them last. I'm not sure. He must have dropped them in the tunnel somewhere."

"So we're doomed," Xander said.

"We're not doomed." Lark pulled out a blaster. "Everybody stand back."

"Are you sure your projectiles will do the job?" I asked.

"Nope," Lark said, "but worth a try."

"But if they don't work, it might bring the guards from the front street."

"So will any explosion," she said.

"But every second counts," I insisted. "Don't worry, I've got this. All of you, if you don't mind, shimmy down the fence a ways so you're clear of the blast."

Lark shrugged, holstered her blaster, then edged away from the frostfire target. I flew back and up to hover about halfway across the street. All I could do was hope it was a safe enough distance. Then I tapped into my umbrix, drew forth a thread of power, and voiced the spell that Jorvun had attempted to cast at the trolls.

"Pyra volatis."

A large ball of fire shot forth from my outstretched paws. It blazed with the intensity of the sun, all orange and red and yellow, maybe even a few purple accents, and the frosted thing was about the size of a roast turkey at Solstice. I couldn't believe I had produced such a volatile projectile! It flew straight at the prison wall and impacted directly in the middle of my frostfire square. The explosion was immense. The humans almost fell off the wall. I was almost blown out of the sky. Not only did the frostfire detonate, the fireball itself broke apart with a thunderclap and showered molten shards all down the wall and into the patch of thornberry. The square of brick that I'd outlined hurtled inward and smashed through the bars of the empty cell.

I shook my head at the devastation while also giving over to an involuntary full-body wiggle. How exciting! I could cast an epic fireball! At the same time, I also swooned a bit from the effort. I'd put a lot of power into that spell.

"Ready?" I shouted to the human trio over the crackling of flames that had caught in the thornbush below the wall. "Right this way."

I was the first to enter the jail. Smoke swirled around me, but from what I could tell, there were still no guards in sight. Lark jumped clear into the middle of the cell with both blasters in hand. Then came Xander, who landed on the rubble-covered bed right below the hole, and when he did, he let out an odd moan. Once Xander was out of the way, Elric came through, also landing on the bed, and he too let out a moan.

No, wait.

Frost's mercy.

The moan hadn't come from Xander or Elric. It was my boss! He was on the little bed. When I'd peeked in through the windows, I hadn't been able to see him. Now he was covered in hot rubble and cinders, plus he'd just been jumped on twice. Holy sleet. I hoped we hadn't killed him.

"Guys," I hissed, trying to be quiet even though we had just announced our arrival with an explosion. "It's Jorvun."

"Oh damn," Xander said.

"Ha." Lark slapped her knee. "Too funny."

"Hurry," I said. "Elric, pull him out of the rubble. Xander, find some boxes or something so we can climb back out. Lark, we'll probably have guards on us in a minute. Cover the corridor?"

"On it," she said.

Meanwhile, Fox was jumping up and down with excitement. I hurried to her cell and checked out the lock. It looked mundane enough. Considering they had put a mage gag or whatever it was over Jorvun's mouth so he couldn't cast, I guessed that they didn't worry about prisoners using magic to get out of their cells.

"*Aperi sesame.*"

My spell took hold, and the lock rattled, but it held. Okay, so it was less mundane than it seemed. There was some subtle trace of magic, but at least it wasn't anti-magic.

"*Nullivar.*" Nope, the spell was locked in some way. "*Nullivar sesame.*" Still nothing.

"What's wrong?" Fox asked.

"I don't know. There's some kind of sneaky magic that is preventing me from unlocking it. I don't suppose you saw the guards stash a key somewhere nearby?"

"No, they keep the keys on them."

"Okay, stand back against the wall over there," I said.

"*Tacitae... mantella... sesame.*" This spell was admittedly an experiment, and maybe this wasn't the time to be making arcane gambles, but it seemed like another explosion was the only option left, so I wanted to do so with a bit less noise if possible. After speaking the spellwords, I had to steady myself. I was using a lot of magic, and it was impacting my strength. But no matter. We had a mission to complete, and we had almost succeeded. I closed my eyes for a second and took a deep breath. I could feel a little sphere of something form around the lock. So maybe the silence spell had worked? There was only one way to find out.

I got up close to the keyhole and blew a little frostfire inside. Then I concentrated on my umbrix, taking great care to only let out the thinnest stream of power, both because I didn't need much and because I didn't have much left.

"Pyra volatis."

The fireball that I created this time was much smaller—about the size of a thornberry, actually. It was bigger than the keyhole, but it impacted directly and then fractured, so plenty of it went right into the lock. The cell door and entire section of bars shuddered and groaned, and although it wasn't silent, the explosion inside the lock didn't make a sound at all.

I hit the ground before I realized I had fallen over backward. The world felt unbalanced, like we were on the deck of a boat in choppy waves. Fox ran over and pulled at the door. The lock caught for a second, but when she gave it another heave, it swung open. Amazing! She ran right over, picked me up, and gave me a squeeze.

"Glad the plan worked," I said. "So far, at least. Now we need to get out of here."

"Definitely." Full-tooth grin.

Fortunately I was too weak to shudder.

"Are you okay?" she asked.

"Just... too much magic," I said. "But I'll be fine."

She carried me over to the others and set me down just inside Jorvun's cell. Elric had pulled the wizard out from under the rubble and had him leaned up against the bars, but his head was slumped in a way that suggested he was unconscious. Oops. He was going to be furious with us. I mean, we were saving him, so he had no right to be furious, especially since he'd betrayed everyone, and yet I didn't think that would stop him from snarking.

He was pretty beat-up, but at least half of his face was protected by the mage gag.

Xander had dragged a desk from the guard station just past Fox's cell. Elric helped him carry it over the rubble and place it on the bed below our escape hole.

"Wait," Fox said. "We can't leave without my whisperglass."

"*Your* whisperglass?" Elric raised an eyebrow at her.

"*The* whisperglass," she corrected. "And we should probably grab the wizard's stuff? It's just in that room."

I opened my mouth to protest, but then Lark fired two shots around the corner. Apparently we had guards approaching.

"Lark," Fox shouted, "can you hold them off for a minute?"

"Brine and Keel," Lark yelled back, then fired off two more shots. "You better hurry up. I'm running out of bullets."

"Can one of you unlock the door?" Fox asked.

"I'll get it," Elric said after taking a look at me.

They left me there on the floor next to Jorvun. The entire scene around me was getting a bit dreamlike. There were shouts from the other end of the building. A faraway shriek of a jungleroo. Another blast from Lark— one of many warning shots, or so I hoped. Elric made an excited yip then disappeared into the storage room with Fox. For a moment I found myself wondering what Aneko had gotten up to and if she was having fun creating creature chaos. My mental image of the flickerkit was so clear, it was like I could imagine her right in front of me, her antennae stiff with concern as she gave me a perplexed inspection, saying...

"Glimm? Glimm, are you okay?"

"Oh, that *is* you!" I shook my head a couple times to clear my vision. "Yes, I'm fine. Just cast a bit too much magic."

"What are you still doing in the jail?"

"Fox is getting her whisperglass."

"A bunch more police just showed up," she said. "Scary-looking ones with armour. Plus a few mages. The creatures are scattered. We need to leave—now."

"I hear you," Xander said, then shouted at the others, "Ready or not! The hour of reckoning is upon us. Move, move, move!" Then he hoisted Jorvun over his shoulder and climbed out through the hole.

"We're good!" Elric shouted from behind me.

He clambered out next with Jorvun's oilskin under one arm. Fox was right behind him, carrying a bundle of her own clothes. Aneko pulled me to my feet, and somehow I found the strength to flap a few times, up and out, but the next thing I knew I was sprawled on the street behind the prison with a bit of dirt in my mouth. Behind us, Lark fired off a few more rounds, then leapt through the hole, over the wall, and landed right beside me.

"Mission accomplished!" Fox said, but then she frowned at the unconscious wizard and added, "More or less."

"Nothing is accomplished if we don't get out of here," Aneko said. "Come on, Minzo found an abandoned house for us to hide in. It's just a few blocks away."

Lark picked me up and carried me. Xander, with Jorvun still over his shoulder, ran across the street to a thick hedge and pulled out Fox's lute case. Then it was all pounding feet and blurred trees and bright sky as they ran. I really needed to get my head on straight, but there wasn't much I could do about that except relax into the pirate's arms. This was as good a place as any to take a rest and recover some of my magic. I would certainly need it again soon. Someone had said they would send police dogs and pigeons out after us. Who was that? Oh well, it didn't matter. Yes, I would get some needed rest, and then all would be well. Better just close my eyes for a few minutes... If they needed any magic, I'd be more than ready—

"Freeze!"

Who was that shouting at us?

"Hands up! All of you. The flickerkit too. You're under arrest."

Oh crap. I gave my head another shake. The party had run around the corner, right into a police patrol—ten cops in blue plate mail trimmed with yellow highlights and a big police crest stamped into the middle of their chests. And of course, all of them were wielding nasty-looking stun sticks.

If only... if only I could remember the magical affix for the number ten. And let me just say—frost's mercy that there were only ten of them. One more and I wouldn't have been able to entertain even this final faint hope.

Unis, duad, tri, then quad. Hmmmm.

Lark slowly set me down with one hand, the other inching toward her holster. Elric was digging around in one of his pockets. Xander was pulling the stopper off a small vial of red liquid. Aneko was poised, her tail ready to flick whatever small amount of fire she could muster. Jorvun made a tiny gurgling sound. And Fox was—oh, Fox actually had her hands in the air.

Sext, septem, octin, novin...

Ten armoured cops against a kitten-moth, a pirate low on ammunition, a paranoid paladin, a pathological liar, and an inventor slash entrepreneur slash rogue who, let's be honest, probably wasn't much use in a fight. The odds weren't looking very good. In a few moments, they would have us all stunned, and then we'd wake up behind bars with terrible headaches, this entire misadventure at a sad, sad end. Unless I could—

Ah, yes, that was it.

"Somno, decem," I said.

And then I passed the fuck out. Excuse my French.

CHAPTER TWENTY

Dragon College or Bust

The first thing I noticed was the smell. Dust and old wood. A bit of mildew. Also something sharp, like a dirty sock. I opened one eye. The room was dim, but not completely dark. Lines of light leaked through the edges of a boarded-up window. There were birds chirping somewhere outside—rock wrens? That was my best guess. The Kippenfolds would know.

My head hurt.

I pushed myself up and blinked a few times. High ceiling. Crown moulding, cracked and stained. Chunks of it missing. Faded floral wallpaper mostly peeled off. The floor was bare wood, covered in dust and leaves. A few old boot prints. Evidence of past squatters—maybe even a failed necromancer, judging by the broken circle scrawled in charcoal by the fireplace.

Someone had thrown a blanket over me. No, not a

blanket. It was Jorvun's oilskin. I pushed it aside and flexed my wings. Still attached. That was something.

Low voices hummed and whispered in the next room. I guessed they were being quiet so I could get some sleep. Much appreciated. I wandered toward them—afoot. I still felt a bit too unsteady to fly.

What a wild adventure had brought us to this point. We hadn't accomplished our mission, but at least we weren't imprisoned. Not yet, anyway. I paused at the door, just gathering myself. I'd led the jailbreak, if nothing else, and our journey was far from over. But something had shifted. I'd come into my magic. I'd discovered the true potential of my frostfire. I'd learned a few things about diplomacy and dishonesty. Leadership too. And I think I'd gained a couple inches, both in height and length.

My biggest goal was still out of reach, but it was coming into focus, like fog burning off with the morning sun. The Aerie. It was out there, somewhere. And for the first time, I truly believed I would arrive. I could almost see myself with a little bookbag and an overstuffed lunchbox.

"And... there we go," Elric said.

I finally came around the corner to find the ex-burglar/inventor knelt next to Jorvun, lockpicks in hand. He had just unfastened the mage gag. The rest of the party was sitting around the wizard on the floor. Aneko was perched in an open window, the view beyond hidden by thick ivy. Minzo was there too, over in the corner, along with a snuffalo and a velvetaur. I gave them all a weak wave as I ambled into the room.

"Hi, Glimm," Lark said. "Feeling any better?"

Just as she asked me, I was overcome with a yawn, which gave Jorvun the opportunity to test the air with his newly freed mouth.

"Is *he* feeling any better," he muttered. "I was half-way killed, and you're worried about whether Glimm got enough sleep?"

"Can you put the gag back on?" Lark asked.

Elric laughed uncomfortably and set the metal anti-magic mask down on the ground next to the wizard. Jorvun scowled and glanced around the room, a certain defensive shame in his expression. Then his eyes fell on the three new creatures in our midst. It was clear from his disorientation that he had also just woken up.

"What are *they* doing here?"

"The bristlegriff is Minzo," I said. "He is my general."

"Introducing Lieutenants Bosho—" Minzo motioned to the snuffalo first, and then to the velvetaur. "—and Liren."

"General?" Jorvun scoffed. "And lieutenants?"

"Yes, you heard correctly," I said. "They are part of the creature army that I freed back on the dreadhull, and they were instrumental in breaking you out of prison."

A stretch of silence followed. Lark pulled out one of her pistols, flipped open the casing, and inspected something on the inside. Maybe the number of bullets she had left. Elric crossed his arms and stared at a clump of dirt on the floor. Fox fingered a fresh scratch on the side of her lute case. Xander twitched when a wren chirped outside the window. And Aneko shot me a sly little wink, as if encouraging me to say something else.

"I suppose we should bring you up to speed," I said, "both on the prison break operation and our next steps, but first... first I think you owe everyone an apology."

Jorvun narrowed his eyes at me. "Excuse me?"

"Don't act surprised or outraged or whatever this feigned indignation is meant to convey." I walked across the room and stood right in front of him. "First of all, you commanded me to lie to everyone from the start of this mission. You tricked them all into coming to Frostvale on a false pretence, and then when we got into the palace, you betrayed them. We could have all ended up in jail."

"You are forgetting yourself, *dragon*. I am your—"

"My boss?" I waved a scolding claw in his face. "Nope. Not anymore. I officially quit as your familiar. As of this moment, I am taking command of the party. Not to be an authoritarian. But to be a voice of reason. Lark, Elric, Fox, and Xander need to get back to Valorica. They are criminals up here now, and they are trapped within the barrier wall. In order to do that, we are going to travel to the Frostvalen Prairies, where, apparently, a good many people hate King Trudera. There, we're going to raise an army, then set off in a wagon convoy to bring the fight across the country to Awtava. And if we can, we will get you installed as the stupid king, but by revolution— not some whiny demand for Trudera to submit to a paternity test. Then you will arrange for them to go home and for me to attend dragon college. Is that clear?"

For what seemed like a year we just stared at each other. There were a couple moments when I thought he would scream at me or burst into laughter. His lips twitched. His eyes narrowed, softened, then narrowed again. Meanwhile, everyone else was dead quiet.

And then, finally—ice me sideways—he said:

"Fine." Cleared his throat. Sniffed. Blinked a few times as if warding off tears. Puffed up his chest a bit, as if that helped him regain a tiny bit of pride or dignity. "My father... he's... well, he's dead to me now. So yes, a new approach is warranted. And... I'm, uh, sorry. Anything else?"

"Yes, actually." I puffed up my own chest, because why not? "You should also know that... that I can do magic. And if I might say so myself, I'm pretty good at it."

Jorvun blanched. He opened his mouth. He closed it again. He swallowed.

"Now that's all out of the way," I said, "I think it's time we found something to eat. I'm absolutely starving."

To be continued!

Stay tuned for the second
installment of Glimm's duology:

We've Come for Your Eggs II
No Country for Old Dragons

Coming in 2026

Thank You for Reading

If you enjoyed *We've Come for Your Eggs*, I'd be incredibly grateful if you left a review on Amazon or Goodreads or StoryGraph. Reviews help other readers discover the story—and they make a huge difference for authors.

Questions, thoughts, or favorite moments? I'd love to hear from you:

53p71mu5.8rown@gmail.com

Your support means everything. Thank you for being part of the journey.

—Septimus Brown

BONUS CHAPTER

The Sparrow War

Excerpt from *The Vengeance of Mal Hook*
Mulg Village, Noreh
Orbit 2120.02.19
Six cycles before the Reth Uprising

Secrets are contraband. Secrets are the root of deceit. So when the Observer extends her palm and fingertip in Mal's direction, eyes locked, he knows that he has been called to take his turn, to tell his truth. The boy rises tall and picks his way through forty-some others who sit semicircle, cross-legged and silent on the dusty wooden floor. But is it boy? Or young man? This is the precipice Mal begins upon.

It's been six days since his last call. Today the Observer is old. Mal can't remember her name or sphere. She is small and her back crooks just below her shoulders. Stringy silver hair with a whisper of long-ago black. Face creased as treebark. She leans on a splintered stick, too small for the purpose, but winter was bitter so there's not much wood to be found. The same ragged clothes as everyone else, but she still wears the full kit issued last autumn, like the chill never left her. Itchy thermal tights visible below her frayed hem, oversized longsleeve protruding from her padded coat. All colours, which were muted to begin with, have been covered over with mud to the knees, and otherwise stripped away by regular applications of fish grease, burnt black and thick to keep out the wind and rain of spring storms. *Squall shine*, they call the grease, and it marks the wealth of their village. Mulg: rich in fish and kelp and salt. In other villages they would have eaten the grease, for hunger comes before warmth.

Mal stops to tie his long black hair in a fisher-folk knot. He bows to the Observer, unhurried, before he turns to the throne in the centre of the room: the Lucent. It's a replica of the Eternal's own throne in the capital, a throne shared with every citizen, for the nation is one and all. And like the Eternal's Lucent, the real throne from which He guides them, the Lucent of Mulg hums with unknowable power. Silver stone, or something like stone, but softer and smoother and lighter. Stone made manifest. It's a remarkable object, for its gentle edges and rippled surface recall the moon—but even more, for the clarity of mind that emanates from the base. There is no other way to describe it. When Mal steps into Lucent Hall, his thoughts grow quiet and then clear. The calm is inescapable: meditative and peaceful. And when he sits upon the throne, the Lucent's full potency shines into every crevice of his soul.

Today is no different. Mal kicks off his slippers and slides into place. At sixteen orbits, he is both large and young for his age. He leans into the splayed seatback, crosses his legs, and closes his eyes. The Eternal is there, immediate, a benevolent guardian somewhere just behind him, within him, before him. The undying presence cannot be seen or touched, yet within the Lucent, the Eternal is more tangible than an embraced parent or a looming enemy. *Only the self can be known as directly,* they say. That's certainly true for most people. But of course, up to this point in Mal's life, he's not yet had a clairvoyant shift—or if he has, the experience was easily dismissed.

"Declarant." The Observer turns to face Mal with hands clasped. "Your trial begins."

"My name is Mal Hook." He opens and again closes his eyes. "And I am a liar."

"Tell us your lies."

Mal doesn't respond immediately. His memories loosen and he can see his recent transgressions. Jealousy: of his brother, Hansol, who is old enough now to have his own travel papers. Anger: at his father, Laon, for sending Hansol inland with their newest batch of smoke-fish, through the valley all the way to Dochen. Alone, to the foot of the mountains and back—Mal's favorite delivery run, and one that had always been shared, father and one son, alternating between the two of them. And the subsequent despair: that his days would now be spent exclusively on the catboat, cold and wet. At least until his brother is called to join the Great Guard, though that won't be for another year at least. But Mal has already acknowledged these failings. He admitted his dark thoughts to Laon and Hansol, and they forgave him, so there is nothing left to tell. He's left no secret hidden, except—

"There is one," he says.

"Only one?" The Observer nods. "Clean heart, young Mal. Go ahead, bare your *one* transgression, then."

"A complaint, I guess." Mal frowns. "A judgement of my parents, maybe—just this morning. Something I could have admitted in the moment, yet I didn't. I brushed it away, but the thought stuck. A criticism, I guess."

"Harbouring judgement against your parents is no small lie."

"I... decided not to say anything, because I saw no solution."

"Go on."

"We had rice in the last ration. We recited our gratitude together—not Hansol, he's on a run—so my parents and my sisters. The Eternal's kindness. But only Dad and I could eat the rice. Nabi asked me for some—a spoonful. I know it's meant for sea strength, but it wasn't much. And she's skinny. They both are."

"And you gave her this spoonful."

"Yes, Observer."

"Even though it went against the allotment."

"Yes."

"Tell us why." She tilts her head back, just slightly, and crosses her arms.

"Because I thought..." Mal relaxes his frown. "I thought it was the right thing to do."

The crowd murmurs. Scattered exclamations, but wordless and hush. Mal opens his eyes, glancing from the Observer to his father seated in the back row. His father's expression hasn't changed, but the Observer's has. Her nose is flared and she's leaning forward, like she suddenly needs a closer look at Mal, as if the nature of his fault can be found in his face.

"The allotments are common good," she says.

"I know, but—"

"And *right* is common good."

Mal tries to protest, or at least to explain himself, but the Lucent has him tight. His mind falls quiet and quieter still. He stares at the Observer, waiting for his resolution, for her wisdom. There is only confession in this space—and from confession comes vulnerabil-ity, impression, and reflection.

"You are Laon's son, it seems. If you lack the strength to fish, you lack the strength to feed your sister. Much worse, you lack the strength to feed the nation," she says. "Is this not true, young Mal?"

"This is true."

"Exceeding your quotas—wouldn't that be a better way to feed your sister?"

"Yes, Observer—and the nation."

"Good." The old woman straightens. "Have you learned from this clarity?"

"I have."

"And are you loyal to the Eternal?"

"I am."

"Very well." The Observer claps her hands together and turns toward the gathered. "We will recess briefly. The next call in a spin."

When Mal finally shakes himself free of the Lucent, the Observer is at the back of the crowd, speaking to his father. Some lies come with consequences. Laon nods twice and bows. As always, his salt-grey hair is braided and coiled—one small detail that marks the man's unspo-ken status as an accomplished mariner, a provider for many. The Observer smiles flatly and returns to her place next to the throne. The villagers seated about the Lucent are basking in the calm until they might be called forward. None looks at Mal as he makes his way to his father.

"I apologize." Mal steps through the doorway and shudders. The Lucent's aura leaves him, suddenly, as the sky presses grey light against his face. "I hadn't properly considered—"

"You've confessed." His father indicates they go right, further into town. "It's done."

Mal relaxes and lets his tamped excitement rise anew. The throne almost made him forget: a projection has come to Mulg. He had been afraid, moments before stepping into the Lucent Hall, that he might be called, as he was, and that he might turn up a lie he had overlooked, which he had, and that the punishment for his lie might cost him the promised afternoon. Mal has only seen a projection once before, five orbits past when all of Noreh was celebrating the end of the Little Famine. He'd been as captivated by the small box that shot a shimmering beam of light against the wall as he'd been by the story the wall revealed—the characters, the danger, the excitement, and most of all, the victory. He'd never seen anything like it. Magic tech from the capital—two charge cells, gleaming silver spheres that the Noreh envoy said contained a sliver of the Eternal's power, and then this box and its impossible light that could make people and places appear like Mal was staring through a window to another world.

His father leads them onward, into town. Toward Common Hall. People will be gathered there and in the park across the street, waiting for their number to be called. The projection runs for a half turn each showing, and the basement of the hall is large, so they won't need to wait for long. Mal sucks on his lip as he wonders what the story will be this time. Some of his friends went after morning oath, but he asked them to keep away until he'd seen it. They will hold their tongues until they can meet this evening, after bean soup, up on the hill beyond the dead orchard. They will meet and discuss every detail, and the discussions will no doubt continue through to the next moon cycle.

Onward into town. Yet his father doesn't turn at the square, and Mal's lungs make two fists within his chest. An emotion threatens to climb from his stomach up into his throat, and he's not sure if it's anger or sadness, but either will make trouble, so he swallows and tries to ignore the surge. A metallic voice rattles somewhere behind them, a farcry from the capital, from Noreh Warren, addressing the Commons crowd. But Mal and his father continue to the market ring, all stalls empty and two seacrows picking through the dust. The scrawny salka trees along the market's edge creak in the breeze, their new pale leaves too small to rustle. Past Dominion Hall with all its glisteningly vestigial poles, wood soaked black with oil—the once-upon-a-time legs of giant galvanic lamps that used to light the entire crumbling street as well as the hall. But Mal has never seen a galvanic light. Or if he ever did, he was too young to remember it. Light in the darkness, and without fire—the mechanism is as incomprehensible as a projection. To think there was such a time of luxury, back before the war demanded every scrap of copper and iron.

"We're not going." Mal looks back at the turn they didn't take.

"No." The father glances at the son, and there is something worse than annoyance creasing his brow and tightening his eyes.

"So then...?"

"You heard the Observer. We must exceed our quota. That was her justice."

"Was it so bad? Giving Nabi the rice?"

"You certainly thought so."

"What do you mean?" Mal pauses, but his father walks on.

Soon the marina is in sight below them. A mud path

down to the water. A rickety dock, half repurposed lumber and half rough-cut logs. Twelve boats that are actually seaworthy. Three more hauled out onto the rocks for repair. Piles of fish net and husk buoys line the shore. The stink of yesterday's fish.

"What do you mean? Because I thought so?"

"If you didn't think it was wrong," Laon keeps his eyes on the ocean, on the waves in the strait, "if your belief had conviction, would the thought have surfaced?"

Mal doesn't respond. He's not sure if his father's angry, but it seems likely. He can't remember hearing his father speak like this before, and he can't decide what it means. He isn't sure if his father is telling him something he knows, or admitting something he doesn't know. And Mal isn't even sure it's okay to be talking about the Lucent in this way, but he doesn't let himself fully consider the implications. The throne is always listening, even in hindsight, and the captive brain learns to bury thoughts before they occur. So he stomps out all considerations and questions and contradictions, and follows a step behind his father, creaking along the pier to their catboat at the end of the second mooring line.

The day is still grey, but brightening. The clouds are breaking up in the north, and the sun promises to simmer off the rest, though it's an empty promise. Mal pushes down his thoughts, concentrating instead on wet rope and slick deck. He unties and folds the waxed burlap that covers the small pilot house, which is nothing more than a bench, a rudder crank, and a low ceiling that poorly protects from spray and squall, but a space just big enough for the two of them to hide from summer sun. He unfastens another ream of burlap that covers the sail, and then helps his father release the mooring lines. They each take up a long oar and begin pushing and paddling the boat away from the pier, and only raise their span of sail once they reach the centre of the bay.

As soon as they're underway, Mal looks back at the town, hoping to catch sight of people up at the Commons, and hating it when he does. The jealousy he feels will need to be measured and confessed, but just now he can't be bothered. As they get more distance from shore, Mulg ascends before them, a bowled-out slope leading up into the Jaka Hills, with squat homes radiating from the four central halls and market streets. The best homes, the homes that survive the most storms, are on the other side of Little River, nestled up to the steep sandstone cliffs.

Cliffs to the south, stony hills to the north: the two earthen arms embrace the oblong bay and the Little's delta, defending them from the worst of squalls in spring and typhoons in autumn. Still, the bay is as protected as anyone could hope for along a battered coast, and the narrow inlet was famously impenetrable in the long-ago days of warlord conquest and raids by the imperialist Solris from across the eastern sea. But the bay is small, so the town is small. The cliffs continue inland all the way to Denu Valley and the Jakun Mountains to the north, the distant peaks where Mal once saw a star tumble from the sky. Mulg has always been isolated. The furthest corner from anything and anywhere.

Beyond the inlet, out into the strait, Mal begins to set a northward tack, but his father stops him with a nod toward the south. Their course is direct as they enter the longer waves of deep ocean and the steady Siber wind. Finally, when the father gives a satisfied nod, the boy ties off the boom and joins him on the bench.

"We're back to redfin?" Mal opens the hatch at his feet, pulls out a stiff blanket to put across their laps.

"No, it'll be darling," Laon says.

"But we'll need—"

"Provisions are in the stern hold. Tent and blankets too. The darling quota came out yesterday, and it's not light, so we might as well get started."

Darling is unexpected. There's been no call for darling in two orbits—it takes the fishers too far south, and lowers the overall haul. All for an ugly, salty little fish. But sometimes, it seems, the world craves strange things of them, and the Eternal will sell Noreh fish to the strange world, and everyone will prosper for it—they learn as such from the Farspeakers. And anyway, there is some relief in a trip for darling. It will be cold, with an overnight on the hook, but at least Mal won't have to face his friends on the hillside tonight. He won't have to hear about what he missed, not when the missing of it is so near and surrounded by dangerous thoughts.

So they sail south, keeping the horizon in view, if only a haze. Then four turns before sundown they set a course back toward shore. There are six small bays between Dagger Rock and Grief Point that will all make for a fine overnight. But as the sky clears before them, a dark threat rolls in from behind, and there is still a long stretch of water to cross. Lashing wind comes first, of course, and then the rain. The waves change eight directions, and all the little catboat can do is run with the storm. Soon the coast disappears, both for the weather and the coming darkness. Father and son hurtle southward, clinging to each other beneath their paltry shelter, ever edging toward land but never arriving.

Coming in 2026
Join my mailing list for updates:
<u>SeptimusBrown.com</u>

About the Author

Septimus Brown writes speculative fiction about alternate worlds, fractured identities, and the strange magic of becoming someone new. His work blends genre energy with  literary experimentation, often dipping into gender-punkery, magical realism, and other liminal realms.

We've Come for Your Eggs is his second novel.

As David Griffin Brown, he is the co-author of *Immersion and Emotion: The Two Pillars of Storytelling* and *Story Skeleton: The Classics*, and runs DarlingAxe.com, a collective of professional editors supporting writers at every stage of the process.

He lives in Victoria, Canada, on the traditional territory of the Xwsepsum and Songhees Nations.

Find him on Threads and Bluesky as @SeptimusBrown and @DarlingAxe.

SeptimusBrown.com